MW01134628

The Perfect Pitch

Seaside Boulevard Series

Karen Cino

Copyright 2017 Karen Cino

A Mandolay Press Book

Women's Fiction
The Perfect Pitch: Seaside Boulevard Series
Copyright 2017 Karen Cino

First Edition: June 2017

Edited by: Em Petrova
Proofread by: Joan Setteducato

ISBN 13: 978-1545254158
ISBN 10: 154525415X

PUBLISHER
Mandolay Press

DEDICATION

This is dedicated to my readers and my fans. Your support is what gives me the inspiration to keep telling my stories.

OTHER BOOKS BY KAREN CINO

Roses

The Boardwalk

Love Challenges and Desires

MYSTICAL WONDERS SERIES

Circle of Friends

Second Chances

The Right Call

Survival

NOVELLAS

Wild Pitch

Midnight Encounter

POETRY

Love Poems

SEASIDE BOULEVARD SERIES

The Perfect Pitch

Chapter One

Richie Raggalio's name was called over the PA system. Everyone jumped to their feet clapping, and Francine's butterflies hatched in her stomach with excitement for her husband. Richie came running out of the dugout, tipping his hat as he waved to the crowd. The press photographers called out to him. He stopped to let them take some pictures. Before going out to the mound, he walked up to the stands to give Francine a peck on her lips.

"This game is for you."

Francine continued clapping and cheering with the crowd along with her friend Amy Mills. Fifteen years earlier, Richie took the same walk out to the mound, except his words to her had been, "Wish me luck" before taking his position on the pitching rubber. Today he stood on the

7

mound, still tall and lean. The only difference being these days, he sported a crew cut.

Her life as a baseball wife, while running her own business, had been far from glamorous. Her foster parents had purchased the business for her after Francine caught them cheating on one another. Their deceit resulted in them paying for her college education, and giving her anything she wanted within reason, in exchange for keeping their secret. Her loyalty to both led her to becoming an entrepreneur.

"Let's all stand to sing the National Anthem, being sung by local musician, Mike Gio," the broadcaster announced.

Francine kept her eyes on Richie. When she sat next to him in biology lab twenty-five years ago, her heart had skipped a beat. The first time she watched him pitching in high school, she had no idea she would become part of his baseball career.

Richie had spent his whole career playing for the New York Pelicans. Most games she attended alone, leaving her two childhood best friends Amy Mills and Toni Belluci to run things at the office. Looking around at the other players' girlfriends and wives sitting in the area, she couldn't help but laugh to herself. The younger the women were, the higher the stilettos and shorter the skirts. Francine never fit in with them. When she wasn't at work, she pulled her long chestnut colored hair in a ponytail, wore jeans and, depending on the weather, flip-flops or flats. Today, she wore flats.

The fans began cheering during the final words of the National Anthem. Since this was Richie's last season, she would cherish the moments spent at the ballpark. This had become her home, her way of living. The only thing that worried her was what Richie would do with his free time. He was drafted during his third year of college and spent the next few years working his way up through the minor-league organization. Since he was a teen, he had devoted his whole life to his baseball career and her. During the off-season, Richie volunteered at the high school helping pitchers, which occupied most of the winter months. Other than that, he didn't have many other interests that would keep him from driving her crazy in retirement.

Amy nudged her. "I just got a text from Toni. Mr. Reynolds signed a binder on the house at Shore Acres for the asking price. He wants to pay cash."

"Woo hoo," Francine sang, causing the people around them to glance over. "That's wonderful news. And cash, even better," she whispered.

"Toni's on the way. She's bringing the paperwork for you to look over tonight. Mr. Reynolds wants to do this transaction by Friday."

"Play ball!" The umpire's voice echoed from behind home plate.

Francine directed her attention to the mound. Before Richie threw the first pitch, his ritual at every game would be to stand tall and roll his shoulders a dozen times. He insisted this helped clear his mind. The ritual seemed to have worked all these years.

Richie held his glove up to his chest, went into his windup and started the game with a strike. The crowd roared, as did Francine. Boy, was she going to miss this. Nothing could come close to hearing the crowd chant Richie's name and feeling the sun beat down on her, with not a breeze to be found, unless you're sitting up in the bleachers. The new stadium didn't have the pizazz of the old one. The ticket booths in the parking lot were gone, just as the two-dollar general admission tickets. A lot had changed since Richie's first game, but the one thing that remained the same were the fans' enthusiasm and food.

The scent of hotdogs, popcorn and beer still lingered in the air and were still being sold by the vendors, the same men who served her the very first time she sat in the box seats on the left of the dugout. The only difference was now she could sit and watch the game with a glass of wine. But during today's game she would pass on the wine and food. The

Pelicans were leading one to nothing with Richie pitching a no hitter, only giving up one walk.

Toni often accompanied her to these games and arrived now, carrying a brown carton with three Coronas. "I thought you might need one," she said, sitting down next to Francine. "I've been listening to the game on the radio. The announcers make it sound so dramatic."

"They always do. If you ask me, the game is boring," Amy said. "There has been very little action going on."

Someone tapped Francine on the shoulder from behind. She turned in her seat to face a gray-haired elderly man holding a scorecard in his hand.

"Your husband has fourteen strikeouts and there are still three more innings left. He's on the way to breaking the Pelicans' record of nineteen."

"Oh. Can I see the scorecard?" Francine asked.

"Sure, but I need it back before the inning starts."

Francine scanned the scorecard. The gentleman was right. In every inning, Richie had two strikeouts. In the forth and sixth inning he had struck the side out.

Francine handed the man back his book. "Thank you."

"I'm sorry I missed such a good game," Toni said.

"Don't worry. You hit the jackpot with the sale in Shore Acres. Good job."

Toni held up her beer bottle. "We work as a team."

By the ninth inning, Richie needed one more strikeout to win the game and break the record. The fans jumped to their feet, their cheers echoing throughout the stadium. Music played in the background until Richie stood on the pitching rubber. The stadium went silent. Glancing up at the Jumbo-Tron screen, she saw the exaggerated look of concentration on his face. Richie was in the zone. He took a deep breath, rolled his shoulders and went into his windup. The pitch flew right by the batter.

"Strike three," the umpire yelled.

"Richie broke the record," fans around her continued cheering.

With that the Pelicans' bench emptied out, as if they had won the World Series. The fans were screaming and Francine jumped up and down along with them. Within minutes, the press and photographers were on the field.

Francine walked with the girls to the Pelicans' Sports Club across the street from the stadium. Outside the bar, they had thick black metal barriers leading to the curb. This was the typical procedure after a game, as fans waited for a glimpse of their favorite players.

They walked up the red carpet to the front door.

"Good evening, Mrs. Raggalio. Congratulations on your husband's achievement this evening," Louie Pinto, the owner said.

"Thank you."

"I have your usual table ready for you."

"Would you mind adding two more chairs for my friends?" she asked, stepping aside to reveal Amy and Toni.

"Not at all. Please take a seat at the bar. I'll be with you in a few minutes."

"Thank you," Francine said. "Order what you want. We have a lot of celebrating to do."

"Yes, we do," Toni agreed, tapping on her handbag. "We just made the deal of a lifetime."

"Yes, we did," Amy said.

Francine signaled to the bartender. He approached them with his long order pad.

"Hi, Cane," Francine said. "I'm thinking dirty martinis for the table. Ladies?"

Amy and Toni nodded in agreement.

"Would you like to see the appetizer menu?"

"No thanks. Louie is getting our table ready. Richie will be meeting us in a bit."

Francine couldn't wait to see Richie. Breaking this record had always been his dream. They would stay for a bit

11

and celebrate with their friends, teammates and fans, and then they'd go home for a private celebration.

While they waited for Cane to make the martinis, Louie returned to bring them to the table. As they sat, Cane returned with their martinis.

"Here you go, ladies." He placed the black leather bill holder on the table. "Enjoy the night."

Louie lifted it. "The drinks are on the house. Enjoy."

Francine waited for him to walk over to the next table to greet the party of four. She lifted her glass. "Let's do a toast."

The three of them held their glass up in the center of the table, leaning the glasses against one another.

"I'd like to propose a toast for a job well done on the Shore Acres house," Francine said.

"You mean the two point four-million-dollar home overseeing the Narrows," Toni explained.

"And Brooklyn," Amy added.

"To a job well done. Salud." Francine took a sip. "This has been one hell of a day. I am so happy for Richie. I hope this last season leaves him with a positive feeling when he retires in September."

"Maybe October," Amy said. "I can foresee a World Series."

Francine waved her index finger back and forth. "Don't even tell me you went to see Shari to get your cards read."

"Maybe I did."

"You know it's a waste of money." Toni shook her head.

"We'll see. She told me I was going to meet someone tall, dark and handsome who will sweep me off my feet by the end of spring."

Toni lifted her hand to stop Amy from talking. "If I had listened to her the first time we went to see her, I would have been married by now. I don't even have a boyfriend and she said I would be married by the end of the year."

"Okay, you two. Stop the bickering," Francine said. "This is a special night. I don't want Richie coming in seeing us talking about all this hocus pocus bullshit. You know how he feels about this."

"Sorry," they said at the same time.

Francine glanced around the room. She heard yelling coming from outside. The guys had arrived in the nick of time.

Richie came from a very religious family, from the gold chain and cross around his neck down to having the crucifix tattooed on his left forearm. When they got married, they had a traditional wedding. Both his parents were from Sicily and attended church every Sunday together, with his mother attending novena every Friday morning.

Both her parents had died in a car accident when she was eleven years old, which led to Francine asking Richie's father to walk her down the aisle. They welcomed her with open arms, teaching her the true meaning of family. The only thing, which saddened her, was that she never learned much about her own Italian heritage. "Here he comes, the man of the hour," Francine heard a man say in a husky voice.

Francine lifted her hand and waved to Richie with her silver bangle bracelets jingling. She watched as he stopped at the tables on the way, shaking hands with the fans and signing autographs.

When he smiled, the dimples she loved since she was a teenager became more pronounced.

With his eyes gleaming, he made his way to their table. Francine placed her hand in his and stood. He gave her a kiss on the lips, slipping his tongue in her mouth to tease her.

"You're such a tease," Francine whispered, slapping his butt as she sat back down.

"Yes, I am." He kissed her again before turning around to acknowledge one of the regulars sitting behind them.

"I'm so proud of you." Francine touched his cheek. "You had me on the edge of my seat the last inning."

"I was just as nervous pitching against Perez, the number two hitter in the league who only stuck out four times last year. You bet your life I was nervous with every batter who came to the plate. Every pitch I made, I prayed when the batter took a swing."

"Even if he did get a hit, you pitched a hell of a game. If you didn't give up the walk, you would have pitched a perfect game."

"I might have come close. But do you know what the best thing to happen today is?" He gave her a penetrating stare. "Having you here with me today beats all of that hands down."

"Richie," Clyde Lewis yelled from across the room over the seven televisions going at the same time with a different game.

"Darling, do you mind?" Richie asked, kissing the top of her head.

"Not at all. Go ahead and enjoy your night. I'm here with the girls."

"You're the best."

Francine held his face between her fingers and gave him a quick peck on his lips. "Yes, I am. Later on, I'll show you."

* * *

Amy swept the loose ends of her shoulder-length blonde hair behind her ears. While Francine and Richie did googly eyes at one another, a gentleman had caught her eye at the bar. He held up his glass, calling her over with his index finger.

He seemed vaguely familiar, but she was pretty sure he wasn't from the Pelicans. Amy slipped out of her chair into her ankle boots, tucking her hair behind her ear as she walked toward him. When she got a few feet away, he stood. The first thing that caught her attention were his broad shoulders that seemed to go on forever. He was tall and muscular, with tribal tattoos on his mocha skin.

As soon as she reached the granite top bar, he extended his hand. Amy eased her hand into his.

14

"Jason Maddock," he said. "Can I buy you a drink, Ms…?"

"Amy Mills." Amy shook his hand before sliding on the bar stool next to him.

"Nice to meet you." He leaned closer to her. "I didn't think you would come over."

She leaned back. "Sometimes I surprise myself."

"What can I get you?"

"A beer would be fine."

"Cane." He signaled to the bartender.

Cane finished making drinks across the bar before walking over. "What can I get you, Jason?"

"A beer for the lady." He held up his glass. "A refill for me."

Jason turned around in his chair and waved to someone by the door. Amy looked over Jason's shoulder to see whom he was signaling. However, the place had become so crowded that it was impossible to pinpoint anyone. A few minutes later the restaurant owner stood by Jason's side.

"What can I do for you?" Louie asked Jason.

"I was hoping you could arrange a table for us."

"Give me a few minutes to have you seated."

When Louie walked away, Jason turned to Amy. "I thought we would grab some dinner and talk. I hope that's all right with you."

Amy nodded. It had been quite some time since she went out on a date. Since her last dinner date had turned into a disaster, she felt her nerves starting to get the best of her. "Yes. That would be fine. I'd like that."

As Cane placed their drinks in front of them, Louie returned. "I'll have the waitress bring your drinks to the table. Please follow me."

They followed Louie across the restaurant to a table for two against the wall. Jason pulled her chair out and Amy slid in. Before sitting, Jason glanced at the baseball game on the television across the room.

A waitress appeared at their table, placing their drinks down in front of them. "Here you go. Would you like to order now, or do you need a little time?"

"How do you feel about buffalo wings, mozzarella and zucchini sticks?" Jason asked.

"That sounds great."

"I'll put your order in. Let me know if you need anything else."

"Thank you." Jason held up his glass, tipping it toward Amy. "To friends."

Amy took a sip of beer. Speechless. She had no idea what to say to him at all. Usually, she talked nonstop. But now, as she sat across the table from this incredible hunk, she felt somewhat intimidated by him.

As if sensing her uneasiness, Jason began the conversation. "I spotted you sitting across the room and I knew I had to have the most beautiful lady in the place across from me at this table. Since you're sitting here with me, I guess it's safe to assume you aren't with anyone." He gave her an assessing stare.

"I came with my friend Francine Raggalio and Toni. We were celebrating her husband's no-hitter."

"That's a wonderful accomplishment. I'm sure Francine is proud of her husband."

"Yes, she is." Amy crossed her legs and leaned on her elbows on the wooden table. "Definitely an exciting game, kept us on the edge of our seats."

"Those are the best kind. But I didn't ask you to join me to talk about your friend and her husband."

Amy rested her chin in her hands. "Oh really?"

"I want to talk about you. What kind of work do you do?"

"If I tell you, then I'll be talking about my friends again."

Jason chuckled. "That's okay. I want to hear all about you."

Amy dropped her hands into her lap. "I'm one of the owners of Rag, Mills and Bell Real Estate on Hylan Boulevard in Grasmere in Staten Island."

"I've passed there many times because it's quicker to take the boulevard then to sit in traffic on the Staten Island Expressway. No matter what time of the day you drive on the expressway, there's always traffic."

"Yeah, got that right. I avoid the expressway, taking the back streets most times. Saves me from doing this," she said in a deep Brooklyn accent as she made a rude gesture with a devilish grin on her face.

Jason's eyes bulged open. "I find that hard to believe."

"Try sitting on the expressway for an hour for a ten-minute ride."

"No thank you. I spend enough time sitting in airports waiting for planes and buses."

Amy leaned closer in when everyone started cheering a play in one of the baseball games. "What kind of work do you do?" Amy asked, tilting her head to the side.

"I work for the New York Rockets."

"What do you do?"

Jason chuckled. "I'm their defensive linebacker."

Amy covered her mouth with her hand, feeling like a fool. "Oh, wow. I didn't recognize you out of your uniform."

"Are you a fan?" he asked, playing with the diamond earring in his left ear.

"Yes. I love sports. My favorite being baseball and football. I don't get to watch as much as I did when I was younger, but I catch enough games. I wouldn't miss the big games for anything."

"A girl after my own heart."

The waitress returned with their appetizers, placing them on the table.

Jason smiled. "Why don't you tell me something about yourself?"

"There isn't much to talk about."

"Sure there is. Tell me how you got into the real estate business. How did you come up with Rag, Mills and Bell?"

"I didn't. Francine Raggalio did. Rag is the beginning of her last name, Mills is the beginning of mine, and Bell is the first four letters of my friend Toni's last name."

"Interesting. Creative at that."

"Francine is. She ran the company for five years alone. When her business picked up, she asked Toni and me to get our real estate licenses and come work with her." Amy stuck her mozzarella stick in the marinara sauce. "Two years later she made us partners."

Jason took a sip of his drink. "You don't find many friends willing to share the wealth."

"Francine is a very generous woman, my best friend."

Amy didn't want to tell this handsome stranger too much information about herself. However, the more she glanced at Jason, the more she knew they had crossed paths before.

Amy finished her food. Before she could push her dish to the side, Jason refilled it.

"They have the best appetizers here. But I'm not too happy with the entrees."

"I usually grab a salad."

Jason stood as Richie walked by the table. "Hey." He hugged Richie. "Congratulations on breaking the strikeout record and the no-hitter."

"Thank you."

"How you doing, bro?"

"Phenomenal. I'm waiting for my social butterfly to make her way back to me. You know Francine." He winked at Amy. "She knows everyone."

Amy turned in her seat. "Tell me about it. We can't go food shopping without being in the store for over an hour. She knows everyone."

"Sadly, that's the truth," Richie said. "What's going on with you?" he asked Jason.

He slid his hands into his back pockets. "Taking it easy, enjoying the spring, and getting to know this lovely woman."

"Good woman. Loves drinking coffee, can't handle alcohol and makes an awesome Italian cheesecake laced in white and dark chocolate."

Richie squeezed her shoulder. He had become a brother to her through the years. Amy had met Francine over twenty-five years ago while she was doing community service at a foster care Christmas party.

"Hey, baby." Francine wrapped her arms around Richie's waist. "I see Amy finally met Jason. You two kept missing each other whenever we had a get-together."

"I'm glad we finally met up." Jason winked at Amy.

"We're leaving. Do you need a ride to your car?" Francine asked.

Amy stood.

"You don't need to leave," Jason said. "I'll take you to your car. I thought we'd have a cup of coffee and dessert." He glanced at his watch. "It's still early." He turned his charm on her with his smoldering eyes.

"Sure, I'm fine. I'd like to stay a little longer."

"Perfect. He's a good guy," Francine whispered in her ear.

Amy glanced at Francine, raising her right eyebrow. "I'll see you in the morning." Amy hugged Francine goodbye. "Again, congratulations on your no-hitter." She hugged Richie.

"Good night," Francine and Richie each said before Richie led her out of the restaurant.

Sitting there, Amy wondered if she had made the right decision in staying behind. But she saw something about Jason she liked, a lot. She wasn't ready to go home yet. The more she gazed at him, the more she wanted to know about him, but it was hard to have an uninterrupted conversation with all the talking going on around them. Despite the loud chatter around them, Amy was happy she stayed. Jason took care of their tab and took hold of her hand.

"What do you say we walk down the street to the Italian pastry shop? We can get a genuine cappuccino and authentic pastry. The place looks like a shop on the streets of Venice." Jason stood and led her out of the restaurant.

"You've been to Venice?"

Jason chuckled. "Of course, via Google map. Haven't you?"

Amy grinned. "Not yet. My trips on Google map have gone exclusively to the Caribbean."

"Am I to presume you are a beach girl?" he asked leading her a few doors down to Larusso's Italian Pastry Shoppe.

"Yes. I love sitting on the beach reading a good book in my hot pink sand chair."

"With a big white cotton hat?"

Amy stopped walking. "Me?" she pointed to herself. "Never."

Jason opened the door. "I didn't think so."

The outside of the bakery was plain, but the inside was spectacular. The space was small, yet quaint. Each table was set with colorful floral Italian dishes, giving the café the feel of being in Italy, complete with soft Italian music playing overhead. What really caught her eye was the selection of pastries and cakes.

"Wow. Look at this." Amy walked over to the glass showcase filled with all kinds of pastries. "There are so many choices, I don't know what to pick."

Jason's hand covered hers. He led her over to a table in the middle of the shop.

"I will make the decision for you. Shelia." He waved to the blonde woman behind the counter.

"What can I get you tonight, Jason?" she asked, in her best Brooklyn accent.

"How about a sampler platter?"

"You got it. Coffee?"

"What would you like?" he asked Amy.

"I'll have a cappuccino."

"Make that two."

"Thank you," Amy said, rolling the silverware onto the table before placing the napkin on her lap.

"This shop is a well-kept secret. People can't imagine how great the sweet goodies are inside." He lifted his thick mocha index finger. "But once they have a nibble, they are back for more."

"Boy, you are building up these goodies."

"He's my best customer," Shelia said, placing a platter of pastries in the middle of the table. "Enjoy."

"Thank you. Please help yourself," he said.

Amy lifted the small plate in front of her and placed a variety of pastries on it. While taking a bite of a chocolate filled cream puff she couldn't help but wonder if he always brought his dates in here, or pickups like her, for a sugary nightcap before taking them home.

Jason's eyes shined. "Yes, I am. Once a week, I send a tray of cookies and pastries to the nursing home down the block."

"Wow. That's quite generous of you."

"A lot of the residents don't get any visitors. When my grandfather lived there, I used to visit him everyday. Sometimes I was the only visitor in the whole place. I always brought cookies. I saw the look on the residents' faces. That's when I knew a simple gesture would make a big difference in their lives." He took a sip of his cappuccino. "I try to stop by there once a week. The men enjoy talking about football."

"That's really nice," Amy replied, taking a bite of the mini-cannoli.

"Promise me you won't tell the paparazzi. I try to keep my personal life private. I'm not looking for any special treatment or awards. I do what I do from my heart."

"That I can see. You're a special man, taking the timeout to make a difference in other people's lives."

Amy ate every piece of pastry on her plate. While she took the last bite of cannoli, she couldn't take her eyes off Jason. His smile was dazzling and teeth startling white against his darker skin tone. She loved his short curly hair, and wondered if his hair was soft or coarse. Under his long sleeve shirt, she knew were tattoos.

Jason took a sip from his tall clear coffee mug. "Thanks for the compliment."

Amy glanced at her watch. "It's getting late. I really need to get going. I have to be at work early tomorrow."

"Not a problem."

"I had a nice time. Would you be interested in doing this again sometime?"

"Yes, I would," Amy said, surprised at his suggestion.

"Good. I'll pick you up tomorrow night around eight."

Amy reached into her handbag. She took out her business card and handed it to him.

Jason looked at the card. "I know exactly where you live. My sister lives in Staten Island not far from you. Gives me an excuse to stop by and see my three nieces before I come for you."

"What can I get you, Jason?" Shelia asked.

Jason lifted the overflowing dish of pastries off the table. "Can you box this up for me?"

"Sure thing. I'll be right back."

"This turned out to be a wonderful evening," Amy said, sipping on her coffee. "This place looks like the shops I've seen in pictures of village squares in Italy."

"I knew you'd love it."

Amy finished her coffee and pushed the cup to the center of the table.

"Would you like another cup of cappuccino before we leave?"

Amy stood. "No thanks. I'll be up all night."

"I hear you. I usually stay away from caffeine at night."

"Here you go, Jason." Shelia handed him the big white box tied in red and white string.

"Thanks, Shelia." He handed her money and Amy the box.

"Oh no. You aren't sending these home with me."

"Yes, I am. Bring them to work with you tomorrow."

Amy shook her head. "Dear God, I know I'm going to be the one eating all these throughout the day."

"Make sure you leave room for dinner."

Jason led her out of the bakery and he guided her back to the stadium parking lot.

"Where did you park?" he asked.

"By the pole over there." She pointed to the lone car in the stadium parking lot.

"Not a problem. I will make sure you make it safely into your car."

"No thanks. I'll be fine."

"I'm not taking no for an answer."

When they got to her car, he leaned down, lifted her chin with his thick index finger and gave her a kiss on her lips. "Good night. I'll see you tomorrow," Jason said.

Jason closed the door and stepped to the side. Her body trembled. That kiss made her feel as if she were floating on air. As she pulled out of the parking lot, she could see him still standing there with his hands in his pockets. Once she got out of the lot and out of his vision, she pulled over to the curb and took a deep breath. What had just happened? Her heart was beating rapidly. This had been the last thing she expected to happen to her. She closed her eyes and touched her lips.

But that kiss? All she could say was wow.

Chapter Two

Francine yawned the whole way to the office. The night before, she had gotten very little sleep. After pitching the game of his life, Richie came home with pains in his right shoulder, which kept him up all night. He had made her promise not to breathe a word to anyone, not even Amy and Toni. He wanted to retire on top of his game, not be forced out because of an injury.

During the past fifteen years, they had been through a lot together. For most of Richie's professional career he had been on top. He had won the Cy Young award five times. As the years went by, his pitching got stronger and faster. Now, he feared he wouldn't be able to pitch up to the standard that he expected of himself.

Francine assured him that everything would be okay—he just needed to rest his arm. Whenever he had a lot of strikeouts in a game, he always had pain in his shoulder the

24

next day. She knew the routine. He wasn't going to say a word to the pitching coach. It was too early in the season. Besides, they were working on a five-man pitching rotation. Usually, they went down to a three-man rotation as the year went on, relying on the relief pitchers.

Before she left, she wrapped a towel full of ice onto his shoulder. Because he pitched the night before, he didn't have to report to the stadium until three o'clock. At that time, he would jump into the whirlpool and when he got out, receive a massage. This was his usual treatment the day after he pitched.

The driver behind her beeped, yelling a curse word. As she made an illegal left-hand turn, Francine stuck her hand out the window giving the famous hand gesture to the woman.

She took her usual spot in the corner of the lot, parking on a slant. Richie had given her a red pearl custom BMW for Christmas when her ten-year-old dented car finally broke down. She had the perfect spot where her car wouldn't get hit or sideswiped.

As she slid out of the car, she grabbed her handbag along with the folder Amy had given her the night before. There were a few things she needed to do at the office this morning before going out to show houses to two new prospective buyers.

Francine pushed the office door open and walked into the small reception area, which was equipped with a Keurig coffee machine along with various flavored K-cups. This morning a plate with assorted pastries replaced the usual tray of mini-bagels. Just what all three of them needed—more sweets.

"Good morning," she sang.

The first thing she saw when she walked into her office was a vase with two dozen red roses. She didn't know how Richie did it, but to this day, he knew how to melt her heart.

"Isn't my husband the best?" Francine reached for the small white envelope attached to the red ribbon on the crystal vase.

Amy appeared, slapping her hand away from the card. "Excuse me, but they aren't for you. You aren't the only one who gets roses around here."

Francine took a step back. "You're shitting me. They're for you."

"Yes, they are."

"Who?"

"Why don't you grab yourself a cup of coffee? I'll tell you all about it."

Francine placed the folder in the middle of the desk and slid her handbag into her bottom desk drawer. When she looked up, Amy's eyes were on her. She stood playing with her hands, rocking from side to side.

"Okay, spit it out."

"I didn't even put it in my mouth yet." Toni stood in the doorway with a cardboard tray with three Starbucks coffees in one hand and some cannoli in her other.

"I wasn't talking about you. Which one is mine?" Francine asked, pointing to the coffee.

"The one I wrote your name on."

Francine lifted hers out of the tray. "Our friend Amy has received those." She pointed at the roses.

"I knew they weren't mine." Toni laughed. "But Amy's? I would have never guessed."

"Okay, you guys, that's enough."

"Tell us. Who sent you the flowers?" Francine asked again.

"Jason Maddock."

"No freakin' way," Toni said. "Are you talking about Jason Maddock of the New York Rockets?"

"Yeah." Amy blushed.

"Oh my God. That is great. He is so hot. Where did you meet him?"

26

"Last night, silly, when we were at the sports club."

"You mean when you disappeared without saying goodbye," Toni said with a mouthful of cannoli.

"I didn't disappear. I walked over to Jason, not even knowing who he was. I had to look him up last night when I got home."

"You mean you didn't know he is a football player." Toni's eyes popped wide open.

"How the hell would I know? I don't follow football that closely. But," she twirled around on the thin heels of her shoes, "I sure know how to pick them."

"I'm impressed," Toni said. "Where did you two disappear to?"

"He took me down the block to the bakery."

"That dive place?" Toni asked.

"It's far from a dive. When I saw the outside, I thought the same thing. But inside, it's like being in a café in Italy. And the pastries are delicious."

"Aw. That's why we have pastries."

Francesca took a sip of coffee and made her way back to her desk. "I don't give a damn about the pastries. I want to know what happened last night."

"There isn't much to tell. After the bakery, he walked me to my car. He asked me to dinner tonight, and gave me a kiss good night."

"That's great," Toni said. "My friend's going out with Jason Maddock. Wow. That just blows me away. I hope you can get tickets for the games."

Amy held up her hand. "Woo. Take a chill pill. I'm only going on a date with him. Let's see what happens. We might not even like each other by the end of the date."

"Oh please. Don't go into this with a negative attitude," Francine said as she twirled in her chair. "Give things a chance. Take yourself back to when you were a teenager. Go out tonight with a carefree attitude. Go with the flow. See where it brings you."

"I didn't realize Richie knew him." Amy said.

"Oh yeah. He's been over to our house a few times."

"How did I miss him?"

"If I'm not mistaken, the last dinner party I had you had gone to Florida to visit your parents."

"Oh yeah, that's right."

Francine glanced down to the folder sitting on her desk. "Before we go any further with our love lives, I think we should concentrate on getting the ball rolling on this contract, especially since they have already been preapproved for the amount." Francine opened the folder. "If this sale goes according to plan, we will be three months ahead of the game."

"That's great news," Toni said. "And I think, I have another house for us too."

"Where?" Francine asked.

"Up on Ocean Terrace. While driving along, I saw a for sale by owner sign. I pulled over, called the owner and stopped in to see the house. We're talking a two and a half million-dollar home."

Francine crossed her legs and sipped her coffee. "No way."

"I don't believe it either," Amy said. "You are never that assertive."

Toni crossed her arms and tapped her foot. "Can you give me credit once in awhile?" She laughed. "Truth being I was sitting in traffic when the sign caught my eye. I made an appointment for eleven with the owner, making us the exclusive seller to sign the papers. Do you want me to handle it or do you want to go?"

"You can take this one. We want an exclusive. If the house is mint, we have the clientele to sell in a matter of a few weeks," Francine said.

"I hate to jinx things, but the past few months we have been taking over the Todt Hill area. I know Circles Real Estate is pissed," Amy said.

Francine stood, walking over to the tray of pastries. "We are a small real estate agency and give individual attention to every customer. That's why I insist that once a week we give our clients a call, keeping them informed of what's going on in the market. Now if we can get the house on Ocean Terrace, the O'Malley's would be the perfect couple for the house. That's the exact area they are looking for." Picking up a mini-napoleon, she broke it in half before popping it into her mouth. "Mmm. You better get these out of my sight or else I'm going to devour the whole platter."

The girls all giggled. Francine took a cream puff off the tray before returning to her desk.

"Are we going to the game tonight?" Toni asked.

"You know where I'm going." Amy giggled.

"I'm going to pass tonight. Richie isn't pitching. I'm going to spend a quiet night at home doing some housecleaning, ending the evening curled up in bed reading a romance novel."

"Once again, I'll be home alone."

"I got an idea, Toni. Why don't you go to the ballpark? I know you love going to the games. I'll call Richie and have him put your name on the list for tonight."

"Thank you. I think I'll take you up on the offer. I just wish you would come."

"I'd love to, but I need a night for myself." Francine yawned. "Truthfully, I want a night alone with my husband when he gets home. I hate this time of the year. I always try my best to stay up but find myself waking up the next morning, having no downtime with him."

"Gotcha. I know exactly what you mean." Amy pulled her hair back in a tiny ponytail.

Francine dropped her gaze back to her desk. The past few weeks had been hard for her. Richie had reported to spring training in Florida a few days before Valentine's Day. Last night had been the first time she had seen him since he left. The Pelicans opened the season in Cincinnati the week before. Last night they'd celebrated Richie's strikeout record and no-hitter. Tonight, she hoped to spend the night making love to her husband.

"Time we concentrate on work," Toni said.

"Now that's a first," Amy said, tapping her pen on the table.

Toni slid her chair back and stood. "I'm going to head over to the house."

"Good luck. Try your best to get a commitment from them," Francine said.

"I hope to be coming home with a signed contract."

Two hours later, Toni stopped at the corner restaurant, ordering a quick burger along with a bottle of beer. She couldn't help but clench both her fists in triumph before walking in. This had been her first two-million-dollar exclusive listing. Every time she had found a for sale by owner sign, she would jot down the address and phone number and gave it to Francine to take care of. Getting this listing had been exactly what she needed.

The past few months she hadn't gotten an exclusive or a sale. Francine never complained, but Toni knew she expected more from her. As the days passed by, her depression deepened. She was good at covering her feelings and keeping her emotions to herself. Ten years ago, she had gone away to her aunt's house in Tennessee. She had lied to her friends, telling them that her aunt was sick and needed help. But the truth of the matter was she had a nervous breakdown after she'd caught her live-in boyfriend in bed with her neighbor's daughter. The devastation of the betrayal put her right over the edge, sending her into a deep depression. Since then, she dated, but never let things go past a date or two, never making a commitment to avoid a repeat performance of the episode.

With her success of the day, she felt confident that things would start an upward spiral. On the way to the restaurant, she had jotted down two more houses for sale by owner, which she would look into while she ate lunch.

"Here you go." the waitress placed the burger and fries, along with a beer in front of her. "Enjoy."

Before she could thank her, she had already approached another table. Opening up her computer, she googled the first address. All the information popped right up on the screen. She shook her head. If she could land the first house, she was looking at an eight hundred and seventy-five-thousand-dollar home. She lifted her oversized hamburger and took a bite. Five years ago, she would have never come out to eat alone. Now, her computer acted as her companion.

After taking the last sip of her beer, within minutes the waitress placed another one in front of her.

Toni waved her hand. "No thank you. I didn't order another one."

"It's from one of the other customers."

"I don't care if it's from the President. My limit is one. I have to go back to work."

"You're telling me you can't play hooky for the afternoon?" A tall brown-haired man appeared next to her table.

"No, I can't."

The tall stranger sat in the chair opposite her. He placed his beer bottle down in front of him. "Why can't you take a few hours off from work to get to know me?"

"I don't know who you think you are, but I'm not in any mood for company."

He reached his hand out. "I'm Eric Summers."

"Antoinette. My friends call me Toni."

"Toni. Does Toni have a last name?"

"Yes. Belluci."

Eric smiled "Nice to meet you Toni Belluci."

"Same here."

"Would you mind if I joined you for a bit?"

Toni met Eric's gaze. "I guess so. But when I'm finished eating, I have to go back to work. I'm loaded with paperwork to do."

"That's fair enough." Eric dropped his hands and stood. "Let me go grab my suit jacket and briefcase."

While Eric returned to his table, Toni closed the top of her laptop and placed it into her bag. She glanced across the room to where Eric stood. He was tall, slim, not athletic at all with shoulders that seemed to go on forever. His short dark brown hair was spotted with gray. When he turned to walk back, she dropped her gaze so he didn't catch her checking him out.

"You seemed quite intense while looking at your computer. Was it work or were you playing a game?" Eric sat down and signaled the waitress, who came right over. "When you bring out my lunch, can you bring it here? I'll be eating with this beautiful young lady."

Toni's right eyebrow shot up. She couldn't remember the last time a man called her a young lady. Usually they would tell her she was too old for them. Hell, it wasn't her fault she had terrible genes. When she stood next to Francine and Amy, she looked like their older sister. At thirty-eight years old, she could pass for fifty. In high school, the other girls would mock her, asking her how many times she was left back. Either this man was blind, or he saw something else in her.

The waitress placed Eric's tuna salad sandwich down in front of him along with a Diet Coke. "Let me know if you need anything else." She turned to Toni. "Can I get you anything else?"

"No thanks." Toni's eye caught the big bag he placed on the chair next to him. "What do you have in that big suitcase of yours?" Toni pointed to the black bag.

Drugs."

Toni jerked her head back. "Drugs?"

"Don't get nervous." Eric opened the bag. "I'm a pharmaceutical rep. I'm the guy who ties up the doctors, making them run late."

"So you're the culprit." She smiled flirtatiously.

"Yes, I am."

"I would say you are the candy man. The one that has all the samples of the latest drugs on the market," Toni joked.

"I can't tell you how many times people ask me for samples. 'Hey, do you have any of those happy pills for me to try?' It's crazy."

"I can imagine, especially with Staten Island being known as the borough with the highest prescription drug use." Toni dipped a fry into ketchup before taking a bite.

"I'd have to agree with you on that."

"So that's what you do all day. Go from one doctor's office to the other?"

"Something like that. I call ahead to see if the doctor is interested in something new he'd like me to bring. But most times, I just show up." Reaching into his bag, he pulled out a composition notebook. "In here, I have all the information on every doctor in the area."

"Now that's old school. Where's your iPad?"

"I don't use electronics. I like writing everything down."

"Wow. Without my technology, I'm lost."

"Then maybe you are the right person to ask for help."

"What kind of help?"

"If I buy an iPad, would you help me set it up? Maybe give me a quick startup lesson?"

"Sure, why not."

"How about I take you out to dinner Saturday night?" he asked.

Toni shook her head. "Sorry, Saturday night isn't good for me. I already have plans."

"Then cancel them." He chuckled. "I'm sure they can't be any more important than having dinner with me."

33

"Sorry," she said again. How she hated when men pushed themselves on her.

"Then what night would be better for you? Tomorrow? Tonight?"

"Friday works fine for me." Toni thought for a few moments. She couldn't let her past experiences deter her from dating. Besides, Eric seemed like a nice guy.

Eric reached into his jacket pocket and took out his business card. Grinning, he flicked the card between his fingers before handing it to her. "Can I have your number so I can confirm and know where to pick you up?"

"I work late on Friday nights," Toni lied, not wanting to give him her home address. Opening her handbag, she took out her business card. "You can reach me at either number."

"Sorry, but I have to get going. I have a few phone calls to make for prospective clients." Toni signaled the waitress.

"Hey, I got this."

Toni raised both her hands waving them. "Oh no, you don't have to do that."

"It will be my pleasure."

"Okay," she agreed, standing. "Thank you."

Eric smiled. "I'll talk to you later."

* * *

Francine pressed accept on her phone. "Hey babe, what's going on?"

"Just got to the stadium."

Francine glanced at her watch. "You're late. What happened?"

"My mom stopped by with some goodies."

"Yummy. Is it what I think?" she asked, licking her lips.

"Manicotti, meatballs and coconut custard pie."

"Two of my favorites."

"I'm coming home straight after the game, so make sure you save me a slice of pie."

"I'll try to this time."

"See you tonight."

"Love you."

"Me too."

Francine hung up. Closing her eyes, she pictured Richie sitting on the round wooden bench with his white pants unbuttoned along with a navy tank top. She couldn't help but smile.

Her life had turned around when she met Richie. Francine tapped her hot pink fingernail against the desk. It had taken Richie's mom over two years to accept her. His mother was old school so she didn't like the fact she had no family structural background, as she called it. But as time went on, Francine slowly opened up to his mom, telling her that she had been in and out of foster homes for years, how she barely remembered her mom and dad. She assured her that she loved Richie and admired the family life he had.

Just when she thought his mother would never accept her, she had been surprised by a family barbecue where his mom invited the whole family, welcoming her into the family. Since then, she called his mother Lena, Mom. Through the years, while Richie was on the road, she always made it a point to have dinner with his mom, two brothers and a sister at least twice a week. After all these years of not having a family, she finally found what she had missed out on since she was eleven.

She found out both her parents were killed in a car accident by her Aunt Cindy. After the funeral, her aunt dropped her off at Child Services saying she was sorry but she couldn't take care of her. That was the last time she saw her. The only picture of Francine with her parents was taken at a family gathering right before the accident.

The bells on the door jingled. Francine looked into the small reception area. An older distinguished man dressed in a business suit with gold and diamond cufflinks approached her desk with an old-fashioned black briefcase.

"Good afternoon." Francine stood, extending her hand. "I'm Francine Raggalio."

"Sam Lockinster, Esquire. Nice to meet you."

"Same here. Please sit down." She pointed to the chair. "Can I get you a cup of coffee and a pastry?"

"No thank you. I will be staying only for a few minutes. Do you mind?" He placed his briefcase on the edge of her desk.

"Not at all."

He unhooked the lock and opened the briefcase like a doctor's bag. Reaching in, he took out an envelope and held it out to her.

"I needed to hand deliver this."

Francine looked at the sealed envelope. "What is this?"

"After looking through the documents, if you have any questions, you can give me a call." His hand disappeared into the briefcase. He handed her his business card. "Good luck with everything."

Before she could open the envelope or answer him, he already had reached the front door. The bells on the door jingled. He was gone.

Chapter Three

The bells jingled again. This time Toni walked into the office waving a file folder. "I just got us another exclusive. Looks like we are on a roll."

"Let me see."

Francine placed the envelope down on the table and took the folder from Toni. She flicked through the papers, smiling. "This is awesome. Good work."

"Thank you. I also have two other leads to check into. Then while getting something to eat, I met someone."

Francine dropped her gaze to the envelope sitting on her desk. Toni continued to talk but she didn't hear a word she was saying. Could it be that Richie had served her with separation papers? Maybe that was the reason why he didn't ask her this year to join him for a few days in Florida for the pitchers and catchers part of the early spring training and account for the reason why he didn't want to make love last night. He said his arm was sore and she believed him. But maybe it was all an act. Why did she always think like this? Maybe it was because her life ran too smoothly.

"Francine." Toni nudged her. "Did you hear a word I've said?"

Tears escaped from her eyes. "Sorry, no."

"What's wrong?"

"Nothing."

"Oh yes there is. I'm telling you about a man I just met, and you didn't make one single comment. What the hell are you staring at on your desk?"

Francine lifted the envelope. "The man, who left here right before you returned, dropped off this envelope for me."

"The one with the big gold chunky cufflinks?"

"Yes."

Toni sat in the chair next to her desk. "What's in the envelope that has you so upset?"

"I don't know. I didn't open it yet."

"Oh Francine. Don't do this to yourself. Open it. What do you think it is?"

"Separation papers."

Toni threw her hands up in the air. "You are sure as hell letting your imagination get the better of you. Richie is your soulmate. Don't go there with that nonsense before you even open the envelope. I'm here. Open it."

Francine took the letter opener off her desk. Slowly she slit the envelope open, took the papers out and sighed in relief. "They aren't separation papers."

"I could have told you that, silly. What do they say?"

"I'll read it to you."

Dear Mrs. Francine Millano-Raggalio,

I'm sure you have forgotten about me after all these years, but I haven't forgotten about you. You were only eighteen years old when I met you. You worked at Revco pharmacy on Bay Street. I would come in twice a month in my wheelchair with six prescriptions. Two were mine, four were my wife's.

I lost my wife many years ago. But I always remembered how you went out of your way for us, picking us up necessities from the store. Your kindness has always touched my heart. This is why I had to let you know how much you meant to me. I have never forgotten your kindness. I know you will use this gift in a way to make me proud.

When you're reading this, you will know I too, have passed on. Words could never describe how thankful we were.

God Bless you. Be happy.
Marvin Peacock

"Wow. Do you remember him?" Toni stood.

Francine stared at the letter. "That was such a long time ago. But I remember the couple. His wife Hannah would call the store asking for me. She would dictate a list of things she needed. I'd take a wagon, walk around the store and deliver the extras along with their medicine."

Toni placed the black mug down in front of her. "Why didn't the wife come?"

"She was paralyzed. They had gotten into a car accident on the way home from their grandson's graduation. That was such a long time ago. I'm surprised I remembered." Francine took a sip of coffee.

"What are the other papers?"

"Let me see." Francine placed the letter down, and lifted up the second sheet. "This is a deed to a piece of property in my neighborhood."

"No way. Let me see."

Francine handed her the deed. "This is on the other end of the Island. If I'm not mistaken this is the building in the deserted lot a few stores down from Katie Lingerie Boutique."

"Are you kidding me? That building has been deserted for years. It's covered by grass and debris."

"I don't remember. I usually always get a spot right in front of her store."

Toni stood. "I think we should go check out the property."

When Francine lifted the envelope, two keys tumbled onto her desk. "I guess these are the keys."

"What are we waiting for? Let's go check it out and make a stop at Katie Lingerie for a couple of sexy outfits."

"You are too much."

"What time is Amy coming back, so we can go?"

"She isn't. I gave her the afternoon off so she can prepare for her date tonight."

"Very nice. Keep this in mind when you let me go home to get ready for my date on Friday night." Toni walked to the door and turned the sign over so the word CLOSED faced the outside world. She pushed open the door with the bells jingling. "Let's go."

Francine didn't hesitate. After locking up, they got into her car and drove up the service road, pulling onto the ramp leading them onto the Staten Island Expressway. Once they got to the top of the ramp it become apparent the highway had turned into a parking lot.

Francine played with the idea of texting Richie with the news, but decided she'd wait to tell him. The beginning of the season was always hectic for him.

"Shit." Francine banged her hands on the steering wheel. "Why is this highway always like this no matter what time you get on it?"

"The worst part is the big concrete walls they put up. There is no way of knowing how bad it is until you get on it."

"Exactly. But this still winds up being the quickest way to get to the other side of the Island." Francine opened the window. "Why don't you get a little closer to me, asshole," she yelled out the window, giving the famous hand gesture.

The old gray-haired woman yelled, "Go to hell," as she continued to cut her off.

Francine shook her head. "I'm so done. I can't wait for all this construction to be completed. We have been doing this for the last few years."

"But it doesn't matter. No matter what time of the day you get on here, there is traffic. Once we get to the West Shore Expressway, we'll make up the time."

"We'll make up the time?" Francine laughed. "We are on no time schedule. The last time I was able to get out of the speeding ticket. I don't want to press my luck. Besides, I have all night before Richie comes home."

"That's why we have to stop at Katie Lingerie Boutique."

Francine smirked, glancing over at Toni. "Oh yeah. Richie loves when I wear a bustier. I'd like to get myself a black and red one."

"I'm sure she can help you with that. The outfit I love is the one-piece purple cat suit you bought last time you went there. Maybe I can borrow it sometime."

Francine giggled. "Yeah, why not."

"But then again, I might buy my own. Maybe this time I'll be able to wear it."

"Like I've been telling you for years. Just take your time. Someone special will come your way when you least expect it. Maybe it's even the new guy you just met, maybe not. But whatever you do, just enjoy life. See where it takes you."

"I agree. Why do you always have to make sense?"

"Who the hell knows? I don't have a clue to where the hell I'm going now. I usually go straight down Hylan."

"Get off the next exit," Toni pointed to the sign. "I'm getting excited. I can't wait to see what Marvin left for you."

"It's probably some small dilapidated storefront. I know at some point, he had told me he had a store down there where he sold garden hardware. When he became disabled, he had his nephew working at the store during the day. Once

41

I left that job, I lost track of him. Totally forgot about him until this afternoon."

Francine put her right blinker on and changed lanes, cutting off the truck in the lane next to her. She couldn't help it. Now she felt even with the old lady who cut her off earlier.

"When you get off, turn left on Page Avenue." Toni pointed, using her hand as a GPS.

"I know where I'm going now."

Francine weaved in and out of traffic. When she spotted Katie Lingerie Boutique, she didn't pull into the parking lot. Instead she continued to the deserted building with overgrown grass covering the walkway and parking spaces.

"Why don't you pull into the lot? It looks like the indentation in the curb is over there." Toni pointed.

"I see it, but not sure if it's a good idea to pull in there. I'm going to stop right here by the curb. We'll walk in."

"In these shoes?" Toni asked, pointing to her three-inch heels.

Francine rolled her eyes as she pushed the car door open and slipped out of the car into her ankle boots. "Thank God we're wearing pants. Look at all this shit here."

"I told you. I should have brought my sneakers with me."

"Too late now. Let's put on our big girl bloomers and dig through this rubbish to find the store."

Francine looked down as she walked through the weeds. The empty lot had turned into a dumping ground through the years. Countless bags of garbage, household objects and bottles were scattered all over.

"Hope there aren't any rats in here," Toni said.

"Geez, thanks. Stop thinking and keep walking. We only have a few more feet to go."

This was the one thing that bothered Francine about Toni. She always made a big deal out of everything they did. Then Toni would go and tell Richie, which would lead into his speech on why she shouldn't be doing this and how they have the money to let other people take care of things like this, so on and so forth.

Francine climbed over the last bag of garbage. Her eyes scanned from one side of the building to the other. Where was the door? She walked along the sidewalk in front and stopped when she realized all the windows were covered with wood. In the middle of the building were also two pieces of wood most likely covering the double doors.

"Toni, come here. I think I found the door."

"That's nice. I'm still fighting with the freakin' garbage. My heels keep getting stuck in something."

"Don't worry about it. I'll buy you a new pair of shoes or a nice outfit at Katie's."

Toni waved her finger. "I'm going to hold you to that."

"I'm sure you will."

After removing the wood, leaning against the door, Francine took the key out of her pocket and tried to slide it into the rusted lock. "Damn it. I need something thin and sharp."

"Just try the key again."

Francine waved her hand. "All right. I'll try again."

This time when she put the key in, she pushed it hard. She turned the key and heard the click. Slowly she pushed the double glass door open.

"What do you see?" Toni asked.

"Shit. It is so dark in there. I don't know how big the area is."

"Do you still have the big flashlight in your trunk?"

"I think I do. I also have the small one in my handbag."

"Give me your keys. I'm going to go and get the flashlight."

Francine handed her the keys. While Toni returned to the car, she pulled out the small flashlight she always carried around with her and shined it around. To her surprise this wasn't just a small store—this looked like a restaurant.

Stepping a few steps into the building, she flashed the light to her right where there was a podium. On the top was an appointment book. Looking up to the last date, she found it read November 1, 2008. Lowering the flashlight, on the side of the podium was a shelf, which held menus. Lifting a menu out, it read Nikki's Bar and Restaurant established 1999.

"Francine," Toni's voice echoed from outside.

"I'm here," she said sticking her head out. "I am so confused. What is this building I was left?"

Toni walked in with the big hurricane flashlight. "Looks like a deserted restaurant to me."

"What in God forsaken name am I going to do with this?"

"We can always sell the property."

"I don't know, Toni. I'm getting this feeling Marvin left me this for a reason because he knew I wouldn't sell the property for a builder to knock down and build more multimillion dollar homes."

Toni nodded her head smirking. "Think of the money we can make."

"Let's walk farther in."

As they wandered around, everything looked untouched. The tables were still set with dishes and water glasses. Francine continued walking through the restaurant with Toni following behind with her hurricane flashlight.

"Look," Toni pointed to some door. "Let's go check what is in there."

With her penlight flashlight, Francine walked forward and pushed the doors open. When Toni came in with the light, Francine sighed.

"Oh my God, Toni. This is a full-size kitchen. Look over there. I see pizza ovens too. What did this man leave me? I was thinking of a small store with rusted tools hanging all over. Instead, this is a huge building."

"Maybe Katie can tell us something about this property. She's been down here for years. I don't remember this place being here at all."

"Neither do I. I think what we need to do is come back with someone who has a generator so we can light up the whole inside. It's just so hard to figure out what's going on in here."

"I'll ask my brother. I know he's working on a house somewhere down in Great Kills. Hopefully he can meet us here sometime tomorrow so we get a better grip on things. Do you have any thoughts?" Toni asked walking back toward the front doors.

"First, we will find out exactly what this building is all about. And then I'll talk to Richie about it. With him retiring at the end of the year, maybe this is something we can look into."

"Can't see that going over very big with Richie."

Francine pulled the glass doors shut and locked the door. "This might be the perfect thing for us opening up some kind of business. He'll go crazy sitting home all day."

"Maybe he can get a job on the pitching coach staff and work at one of the local colleges."

"I know my husband. He can't sit still. He has to do something." Francine walked back to her car and slid in. "Let's take a ride around the corner, see what's behind this place before we stop at Katie's."

"Works for me."

They drove to the back of the building. "Hey, look at this," she said, pulling into the small dirt driveway behind the building. "There is another entrance to the back."

"Do you want to check it out?"

"Nah. We'll come back tomorrow with our sneakers and jeans. Try to get the generator from your brother."

"I'll call him now."

Francine drove around the back of the building, making her way down the street to the front of the strip mall. She slipped right into the spot in front of Katie Lingerie Boutique. Francine got out of the car, leaving Toni still talking on the phone with her brother.

"Hello," Francine called into the store.

"Oh my God. I can't believe it." Katie opened her arms. Francine hugged her.

"I was in the neighborhood. You know I couldn't pass here without stopping in to get something sexy for Richie."

"I know exactly what he likes. And that game he pitched the other night, oh my freaking God. I was on the edge of my seat. Twenty strikeouts, that's a new record. Then to add to the excitement, he just missed pitching a perfect game."

"I'll take the no-hitter anytime. That first inning was the first and only time a runner saw the first base line." Francine lifted both her hands. "By the top of the eighth inning, it's all everyone was talking about."

"Richie must have been nervous."

"He never is." A black and white lace outfit caught Francine's eye. "Richie never takes things like no-hitters and one-hitters to heart. His main concern is winning the game."

Francine took a size medium off the hook. "Now this is my main concern. I can see Richie's face lighting up as I open the door for him later on."

Katie pinched Francine's cheek. "That's what I love about you. You come here to buy something to seduce your husband with. Most women after being married all these years would be buying one of these for their lover."

"Oh stop it." Francine laughed, and then pointed. "I see something else in the front of the store."

"I bet it's this one," Toni said, holding up a black one-piece cat suit.

"How well you know me."

"That is one of my best sellers," Katie said. "I just got the black one in. A few women have already come in here complaining that the only color I had it in is purple."

"Then it looks like I am the only one happy." Francine took the hanger from the rack and flicked the tag in her hand, making sure it said medium. "Didn't you find something?"

"I did." Toni turned and lifted four hangers off the small white wooden table. "I found two bras. One black and the other nude." She held them up. "Then I found this cute zebra print nightgown with a matching short silk robe."

"Nice. I love the zebra print." Francine reached for a red and a black bra off the rack. "I'm going to try these on too."

Toni gave her the thumbs up. "You go, girl. You are going to make Richie a very happy man later."

"I sure as hell hope so, especially when he sees the bill."

"Just remind him of how good the sex is while he's opening the bill," Katie threw in.

Francine giggled as she walked to the small dressing room in the back of the store. After removing the black and purple cat suit off the hanger, she slid it on. Turning sideways she held her hand over her stomach. The cat suit actually looked good on her. She would definitely be able to wear it under her jeans and shirt later on.

Rubbing her stomach, she whispered into the mirror, "If only." Francine squeezed her eyes shut. *Don't even go there.*

Everyday she thanked God for giving her the life she had. She had a wonderful husband who stood by her side. At twenty-five years old, she had been pregnant with twins. They were so happy. But the outcome was one they never expected. By the seventh month, she went into premature labor. Both babies were stillborn. Francine insisted on a burial. To this day, she still visited her daughters once a week, bringing flowers and stuffed animals to their grave. A few years later they had tried again, but each pregnancy ended in a miscarriage within the first two months.

Francine ran her fingers through her hair taking a deep breath. Time to push those memories back into the vault. Why move backwards, when the future held so many more opportunities to reach out for.

Outside the dressing room, she could hear Katie and Toni talking about the new bakery shop across the street that made all kinds of cupcakes. When Katie mentioned the old dilapidated building down the block, Francine rushed to get dressed. She wanted to find out about the building. But Toni did what Toni did best, she quickly readjusted the conversation back to a pair of thongs she had missed on the wall behind the register.

Once she was dressed, she pushed the dark brown curtain to the side and walked out to the counter where Toni had placed a nice sized pile of lingerie.

"How'd you make out?" Katie asked. "We were waiting for you to come out and model for us."

"Never. You know I don't like parading around with bedroom gear in the store. You never know who will show up."

Katie laughed so hard she had tears in her eyes. "My favorite time was when you were standing here in the nude colored bustier, when a photographer from the Enquirer walked in. You grabbed the silk bathrobe off the hanger and ran into the back, tying it as you went along."

"You're lucky he didn't get a picture of me. Richie would have killed me."

"His last words to you were, 'next time you want to go down to Katie's, we're going together,'" Toni mimicked.

"Hell. He's at the ballpark. I can't sit home or in the office all day long. Besides, no one cares about us. We just blend into the crowd."

"You girls should love the publicity." Katie lifted up her black thigh-high boots, which had fallen below her knee. "Who wants to be another face in the crowd? I know I don't."

All three of them laughed until tears escaped from their eyes. Every time they visited Katie they left in good spirits.

"Katie, about the abandoned building down the street, do you know the story?"

"Only through hearsay." Katie took the thongs off the small clear plastic hangers, folding them neatly into a square. "From what I understand, when the hardware store closed twenty years ago, it remained vacant until the restaurant opened. It only lasted a couple of years. A few years ago, two men started construction on the building but soon abandoned the project."

"I wonder why?"

"The place is an eyesore. I wish someone would do something with it or knock it down," Katie concluded.

Toni placed a bottle of sandalwood scented hot oil on the counter. "Add this too."

"Gotcha." Katie looked at Francine. "What were we talking about?"

"The building down the block will not be looking like that for much longer."

"Did you hear something I didn't?" Katie asked her eyes bulging open.

"I'm the owner of the property."

"You're kidding me."

"Nope." Francine went on to tell Katie the story of how she acquired the property. "We're
going to be neighbors." Katie's face shined.

"I didn't make any decision yet on the property. I'll have to discuss it with Richie after the game. I sent him a post earlier but I must have just missed him."

"Keep me posted."

"I will." Francine placed her outfits on the counter next to Toni's. "Time to roll." She twirled around, removed red, black, navy and white thongs in different styles, and placed them on the counter with her things.

"Anything else?" Katie asked. "A new vibrator, cock ring?"

Francine pushed her merchandise closer to Katie. "Please."

Toni pointed at Francine. "Look at her blush," she said to Katie. "She acts like she had never seen an adult toy, or used one."

"That's it. Ring me up. Time to go."

"She's such a prude," Toni joked.

"Don't listen to her. Start talking dirty in front of her," Francine pointed at Toni, "and she'll turn red as an apple."

"I'm done here too."

"Everyone who walks into my shop always leaves here smiling." Katie readjusted her headband, pushing her blonde hair out of her eyes. "This is a happy place. Good things always happen in here." Katie glanced at her watch. "I didn't realize the time. I have to get ready. I have a psychic coming in tonight. She's booked until two o'clock in the morning."

"Would you like me to grab you a bite to eat from the diner?" Francine asked, handing Katie her Visa card.

"No thanks. I have a cheese and crackers platter coming later on."

"I'd love to come in for a psychic reading the next time she comes. Just give me a call, let me know," Francine said.

"I will."

Francine took her bag from Katie and hugged her goodbye. "I will let you know how my two outfits pan out." Francine opened the door to the shop and turned to Katie, who sat on the bar stool behind the counter. "I'll have Richie leave you two tickets for Saturday's game at the window."

"I'll try to get there. Saturday is usually my busy day."

Francine blew her a kiss. "Hope to see you. Richie is pitching on Saturday."

"Can't make you any promises, but I'll try my best."

Chapter Four

Amy chose a tan skirt, which fell right above her knees, complemented by an electric blue button-down silk shirt and black pumps. After leaving the office early, she spent the day shopping for the perfect outfit. Now, looking at herself in the full-length mirror on the back of her bedroom door, she wasn't sure if her outfit was the right choice.

Jason Maddock wasn't like the guys she had recently met. The big-shots who bragged about themselves before leaving her with the bill were the kind of guys she kept meeting.

Earlier, she did some research on the Internet at work, checking on the kind of women Jason had been involved with in the past. The line of women kept on getting longer and more sickening. In every picture, Jason was seen with a model, actress or singer. There wasn't one picture of him with a real estate broker. Amy sighed. Why did she always second-guess herself? She deserved to meet a good man.

Amy took her jewelry box out of the closet, opened it and chose a sterling silver heart pendant necklace with matching bracelet and earrings. Taking another look in the mirror, she shook her head. She had to have faith in herself.

When Jason called her in the morning, she'd thought he was canceling their date. Instead, he called to tell her he'd pick her up at eight o'clock since they had reservations at La Fontana at eight-thirty. After stressing out all day on what to wear, the thought of what to talk about now became her obsession. Knowing the game of football would be a plus, but she was sure it wouldn't be the first thing on his conversation list.

"Stop it," Amy said out loud. She had to just go with the flow. Let Jason take the lead. Maybe Francine could enlighten her on what to say when the conversation started to go south. As she reached for the phone, the doorbell rang.

Amy took a deep breath before walking to the door. The moment she opened it, she smelled Jason's cologne. Jason wore a navy suit with a white shirt and blue striped tie and a smile on his face. His hair was cut short and the five o'clock shadow that appeared on his mocha cheeks the day before was now gone.

"You look stunning." Jason leaned over and gave her a kiss on her cheek. "I'm generally not a flower and candy kind of man. But I know the way to a woman's heart."

He handed her a hot pink gift bag with neon green tissue paper sticking out of the top. Amy separated the gift paper and took out a Sephora eye shadow and blush palette.

"I love it, Jason. I'd take this any day over candy and flowers." Amy slid the box back into the bag and placed it on the half moon-shaped oak table sitting by the front door. "Thank you." She reached on her tippy toes to kiss him on the cheek.

Jason squeezed her shoulder and smiled. "Sorry I'm a few minutes late, but the traffic on the Staten Island Expressway is backed up in both directions. That's why I'd rather arrive early and have a cocktail at the bar."

"That sounds nice."

They walked out to the car. Jason opened the door for her, waiting for her to settle in with her seat belt before closing it. She watched him walk around the front of the Jeep. He slid into his seat and stretched his seat belt over his firm muscles.

"Have you been to La Fontana recently?" Jason asked.

"I haven't been there in years. The food in phenomenal."

"Yes, it is. I'm hoping the piano player is there. That would make the night more intimate. I asked for the table in the back room so no one interrupts us while we're eating."

"I can imagine."

"Don't get me wrong. I love giving autographs, especially to the young kids. That's why I do a lot of charity work on the Island."

"Why Staten Island?" she asked, pushing a few loose hairs behind her ear.

"Because it's now my hometown."

"Really?"

"You seem surprised. I moved here six years ago when I got traded to the New York Rockets. I was born and raised in Boston. I now live off Ocean Terrace."

"You know where I live. I was born and raised in Staten Island."

"And I bet you went to Catholic school too."

Amy giggled. "Yes, I did, from kindergarten through high school. How about you?"

"I went to public school. I lived in a two-bedroom apartment with my mother, two sisters and grandmother. Some nights we were lucky if there was food on the table."

"I grew up in the same house my mother grew up in. I go every Sunday for dinner and have to make the daily phone call to my mom every night at six."

"Is your dad still alive?"

"Alive and driving my mother crazy everyday."

"Sounds like my family."

The more they talked, the more their family lives seemed to run parallel. Every so often, Amy would sneak a peak at Jason's forearms, which flexed as he glided the car through the traffic

Jason pulled up to the valet sign. When the valet approached the car, he got out. By the time she took her handbag off the floor, Jason had her door open. He held out his hand and she placed hers in his as he led her down the navy-blue carpet. When they reached the door, he let go of her hand.

Jason opened the glass door. "I am so glad you accepted my dinner invitation."

"Why wouldn't I?" Amy asked walking in.

"You're a beautiful woman. I've had my eye on you for quite some time. You always walk into the club with Francine. I tried to make eye contact with you numerous times, but you never noticed."

"Good evening, Mr. Maddock." The tall gray-haired man dropped his eyes to the appointment book. "Your table is ready. If you would follow me."

Jason placed his hand under her elbow, leading her to their table in the corner. He held out her chair, waiting for her to settle in before sitting next to her. By the time he sat down, the waitress stood at their table.

"Good evening, Mr. Maddock. What can I get you from the bar this evening?"

"Ketel Vodka and cranberry juice," he said to the waitress. "What's your poison?"

Amy giggled. "I'll have a mimosa with a twist of orange."

"Hmm. So you're a champagne kind of a gal."

"Not at all. I never drink champagne straight. I really don't drink anything straight except for Sambuca."

"Now you're talking. I like Sambuca too." Jason hesitated for a few moments. "I enjoy my drinks during the off-season. But as soon as preseason begins, the only time I drink is after the game. I have to make sure I keep in shape."

"I'm really not a big drinker either. I drink socially. If told I could never drink another day in my life, I wouldn't lose any sleep."

The waitress returned with their drinks and a basket of bread and handed each of them a menu. "I'll give you some time to decide what you'd like."

"We'll start with a hot and cold antipasto platter. Extra mozzarella and stuffed mushrooms."

"Not a problem, Mr. Maddock."

As Amy looked around the restaurant, she made eye contact with a few people, who smiled. She was sure they recognized Jason and respected his privacy. Crossing her legs, she leaned back in her chair, feeling a little more comfortable having her drink in her hand to play with.

"Besides going out for dinner, what else do you enjoy doing?" Jason took a piece of bread out of the basket and took a bite.

"I'm pretty easy." After she said it, she covered her mouth with her hand.

"It's okay." Jason reached over and ran his finger along her cheek. "Has anyone ever told you how cute you look when you blush?"

Amy dropped her hands to the table. "No. I usually don't put my foot in my mouth."

"I know what you meant."

"People think I'm a diva. But I'm not. So in answer to your question, I'd have to say that the best things in life are free."

"Hmm." He rested his chin on his right hand. "Interesting cliché. Tell me more."

"I love going to Central Park, stopping by Strawberry Fields and sitting by the fountain. Coney Island is another one of my favorite places to go to." Amy took a piece of bread out of the basket and spread a thin layer of butter on the top.

"Do you like the theater?"

"I don't mind the occasional movie." Amy lifted her glass. "I usually fall asleep in the movie theater. Anyway with Netflix, I can watch a movie anytime I want."

Jason laughed a little too loud, causing the couple at the table next to them to look over.

"Sorry for interrupting your dinner," Jason said nonchalantly to the elderly couple.

The gentleman reached out to shake his hand. "It's okay. I didn't forget what it felt like to be a young couple in love."

Amy bit her bottom lip. For the first time that night she felt awkward. She dropped her glance to her fingers wrapped around her glass and relished the intrusion of the waitress placing the two platters down on the table.

"I can't believe we're on our first date," he said, picking up the fork. "Please help yourself. I can assure you that everything here is delicious."

Amy's eyes shot wide open. "Everything smells awesome."

"I wish I could take a picture of your face."

"Why?"

"When I said first date, you look surprised."

"Yeah, I am." Amy played with the cloth napkin on her lap.

"I'm hoping it's a good one. Because I would like to have a second date."

"You would?"

"You can't understand how refreshing it feels to be here with you. Most women by now are all over me, looking to show me off to their friends. You are different."

"What I really love doing is throwing on a pair of jeans and sneakers and going to a rock concert."

"No way." His eyebrows shot up. "Now you're talking my game. I love going to concerts. Last year I took my sister's kids to Warp Tour. I think I had more fun than they did."

"I'm sure you did. I love listening to all kinds of music. Music soothes the soul."

"Oh, a woman after my own heart. I had a music system installed throughout my house. I can listen to music in every room. I enjoy Motown and R & B."

"So do I. But I also like my classic disco and rock."

"Oh yeah." Jason pointed to the corner of the room. "Looks like I picked the perfect night to take you out.

"I think you are right."

The chatter of people's voices was drowned out when the piano music started. In a way, Amy felt relieved. This would give them a chance to gather their thoughts. Now that they covered the music, what could they possibly talk about?

Jason slid his chair back and stood, removing his suit jacket. He reached his hand out to Amy.

"Let's dance."

Amy looked around the restaurant. There was only one couple whirling on the small dance floor surrounding the piano.

Placing her hand in his, she stood and he led her out onto the dance floor. He slid his free arm around her waist, while Amy rested her hand on his shoulder. She hadn't realized just how tall and muscular he was. Even with three-inch heels on, Jason still towered over her.

They danced for the next two songs. By the end of the third song, Jason held her tightly against him. He stepped back, leaned down and softly kissed her lips. Amy, surprised by his gesture, didn't resist. When their lips parted, he rested his hands on her shoulders.

"Thank you for the dance."

What Amy wanted to say was the kiss had made her whole night. But instead she said, "Thank you."

"We'll be up again to dance."

"I sure hope so."

For dinner Francine ate her mother-in-law's manicotti and meatballs. She sat on the couch with a glass of red wine with her feet up on the black granite cocktail table. Earlier, she had strategically placed candles throughout the living room, with her favorite being a six-tier spiral tea light candleholder. She had gotten that from her friend Flo for an engagement present. Each time she used it, she remembered her friend.

Flo's natural strawberry blonde hair and big blue eyes always had the guys going crazy. Though the way Flo's life had ended always brought sadness to Francine's heart, she couldn't help but have happy memories of the time they had shared in college.

The car commercial ended. It was now the top of the ninth, with the Pelicans up by two runs. All Andy Napoli had to do was get three quick outs, and Richie would be home within an hour, as long as there was no traffic.

Each time Richie came home from a road trip, Francine would find a different way to set the scene. Keeping her marriage fun and alive had been the easy part. Money had never been a problem either. While Richie went through the minor-league system, they lived in a small apartment while Francine worked on building up her real estate company.

Francine looked at their wedding picture. At times she would swear their marriage was the perfect fairy tale. The only thing missing was the pitter-patter of kids running up and down the spiral staircase. They had come close but decided not to try anymore. The emotional stress had been too hard to bear.

They accepted that having kids just wasn't in their cards with both of them being content in their lifestyle. Besides, Richie's older sister had four, three boys and one girl, that would come and stay with them when his sister went on business trips with her husband. Francine loved when the kids came so she could spoil them.

Glancing up at the television, her eyes fixated on the upper left hand corner of the screen where the score remained the same. However, there was one out, with runners on the corners, the leading run at the plate.

"Come on, Andy. I want my husband to come home."

The manager walked out to the mound, tapping his right arm. The camera immediately panned to the bullpen where Bob Appleton threw his last pitch before walking over to the outfield gate. As the camera followed Bob, she spotted Richie standing up in the bullpen dugout calling something out to Bob.

"Let's go, Bob. Get out of this inning. I want my man home with me," she yelled at the television.

Francine stood, pacing around the candlelit living room, as Bob took his eight warm up pitches. The batter walked up to the plate, swinging his bat. Bob's first pitch was low. The second pitch the batter hit up the third base line, going foul. This caused a stir from the opposing team's bench. Watching the replay, it was apparent the umpire made the wrong call.

Crossing her arms, Francine sat on the edge of the couch. She rocked back and forth. The last time this happened, the other team tied the game and Richie found her fast asleep on the couch when he got home after two in the morning. But tonight, she worried for nothing. The batter hit a ground ball to second base. Neil stepped on second and threw the ball to first for a double play. Francine leaped off the couch. She had less than an hour to get things in order.

The first thing on the list to do was to get ready. Grabbing the basket of folded towels off the sofa, she carried it upstairs. Richie and she hardly argued, but they could not agree upon hiring a live-in housekeeper. Francine was totally against it. She didn't mind doing laundry or even cooking their meals. Most of the time Richie was on the road, so takeout had been her main form of eating. She didn't see any sense in dirtying the kitchen for herself.

Francine took the sky-blue plastic Katie Lingerie bag off the leather lounge chair in the corner by the window. The first thing she pulled out was the black and purple cat suit. She struggled to get it on. Every time she brought something home it never fit the way it did at the store. Tonight, everything had to be perfect.

In her walk-in closet, Francine chose a pair of black tights and an oversized black shirt. She slid on a pair of flats but took the black stilettos off the shelf and carried them downstairs with her, leaving them behind the couch.

Soft music echoed through their house when Francine turned the switch on. They loved their music. During the off-season, they even took ballroom dancing classes. Many a night, they danced around the living room, not leaving each other's arms. Her life couldn't be any more complete.

Francine checked all the candles, making sure none of them had gone out. The room smelled of vanilla, their favorite scent. She'd wait for the morning to tell him about the building, something else she had to figure out what to do with. Hopefully Toni's brother came through with a generator so they could see exactly what was in the building.

Once she had everything in order she went upstairs to take a hot bubble bath. Before getting in, she moved her glass of red wine to the edge of the tub and turned on the soft music. The moment she stepped in, she moaned in delight. This had always been her routine all these years while waiting for Richie to come home; a long hot soak, complemented by vanilla body scrub to soften her skin. Once the hot water started getting warm, she turned the water off. Francine rested her head on the back of the tub and listened to the music. After taking her last sip of wine, she lifted the plug covering the drain and got out.

Francine slipped into her thick white robe and began tackling her long, wet hair, which always took forever to dry. With the round brush she pulled her hair so that the curls dissipated. Richie loved the curls, but when she dressed up, he loved her hair when she straightened it. The last thing to do before getting dressed was to carefully apply her makeup. Francine took pride in always looking perfect for Richie. Once dressed and satisfied with the way she looked, she returned downstairs.

The sound of the key in the door made her heart skip a beat. Standing in the middle of the living room, Francine turned to face the doorway. She could hear above the soft music the sound of his sneakers squeaking on the marble hallway floor.

"I'm in here," Francine called out.

Richie walked in with a bouquet of red roses. "I couldn't wait to get home," he muttered.

Francine read the disappointment in his voice. No doubt he expected her to be wearing something sexy and laying on the couch.

"I waited all night too. Let me shut off the television."

"You were watching the game."

"Yes, I was. I wanted to be ready for you when you got home." Francine walked to the side of the couch and slid her feet into the stilettos.

Richie held out flowers. "I thought you would like these to start the evening."

"Yes. I love them." Francine walked over to Richie and kissed his lips before taking the roses from him. "I'm going to run these into the kitchen to put them in water. I'll be right back."

"I'll be waiting for you."

Francine bit her bottom lip to stop her from laughing. Boy, was he in for a big surprise when she walked back into the living room.

Quickly she placed the roses in the vase. Next she slid out of the black tights and pulled the oversized black shirt over her head. Folding them neatly, she placed them on the kitchen table.

"Can I get you anything while I'm in here?" she called out, pouring red wine into their glasses.

Francine placed the cork back into the bottle. Just as she was about to turn around, she smelled Richie's cologne, meaning he stood in the kitchen. She twirled around on the heels of her four-inch black stilettos to see Richie grinning at her.

To her surprise, he too had a surprise for her. He wore black silk boxers with a black tank top. His green eyes glared right through her. To this day, when he looked at her, she felt the same sensation she did the first time they met.

Richie pointed to her. "You look absolutely delicious. It looks like we both had the same idea to surprise one another."

"Yes, it does." Francine went to take a step toward him, but he held up his hand.

"Not yet, sweetheart. We have all night."

"We do?" Francine asked, crossing her arms. "I don't understand."

"The good news is tomorrow is an off day."

"And the bad?"

"We don't have another day off for twenty-two days."

"Bad news," she shook her head, "but I say we live for the day." Francine dropped her hands to her hips. "I can come meet you anytime I want."

"Always. I especially love when you come and surprise me when I'm on the road."

Francine took the two glasses of wine off the counter and handed one to Richie. "My business also helped pay the bills while you played down in the minors."

"For that I will always be grateful to you. You have always supported me through the good times and bad. That's why I would like to discuss what we're going to do when I retire at the end of the season."

"Can't we have that conversation later?" Francine tapped her glass into his before taking a sip.

"We can."

Francine placed her glass on the kitchen table and slowly turned to face him. "I waited all day to see you, feel you, taste you." She licked her lips. "We have the rest of our lives to talk about what the future holds for us once you retire. But for now, I want to feel your body pressed against mine."

Richie extended his arms. Slowly, Francine walked over to him, taking his hands and placing them around her waist. Lifting her head, she leaned into Richie. The taste of wine still lingered on his lips.

She ran her fingers up his muscular chest. As they kissed, Francine played with his nipples. Within seconds they were hard.

After all these years, his sparkling green eyes still set her on fire along with his dimples. He had recently cut his hair short, as he did at the start of every season and she couldn't wait for his thick black hair to grow back in.

Richie moaned. "You know how that makes me feel," he softly spoke in her ear.

Sliding her tongue down his neck, she pushed his wife beater tank top to the side. Her tongue glided over his nipple, causing him to grab onto her ass. "Yeah, I know." She went from one nipple to another, keeping her hands firmly on his muscular chest.

"Oh just like that. You are driving me crazy."

"I can tease you all night long, just like when we were kids."

"We can, but we won't."

He gathered her into his arms, carrying her up the spiral staircase with her black stilettos dangling over the railing. The last time he carried her up the stairs was when they moved into this house over ten years ago. Usually they chased each other up the stairs, collapsing on the bed.

Love and passion shined in his green eyes. Every time he looked at her, she remembered the first time their eyes met. He'd glanced at her over the Bunsen burner in the chemistry lab. She thought the orange flame had blended with his eyes, making them look greener. When her lab partner turned it off, their eyes met again, and she felt a surge of electricity travel throughout her. After lab, he'd followed her to her locker and asked her if she'd like to catch a burger and fries at A & W. She accepted and they had been together ever since.

Richie pushed the bedroom door open. Inside, Francine had already lit the candles and had adjusted the music to just the right volume. Gently, Richie placed her down on the bed.

"You have made everything perfect, setting the scene, looking beautiful."

Francine kept her eyes on Richie as he lifted his shirt over his head. Tan lines were evident from the six weeks he had spent at spring training camp. Richie's feet were always white, with tan lines above his knees and at the end of his biceps.

"I waited all day to come home," he whispered. Lifting her right leg, he slid her right shoe off, before proceeding to remove her left. "You make each time we're together special."

"I don't ever want to lose what we have together."

"Oh baby, you never will." Richie lay down next to her, pushing her chestnut color hair out of her eyes. "Why would you say that?"

Francine dropped her gaze to the bed. "I don't know. I just worry when you retire…"

Richie put his finger over her lips. "You have nothing to worry about. Once I retire we are going to enjoy life. Travel. Do all the things we wanted to do but couldn't. Why the insecurity, Francine? Did someone say something to you?"

"No. It's our fairy tale. We have beaten all the odds. High school sweethearts never stay together for all these years."

"We're not everybody. Now get these ridiculous thoughts out of your mind or else I'm going to put you over my knee and spank you."

"Yeah, yeah, keep teasing."

They both laughed. Richie always knew what to say to lighten up any mood. He always teased her about spanking or tying her up. But deep down, he was the kindest and gentlest man she had ever met.

Richie ran his long fingers along her cheek, outlining her lips. He played with the Spandex lace on her cat suit as his lips crushed against hers, making her body shake in excitement. Standing up, Richie reached his hands out to her. She took them and stood inches away from him.

"I want to look at you, my beautiful Francine," he whispered. "You are more beautiful than the day I met you."

After he said it, he pulled Francine against him. Francine put her arms around his waist, dropping them down to his rock-solid butt. Her husband did not have a flat ass. Instead he had enough for her to squeeze, which was exactly what she did as he kissed her neck.

Pushing the cat suit over her shoulders, he kissed her shoulders. The further down he pushed the Spandex, the more excited she became as the sensation of his lips capturing her body drove her excessively wild.

Francine's breathing became heavy as her wetness dripped down her inner thighs. Francine pushed Richie's silk briefs down before stepping out of the cat suit, and then leaped into his arms, wrapping her legs around his waist.

Richie lowered her onto the bed. "Tonight, it's just you and me."

Chapter Five

The sun peeked through the small opening in the drapes, shining directly into Francine's eyes. She turned onto her side, reaching out for Richie only to feel the empty pillow under her fingernails. Once spring training started, unless they were the home team, Francine woke up to an empty bed.

Disappointed, Francine turned back over and threw the blanket over her head. Through the blanket, she smelled the faint aroma of coffee. But the other smell, what was it? Giggling under the covers, she knew what she smelled—a total mess in the kitchen.

Whenever Richie was home, he insisted on a big breakfast, consisting of bacon, eggs, potatoes and toast. A big breakfast for her was a large cup of Starbucks coffee and a Special K bar. Francine never had bacon or eggs in the refrigerator, so most times they would go out to the corner diner for breakfast.

"Get up, sleepy head."

Francine threw the covers down and gasped. Richie stood at the edge of the bed holding a long, rectangular floral tray.

"Wow. I'm at a loss for words." Francine sat and crossed her legs.

"Now that's a first." Richie chuckled. "I thought we would spend the day in bed."

Richie placed the tray in the center of the bed, before sitting down next to her.

Francine lifted her coffee mug off the tray, warming her hands. "Baby, I wish I could. But I have a lot of things to do at work today."

"Not a problem. I already spoke to Amy and Toni. They'll handle things today." Richie took a sip of his coffee. "Amy did say she would call you in a bit to tell you about her date last night. And Toni said she couldn't get the light you needed."

"That's right. Amy had dinner with Jason," Francine said ignoring the part about Toni.

Richie pulled his head back. "An unusual match, don't you think?"

"Not at all. Amy loves her football. Besides, she has a heads-up watching how I've lived all these years. She will do just fine."

"He's a ladies' man. An eligible bachelor with women constantly swarming all around him."

"Yes, you're right. But it was Amy he asked out. And I really don't think he would do anything to hurt her, especially being our friend."

"I agree with you there." Richie took a slice of toast and dipped it into his poached egg. "Jason is a good catch for the right woman."

"I'm sure it's hard trying to separate the women who like him from those who pursued him because he is a star football player."

"That's why we are lucky. Who would have thought high school sweethearts would still be together after all these years?"

"Sometimes love is a fairy tale with many major bumps along the way."

Richie leaned over, kissed the top of her head. "We've been together from the start. You supported me during the darkest time of my career."

"Yes, I did. But you were always there for me too. We grew from two crazy teenagers in love to even crazier adults." Francine lifted a piece of bacon off her dish.

"That's why when we get days like this, we need to enjoy them, relish every moment we can spend together."

Holding up the half-eaten piece of bacon, she asked, "Turkey bacon?"

He patted his six-pack abs. "Have to watch the weight."

"Of course. Unless your mom sends you over another tray of manicotti or lasagna stuffed with meatballs and sausage."

"Hey," he opened his arms. "Who could pass up a home cooked meal from their mother?"

"You make it sound like I don't cook for you." Francine bit on her bottom lip to prevent herself from going into a fit of laughter. They very rarely ate home during the season.

With a grin on his face, he pointed his index finger at her. "Don't even go there."

Francine leaned into Richie. "I'm not even going to touch that. I'm going to just eat my breakfast."

After eating the last piece of toast in her dish, Richie removed the tray from the bed and placed it on the triple dresser. Francine kept her eyes on him. He hadn't aged a single day. He was still the high school superstar she had fallen in love with.

"So," he plopped down on the bed, "what do you want to do today?"

"I guess," she hesitantly began, "I should tell you about what happened yesterday."

"I don't like your tone. Should I ask?"

"Nothing bad. I didn't have a fight with the bitch from the real estate agency down the block. To be honest, she has been very nice to me. I guess she's afraid I'll have her business closed."

"Don't even go there. The last time you caused a rumpus with her, the story hit the newspapers."

Francine made a cross over her chest. "Cross my heart, hope to die. I will never again intentionally have us hit the tabloids."

Richie stretched his long legs under the blanket, turning sideways, leaning his head against his hand and glaring down at her. "Now that we got off the original subject of what happened yesterday, maybe you can enlighten me on what I should expect."

"This is really a unique story."

"Oh no. I know the vibe. What did you do?" he asked, sitting up.

Francine threw her feet over the side of the bed and stood. "You can give me more credit than that. This time it fell right into my lap."

"I hate the word 'it.' There is always a story behind 'it.'"

Francine giggled. "Yesterday, while I sat in my office minding my own business, Sam Lockinster, Esquire stopped by my office and handed me this." Francine lifted her handbag off the chair and pulled out the envelope.

Richie extended his hand. "Let me see."

Francine handed him the envelope and sat down on the edge of the bed. Keeping her eyes on Richie, she watched his right eyebrow shoot up as he read the letter. He looked up at her, not saying a word before lowering his eyes to the next paper—the deed to the building.

"Are you kidding me? How the hell did you meet this man?"

"I was a kid working at a pharmacy. He used to come in everyday with his wife who was in a wheelchair. When he became ill, he would call me with a list. I'd do his shopping and he'd pick it up. But as his health started to fail, I hand-delivered it to his apartment."

"So I see." Richie returned the papers to the envelope and handed them back to her. "Looks like we have our afternoon planned."

Francine smiled. "You're not going to yell?"

"Not yet. First let's see what this piece of property looks like before we make any decisions."

Francine turned her head to face the window. She didn't want him to see the smirk on her face. He would immediately know she had already been there. But who was she kidding? She needed him to help her.

"You were there. I know it. So now you can turn around and look at me."

Francine sat down on the edge of the bed. "You caught me. The only problem is the windows are boarded up. We went in there with a flashlight."

"Don't tell me that small little light you have in the glove compartment of the car."

"You got it." Francine clenched her hand in triumph.

"Okay. We'll go and look at the property. But I'm not making any promises. This still smells fishy to me."

"I got the deed."

"We have to have an attorney look over this to make sure it is authentic. But let's take this one step at a time. Let me call Jason. I know he has a generator for when he has his big bashes in the summer. Maybe I can get him to tag along."

"Sounds perfect."

Francine knelt next to Richie on the bed. "Hopefully later when we get home, we'll pick up where we left off last night."

"Hopefully," he said, lifting her up. "My shoulder is on fire."

"What's wrong?" she asked, getting off the bed.

"My shoulder is shot."

"Since when? You never told me this before. Keeping secrets?"

"Yeah, the way you went to see the property without telling me."

Francine bobbed her head in agreement. "Okay, you're right. But I'm worried about your shoulder. What's going on?"

"Listen." As Richie lifted his arm and rolled it around, she could hear his shoulder crack.

"What are you going to do? That doesn't sound very good."

"This is why I made the decision to retire after this season."

"Why didn't you tell me about this sooner?"

"Babe, I wanted to get in one last season. I know you would have talked me into retiring over the off-season."

"You're damn right I would have."

Richie slid off the bed. "I don't know anything else but baseball. What am I going to do?"

"Please. We have everything we need right here. We invested your money. There is nothing to worry about."

"I'm not talking about money. I need to do something to keep myself occupied."

"You can't worry about that right now." Francine stood. "My job is to make sure we grow old together. It will be just you and me to conquer the world."

Richie opened his arms and Francine walked into them. She knew what he meant. But he would have no problem finding work. He always talked about helping the kids down at the community center. By helping these kids, he would be giving back for all the good they were handed throughout the years.

Growing up in foster care had been hard for her. She had no mementos of her teenage years. But being in Richie's arms made all the material keepsakes seem irrelevant. All her happy memories revolved around him.

"Everything will be fine. I promise you I'll take care of myself. Right now, we are on a five-man rotation. Which gives me a few days to rest my arm in between."

"Please promise me you won't overpitch."

"Babe, it's too late." Richie frowned. "I don't want you to worry about this."

"But I do." Francine stepped back. "I know you better than you know yourself. I know you're hiding something from me. I had this feeling over the winter. What are you hiding?"

Richie spun around. The silence in the room was deafening. As much as she tried, she couldn't stop the tears from appearing. They had shared everything together, never concealing anything. She sniffed a few times as her nose got stuffed from the tears. This caused Richie to turn around.

"Why are you crying?" He pulled a tissue out of the box on the night stand, wiping her eyes.

"I don't know. You never hid anything from me before. Are you cheating on me?" she asked between sniffs.

"No," he shook his head. "No." He handed her a few more tissues before gathering her in his arms. "I didn't want to worry you. I know how you get."

"What do you mean?" she asked rubbing her eyes against his soft bare skin.

"My shoulder." He stepped back, took her hand and led her into the bathroom. Picking up the teal washcloth, he wiped her face. "At the end of the season, I'm going to have shoulder surgery."

"Then maybe you shouldn't be pitching anymore."

"It's okay. The trainer said as long as I take it easy, I'll be okay. He would have taken me out of the game the other night, but since I was pitching a no-hitter, I wanted to finish the game." He lifted her chin up with his thick thumb until her eyes met his big green ones. "I don't want you to breathe a word of this to anyone. Not even your friends. This is between the trainer and me. I want to go out on a high note. I want you to promise me."

Every time she looked at him she got lost in his eyes. The first time he looked at her with those big green eyes, he had captured her heart. This time was no exception. Through the years, they always had each other's backs, and this would be no different.

Francine held out her pinky. "Promise."

Richie took hold of her pinky with his. "Promise."

"Now if you want to make it official, I can get the pin."

"We did that over twenty years ago. I think we are still bonded forever by blood."

The memory was priceless. They had been sitting in his mom's kitchen with her sewing kit. On his mother's white tablecloth, they pricked each other with the pin then held their index fingers together so their blood mixed.

"Do you remember how your mother yelled at us because we ruined the brand-new tablecloth her cousin sent her from Italy?"

"How could I ever forget? You know how she always brings up that incident every holiday."

"And it's good for a laugh from everyone. That's what I love about being a part of your family."

Richie leaned down, kissing her lips. "Go take a shower while I clean up the mess I made in the kitchen."

By the time Francine got out of the bathroom, Richie had already cleaned up and showered. He dressed in her favorite pair of jeans, the ones that were a tad too tight, with the white button-down shirt. After all these years, he kept his weight down and still had a full head of hair. Not bad for being close to forty.

"Keep standing with your hands resting down your pants and we aren't going to make it out of the house," Francine warned.

"Oh really. You're not looking so bad yourself. Don't be getting your libido on high speed, or else we'll be spending the day in bed."

"You are no fun." Francine turned around and rubbed her hands along her butt. "You'll just have to wait to get a piece of this later."

Richie wagged his head side to side. "You are so bad."

"Wouldn't be me if I weren't."

Richie walked down the spiral staircase with Francine walking behind.

"I called Jason. He'll meet us there."

Francine smiled. "That's great, thank you."

"I hope the kitchen is to your liking."

"Oh boy," Francine mumbled as she rounded the corner. She gasped. "The kitchen is spotless. How did you do it?"

"That's my other surprise."

Francine crossed her arms and leaned against the island in the kitchen. Her eyes stayed focused on Richie, who didn't flinch.

"I know you are old-fashioned and you don't want anyone in our house," he said, making quotes with both his hands, "but I came up with a feasible solution."

"Okay, I'm waiting."

Richie walked to the side door and opened it. He stepped aside and his mother came in.

"Hi, my dear." Richie's mom walked in giving her a kiss hello. "Dad and I will be here for a week or so, while we have our wooden floors scraped and house painted. Your father will be joining us later on."

Francine threw daggers with her eyes. Now the pieces were all coming together. She should have known the minute he walked into the bedroom with a perfectly made breakfast on the tray. Now she needed to act excited.

"That's wonderful. I'm so happy to have you here."

"Dear, I'm going to break in your kitchen. I've never seen such clean pots and utensils in my whole life. You have top of the line appliances in here that look hardly used. Don't you cook?" she asked Francine.

"Sometimes."

"Okay, Mom. We will be back later on. We have a few things we need to do this morning."

She blew a kiss. *"Arrivederci."*

"Bye, Mom." Francine walked out the back door.

"I'm going to put up a pot of chicken soup. It should be done by the time you kids get home," she yelled out the backdoor.

As soon as the car pulled away from the curb Francine went ballistic. "Are you kidding me?" she hollered. "Your mom and dad are staying with us for a week? When did you plan on telling me?"

"I just found out this morning. What was I going to tell her? She was already on her way."

"Oh dear God. It took me months to get the scent of garlic out of my house. Now with her cooking for a week, well, my house is going to smell horrendous for a year."

"Calm down." He patted his hand on her knee, not taking his eyes off the road. "It's only for a week."

"Yeah, and you'll be leaving in a couple of days."

"Everything will be fine."

"Because your parents are here doesn't mean we aren't having sex tonight."

"No, it doesn't."

Francine didn't say another word on the subject. There was no sense in getting upset because it wasn't going to change anything. His mom always went out of her way for her, knowing her story of going from foster home to another, having no family security. Once Richie's mom learned of her childhood, she lightened up, turning out to be a vital part of her life.

Twenty minutes later Richie pulled up to the curb behind Jason's truck. She got out of the Jeep, joining Richie on the sidewalk.

"Hey, Jason. Thanks for helping us out."

"No problem. I always love when I get to go out on an adventure with the two of you. It always turns out interesting." He punched knuckles with Richie. "I envy you, brother."

"Try living with her."

The two men chuckled. Francine stuck her tongue out at them before walking through the weeds to the front door. The lot in the front of the building was large enough to fit around twenty cars. However, she wondered how much property on the side belonged with the building.

Looking up, she saw where the diner's sign had hung. The outside of the building needed one hell of a painting job with graffiti covering the front and side of the building. Once she got inside she hoped the windows weren't broken.

Francine unhooked her keychain off the loop of her jeans and opened the two locks on the door. Richie and Jason were directly behind her with the generator. While they added gas to the generator, Francine walked around inside with the flashlight she had thrown in her handbag.

"Babe, where are you?" Richie called in.

Francine shined the flashlight in his direction. "I'm over here."

"Stay there. I'll walk over to you."

"Here we go," Jason said.

In seconds, the generator lit the room up. Francine gasped, covering her mouth with her hands. This wasn't a diner, but looked more like a supper club. A quick scan of the room, led her to believe the room had been recently renovated.

"Wow. This is some room." Richie walked around the open space, around the tables. "I see so much potential in here."

"This could be Staten Island's new hot spot," Jason said. "I wonder what kind of a kitchen they have in here."

"Let's go check it out," Richie said.

They walked through the restaurant, leaving her standing in the middle of the room. "Hello. Did you guys forget about me?" Francine lashed out.

"Of course not." Richie held out his hand. "Just jumping ahead of the game," he mumbled.

Francine knew her husband's mind was running.

Jason pushed open the kitchen door. "Holy shit. Let me bring the generator back here. If I'm seeing right, it looks like there's a pizza oven in here."

Richie leaned into Francine, kissing the top of her head. "What do you think?"

"Think about what?"

"This," he said turning around in a circle.

"What about it?"

"I hate to jump ahead of the game until we verify the authenticity of this deed, but I have a lot of ideas for this."

Francine took a step back. "This property is in a high traffic area. I could sell it in under sixty days."

"Sell? That was the last thing I was thinking."

Jason brought the generator to the back of the restaurant, in line with the kitchen doors. Richie grabbed a chair to keep one of the doors open, while Jason repeated the process on the other door.

"That is a pizza oven." Jason walked over to the oven, opening the oven door. "Bro, come look at this." He reached up and took a pot down. "They look brand new. I would bet my life this pot was never used."

"What a perfect way to keep your parents busy," Jason said.

"You're right."

Francine put her hands on her hips. "Okay, bros, what's going on here? I have a feeling you two have something up your sleeves. Care to share?"

"I hate when she stands with her hands on her hips," Richie said. "I know that means if I don't come up with the right explanation, I'm not going to hear the end of it."

"Tell her our idea."

"What idea?" Francine dropped her arms. "And when did you two have time to brainstorm?"

Richie bit his bottom lip. "While you were taking your shower this morning."

"Are you kidding me? You two were making plans on my property that you hadn't even seen yet."

"Look what I found," Jason interrupted, placing a tall white chef's hat on his head.

"That is so cool. Is there anything else around here?"

"Guys. What are you doing?" Francine shook her hands.

"This is it, babe. We can build this up. Make it into a sports bar, restaurant."

"And the location is mint," Jason added.

"Why do I feel like it's two against one and in the end, I'm going to be the one cleaning the toilets in here?"

"She's in." Richie high-fived Jason. "I think I have found the perfect retirement plan."

"We can get this place together in a few months."

"What are you guys talking about?" Francine took the chef's hat off Jason's head and plopped it on hers. "How do I look?"

"You might look like a chef, but baby," he put his arm around her shoulder, "your cooking leaves a lot to be desired."

Francine grabbed a wooden spoon out of the utensil holder. She pointed it toward Richie. "Now that's so unfair. I might not be able to cook well, but I sure can talk customers into making big purchases." Tapping the spoon on Richie's tight butt, she asked, "So what does all of this mean?"

"It means we're going to see our attorney to show him the letter and deed. If everything pans out, then we have some major decisions to make."

Jason sat on the stainless steel counter. "This could definitely work, keep us busy after we retire."

"Retire? You're retiring too?" Francine asked sitting next to him.

"After next season. Like Richie, I want to leave while I'm still on top. I don't want to hold on for a few more years. One of the new defensive ends who joined the team this year is young enough to be my son."

Richie leaned on the stainless steel island in the middle of the kitchen. "Sucks getting old in our profession."

"Okay, so let me get this right. You two love the idea of reinventing this place."

"Absolutely." Richie rubbed his hands together. "From what I see, the place looks to have been abandoned. Hopefully the attorney can give us the background on the building."

"I'll have Toni research the property. See if you can get us in to see Alan this afternoon."

"I'm going to take out the generator." Jason slid off the counter. "Once we're sure the property is yours, we'll turn on the electricity so we can see what we can work with and what we need to get rid of."

"This is the perfect weather too. Not too hot, not too cold," Richie said.

"Richie, are you forgetting you're leaving to go on the road?" Francine asked.

"I didn't. Jason can take care of things."

"Let's not jump the gun." Francine hopped off the counter. They didn't even know if they really owned the property and the men already had a game plan. "Then let's get moving, boys." Francine clapped her hands. "We have a lot of work ahead of us."

Chapter Six

An hour later, after sitting in traffic on the Staten Island Expressway, Francine and Richie pulled up in front of the real estate office with Jason following behind in his truck. The whole way back home, Richie rambled on about what he wanted to do with the restaurant providing the property really belonged to them. She couldn't remember the last time she had seen him this excited. Hopefully everything panned out when they went to the attorney's office later.

Francine opened the car door. "I'm just running in for a few minutes. I promise to be quick."

"I know you're going to try to be quick, but I am pretty sure I'll have to come in at some point to get you."

"You're being overdramatic." She waved him off. "By the time Jason gets here, I'll be in the car with you, waiting for him."

"We'll see about it."

Francine walked into the reception area. The flowers Jason had sent to Amy were in full bloom, blocking her view from Amy and Toni, who were both talking on the phone.

Amy held up her index finger. "Yes, I totally understand. I will add the addition to my notes." She shook her head. "Yes. I changed your preference to two full baths and a half bath." Shaking her head again, she said, "I will look through the listings and see what I can find in the area at the price range you are looking for."

Francine loved the way Amy handled the clients. The tranquil side of her personality came out, especially when the clients became extremely frustrated. On the other hand, her business would have never survived without Toni's expertise with the computer. Both her friends had been the best additions to her business.

Amy hung up. "Boy, does Mrs. Fischer have a lot of pep."

"Is she changing her mind again?" Toni asked, rolling her chair around to face Amy.

"Of course. She's looking for the best, but penny pinching, looking for more."

"You handled her beautifully." Francine slid her handbag off her shoulder and placed it on Amy's desk. "What's going on for today?"

"Not much," Toni said. "I'm waiting to get verification on two certificates of occupancy before I can contact my clients."

"How about you?" Francine asked Amy.

"I have two appointments later on. The houses on Clements and Fairbanks."

"What's going on with you? Any information on the property?" Toni asked.

"Toni told me about it. I'm excited to hear what happened," Amy said.

"I just came back from there. Richie is outside waiting for me. We have an appointment with Richie's attorney in a little while."

"What did Richie say?" Amy asked.

"Richie and Jason are excited. They were making plans on what they were going to do with the place."

"Jason went with you?" Amy's eyes opened widely.

"Yes. He provided the generator." Francine stopped for a moment. "Oh, wait a second. Tell me about your date last night. Did everything go okay?"

Francine saw the sparkle in her eyes. She had totally forgotten about the date and wondered why Jason didn't mention anything to her.

Amy bit down on her bottom lip, a nervous habit she had since she was a kid. "I thought everything went pretty well. We went out to dinner. Jason was the perfect gentleman. Instead of bringing me flowers, he brought me a makeup palette from Sephora."

"Now that's a man. I bet Richie gave him the heads-up on what a woman likes. But that's irrelevant. Tell me, do you like him?"

Amy blushed. "Yeah, I do. I just don't want to get my hopes up. You know my track record with men."

"Jason might be the one you've been waiting for."

"Yea," she bobbed her head, "just like my ex-husband."

"That was a very long time ago. We've all changed since we were twenty-one." Francine lifted her appointment book off her desk and skimmed through the pages. "I have a busy day tomorrow, so I'm going to try to get everything done today."

"If there's anything you need help with, let me know," Toni said.

"I do have a mini project for you this afternoon." Francine walked over to her desk. "I need you to research the property. Find out who rented the building and why it was abandoned. There has to be a reason to pick up and leave your business with everything intact."

"You're right. In all the times I stopped by Katie Lingerie Boutique, I've never noticed the property, let alone it being a restaurant." Toni scribbled something down on the pad in front of her. "I'm going to give Katie a call later and find out if she found anything out. If not, I'm sure someone in one of the stores in the strip mall has information."

"Good thinking," Amy said. "Toni is finally on the ball, now that she has a date on Friday."

"Oh stop it." Toni blushed. "It's just dinner. I'll see where it goes from there. But for now," she stood walking over to the coffee machine, "finding out information on this property is more important."

"Were you able to see anything more than yesterday?" Amy asked.

"Yes. Jason brought his generator to light up the restaurant. Someone picked up and left pretty damn fast. The tables were all set. In the back is a kitchen to kill for. It has two pizza ovens, utensils, pots and pans that were sparkling and…" Francine stopped in midsentence. Something wasn't right. She didn't remember seeing any nonperishables at all. Not even any salt and pepper shakers. The stainless steel counter was also sparkling.

"I'm going to get right on it. This is like some unsolved mystery."

"Yeah, one that I got stuck with, Toni." Francine nodded.

"What did I tell you?" Francine heard Richie say. "She's in here having a cup of coffee and gabbing while we're sitting outside waiting for her."

Francine twirled her hair around her index finger as she turned to face Richie and Jason. "I was just coming out. I just finished telling them about the property."

Toni immediately came to her rescue. "We went through some of the paperwork. You know me—I can be ditsy at times."

"The three of you," Richie pointed, "are always covering for each other. I know exactly what you were doing in here."

Jason walked passed Richie, straight to Amy. He leaned over, giving her a kiss on her cheek. Francine watched Amy turn red.

"Why don't we get going?" Francine suggested. "Amy, why don't you take a lunch break with Jason." She turned to Toni. "I'll be back in an hour or so. Hopefully we don't have to wait long for the attorney. When I get back, you can go shopping for an outfit for your date on Friday."

"Thank you. I'll try my best to have the information you ask for by the time you return."

"Ready, babe? Hopefully we don't have a long wait."

"I sure hope not."

"We'll have another round of drinks," Jason told the waitress.

"I can't get too crazy with the cocktails. I still have to go back to work."

"Can't condemn a man for trying to get you drunk in order to take advantage of you."

Amy shifted her head back. "You are so bad."

"I know. But the best part is seeing the look on your face."

Amy flashed him a huge smile, feeling the heat swell in her face.

"I can't believe I made you blush." Jason touched her face. "You are so damn cute."

Amy looked down at the menu in front of her. "Thank you."

"I had a wonderful time last night. I was sorry to see the night end. You're an angel from heaven dropped into my lap."

"Oh stop."

"You are so real. Now don't take this the wrong way, but you are natural. You don't cake your face with an inch of makeup, or take me to places where you show me off to your friends."

"Now that would have been immature."

"Sweetheart, you can't imagine the things I've gone through. That's why I chose to remain a bachelor."

"That's a shame."

"I came to terms with my future years ago. I'm like any other guy out there. I have faith that one day I'm going to meet the right woman."

Amy sat back and crossed her legs under the table. "I understand where you're coming from. For years, I have watched Francine, always wishing I could have a life like hers, married to the love of her life. Then I take a step back, thankful for what I have."

"I'd be lying if the thought didn't cross my mind either. I just miss not sharing my successful career with anybody."

"That's where you are wrong. You have shared your successful career with millions of fans."

"It's not the same."

"Who am I kidding? It's tough finding someone who loves you for you. I'm sure it must be a challenge for you, especially because it's a nightmare for me."

"Dear God." Jason raised his eyes looking up at the ceiling. "Where did you come from? I feel as though I've known you forever."

Amy smiled. "You know how to keep boosting my ego."

"But that's it. I'm not. I am so glad we found each other."

"I don't know how we missed each other, especially since we have been at the same places." Amy pointed her fork at him. "Were you at Francine's New Year's Eve party this year?"

"Yes, I was. But if my memory is correct, she had over seventy people coming and going. Besides, I had a date with me, so that's probably why I didn't run into you. Because if I did, I would have snatched you up back then."

Amy dropped her gaze to the table. She could feel the heat building up in her face. Jason had some affect on her. But keeping her cool had to be essential. She didn't want him to know how much she liked him. Every time she got her hopes up, something would happen to ruin things.

"Hey, sorry if I'm making you feel uncomfortable." Jason reached over and placed his hand over hers. "Right now I'm feeling like a teenager. I want to scoop you up and take you on an afternoon escapade."

"Oh no. I can see it now. You are going to be the man who gets me into trouble on the job."

"I can go for some fun. I want to experience the little things in life that I missed all these years."

"I know what you mean. I would love to go to a waterpark and spend the day on the rides," Amy said.

"I always wanted to go to Cooperstown, even Las Vegas."

"You have got to be kidding me. You have never gone to Vegas?"

"Nope. I am not a gambling man. I want to go to Vegas to walk around, checkout the hotels and checkout the Pawn Stars shop."

Her eyes bulged open. "You watch Pawn Stars?"

"Yes. I also like Storage Wars."

"Oh boy, a man after my own heart. I love those shows. I've just recently started watching the Investigation Discovery Channel too. I enjoy watching the crime shows."

"I have a feeling we are going to get along just fine."

The young blonde waitress stood at the end of their table and handed each of them a menu. "I'm so sorry. All at once we got a rush of customers."

"Not a problem, Leslie."

"What can I get you two to start?"

"I'll have a beer," Jason said.

"Mimosa for me."

"I'll be right back with your drinks."

Amy opened the menu. "I don't know why I even bother to open the menu. I love the fresh mozzarella cheeseburger from here." She closed the menu, placing it on the edge of the table.

"I like the sharp cheddar cheese and bacon burger." Jason patted his stomach. "I do have to watch my figure." He chuckled. "I still have to watch my weight during the off-season."

Leslie returned, placing their drinks in front of them. Before taking their order, she slid a football card in front of him. "The little boy over there wanted me to ask you for an autograph."

"Not a problem," he said.

Jason turned to the blond-haired boy who couldn't have been anymore than ten years old. Amy smiled when Jason stood and walked over to the table where the young boy sat. He said something to the boy, causing the boy to smile. After signing the card, he ruffled the boy's hair and they bumped knuckles.

Amy was impressed with Jason's kindness. Through the years, she had witnessed a few of Richie's friends getting annoyed at being interrupted. She understood but couldn't understand anyone turning down a young impressionable kid.

"Sorry about that," Jason said, sitting back down. "I can never turn down a kid."

"I loved watching how you interacted with him. I think it's wonderful."

Leslie returned holding her pad. "Are you guys ready?"

Jason ordered for both of them, adding sweet potato fries to the order instead of regular potatoes. When Leslie walked away, he held up his bottle of beer.

"I'd like to see more of you. For the first time in my life, I feel comfortable sitting here being myself. I don't know why it took so long to meet you, especially since we've been in each other's company before, but I'm happy to have finally found you. Here's to more days together."

Amy clanked her glass against his bottle before taking a sip. She needed a few minutes to digest what Jason had just said, shocked how open he had been with his feelings. Opening up like he did was something she never did. How could she tell people her marriage only lasted nine months with her husband still sleeping with the woman he was cheating on her with while they were engaged? Why did he even bother marrying her?

"I'd like that," Amy finally answered. "I'd love to spend more time with you."

"How about Saturday? Would you come to the game with me?"

"I'd love too."

"The only thing is, the seats I get aren't near Francine's. That's why we never ran into each other at the games either."

"Isn't that something?" Amy lifted her glass and took a sip. "I believe in fate. We weren't meant to meet until now."

"I couldn't agree more. And fate will bring us even closer together if the building Francine was left is indeed hers. It will open up endless possibilities for Richie and me when we retire after the season."

"I can't believe you're retiring."

Jason reached over and touched her cheek. "Sweetheart, I'm going to be forty-two. My body is shot. I just hung in there for this season because I am uncertain what I want to do once I retire."

"What did you take in college?"

"Architecture. But I never finished. I got drafted during my sophomore year of college. That's why I'm keeping my fingers crossed things will work out with the building. Richie and I were talking about all the possibilities."

"What do you two know about running a business?"

"We don't. We will learn as we go along. Besides, we have you and Francine to help us out."

If Francine had any idea what the guys had planned, she would be freaking out. Amy knew exactly what the conversation would be between the two of them later.

"Excuse me." Leslie interrupted placing their dishes down in front of them. "Can I get you two a refill?"

"That would be fine, thank you."

Amy held up her hand. "I have to go back to work."

Jason waved her off. "She'll have another mimosa." He turned to Amy. "It's mostly orange juice anyway."

"Oh yeah." Amy giggled. "You're going to get me in trouble. I can feel it."

"Just sit back and enjoy the ride. I have a lot of things in store for you. Just wait and see."

"I look forward to sharing things with you. But, there are a few things about myself I'd like to share with you now."

"Sweetie, your past is your past. What you did before you met me doesn't matter."

Amy lifted a sweet potato fry out of her dish and took a bite. "I know that. But I do want you to know I was married for a very short time."

Jason pulled his head back. "A very short time?"

"Yes. I was stupid, not paying attention to what was going on around me. I had put my heart and soul into working with Francine and I missed all the warning signs."

"What happened?"

"I'm so embarrassed."

"I'm sorry for questioning you. I was totally out of line."

"No, you weren't." Amy took a bite of her hamburger. "Mmm." Lifting her napkin, she cleaned the ketchup she was sure had escaped from her mouth. After wiping her mouth, she glanced at the napkin. Yes indeed, her hunch on the ketchup had been right. "All I will say, is, I never totally got over the shock of deceit. Who would have thought my husband would continue his relationship with his high school sweetheart?"

"I'm so sorry."

"It's all right. That took place a long time ago. I try not to look back when the future looks so alluring."

Jason lifted his half empty beer bottle. "A toast to the future."

"Salud."

They clinked glasses. This time, when his hand grazed hers, she felt a feeling of peace flow through her. Could Jason be the man she had been searching for all these years?

Francine and Richie sat in Alan Davis's office. Alan and Richie had been friends since high school. Alan attended New York University Law School and Richie became his first client after Alan passed the bar exam.

Alan walked in. "Sorry for keeping you waiting."

After they all greeted each other, they sat back down. "I can't tell you how much I appreciate you seeing us on such short notice. I know how busy you are, Alan," Francine said.

"Never too busy for my friends."

"Can you get away for the game on Saturday? I can have two tickets for you and your wife left at the box office."

"I'll ask Sandy. But she likes Saturday night to be our date night. She doesn't give up her night so easily. If she's cool with it, I'll give you a call."

Francine crossed her arms with her left leg shaking up and down. The two were talking complete nonsense while she sat there waiting for the results from his research on the property. She let the boys shoot the breeze for a few minutes before she stood.

"Okay guys. Enough," Francine snapped. "I've been dying to hear about the outcome of your search." She looked from Richie to Alan. By the look on their faces, she already knew Alan had been the texting culprit on their trip there.

Four times she had to yell at Richie to stop reading his text messages while driving.

"I'm sorry, baby. Alan had to check into a few things before being able to give us an answer along with additional information." Richie patted on the black leather seat next to him. "Sit. Alan will explain everything."

Francine slid back into her chair, crossing her legs. "I'm all ears."

Alan stood, walked around to the front of his desk and leaned against it. "Francine, the deed to the property is indeed authentic. Not only do you own the building, but you also own the property in front, behind and to the left of the building."

Francine's mouth dropped open. "Are you kidding me?"

"Absolutely not. Mr. Peacock was an extremely well-off man."

"Wow. I don't understand why the restaurant is abandoned."

"I checked into that too." Alan took a folder off his desk and handed it to Francine. "The restaurant was rented out to Leon Vance and Doug Sussman. They opened it five years ago, but abandoned it seven months later. Mr. Peacock decided to leave it be. He had the glass windows boarded up and the place has remained like that for years."

Francine bobbled her head. "I don't believe it."

"Even better, Mr. Peacock continued to renew the liquor license, saving you a lot of red tape. You must have left some impression on him."

"As a kid I helped him with his shopping and even delivered him his medicine. That was over twenty years ago."

"He didn't forget your generosity. The quality I fell in love with." Richie winked.

Francine blew Richie a kiss. "Where does this leave us Alan?"

"It leaves you a piece of property worth over two million dollars."

Silence filled the room. Francine didn't have a clue as to what to say. This had been so surreal, a complete stranger whom she'd helped years ago, leaving her such an expensive gift.

Richie leaned. "I still find it hard to believe."

"Yes, but this leaves you in a very good position, offering you a new career after retirement."

"And if I decide to sell?" Francine asked.

"You'll have to take that up with your husband. He has already written out a proposal on his new sports bar restaurant."

"Richie?"

"Baby, we don't need the money if you sell it. I see this as a business venture. We'll make up for all the time we were apart."

"What about my real estate business?"

"I think it's time you think about giving the business up. We don't need the money. I'd like to start this new journey in my life with you by my side. What do you think?"

"For one, thank you for putting me on the spot. But for two, I'd like nothing better than to do this by your side."

Richie stood. After saying their goodbyes, they were on their way back to her office. A half hour of traffic later, they pulled up in front of her building, pulling in behind Jason's truck.

"Looks like Jason's still here."

"Perfect." Richie shifted the car into park. "Jason will be excited. This is great having our retirement already planned."

By the time Francine slid out of the truck, Richie had already gone inside and was sitting behind her desk. Jason had a big ass grin on his face, meaning Richie had already told him the news. Seeing Amy's eyes sparkle made her day. Francine hadn't seen Amy this happy in a very long time.

Francine sat behind Toni's desk. "Did you talk to Toni?"

"Yes, I did." Amy giggled. "She called me between outfit number seven and eight."

Lifting her cell phone, Amy handed it to Francine. Hitting the photo widget on the phone, she went through the pictures. "Honestly, I'm not crazy about any of the outfits she tried on."

"I told her the same thing. She's on the way back to the mall to get herself a pair of black dress pants, a white shirt and jacket."

"Don't you think that's a little too conservative for Toni?"

"Yes, I do. Eric dresses very conservative and seems somewhat old-fashioned. Besides, Toni wants to try a different approach with Eric."

"I just hope she stays alert. Sometimes she's too trusting of people."

"I agree. I told her to keep us posted throughout the night."

"You can forget about that. The only time we hear from her is if she gets herself into trouble."

Amy walked over to the coffee machine. "And that's been one too many times."

"Forget about your putrid coffee." Richie jingled his car keys. "Let's go grab some lattes down the street before I have to head to the stadium."

"Sounds like a plan," Jason said. "It will give us a chance to talk about our future."

Chapter Seven

The whole trip over to the diner the four of them laughed like teenagers. Francine couldn't believe how well Amy and Jason got along. They look so natural together like they had been dating for years. Looking at them reminded her of her early years with Richie. They met in high school and fell in love, with the passion between them growing more and more each year. She wondered if they would have had kids if their relationship would have been challenged and would they still be together.

When they walked into the diner, the staff knew them, greeting them like celebrities. Maybe Richie's fans saw him as a celebrity, but to her, he was like any other man. They didn't do anything different than the next person. Francine always took coupons when she went food shopping, and even bargain shopped for things for the house, despite Richie's insistence it wasn't necessary to live like that.

At holiday time, she volunteered at the church, even adopting a few families, making certain they had food and toys from Santa for their kids. This had been Richie's and her secret. They always gave anonymously, not wanting to draw any attention from the paparazzi. Their giving came from their hearts. The last thing they were looking for was recognition.

All four of them slid into the round booth in the back left hand corner of the diner. By the time they settled in, the waitress had four cups of coffee waiting in front of them along with half and half.

"Thank you, Josie."

"You're welcome." She handed each of them a menu. "Glad to see all four of you here together. You just missed my daughter, Jason. She would have gone ballistic if she saw you."

"I keep on missing her. Tell her I said hello. Next time I see her, I'll treat her for lunch."

"She's going to go nuts. You know how crazy teenagers are."

Francine held up her hand. "Thank God, I don't."

They all laughed.

"Do you know what you want, or do you need more time?"

"We just finished eating breakfast not too long ago. I think I'll go with the fresh fruit and fat free frozen yogurt," Francine said.

Amy handed her back the menu. "I'll have the same."

"Maybe you ladies aren't going to eat, but I sure as hell am," Jason said. "I'll have three eggs over easy, rye toast, home fries and a side of sausage."

Richie licked his lips. "I think I'll stay on the same line as the ladies with fresh fruit. So I'll take a slice of apple crumb pie."

"What are you talking about?" Francine asked. "That's not fresh fruit."

"Yes, it is. The sign says pies made daily, which means there are fresh apples in the pie."

"I'm not even going to go there. I don't want to hear you gained a few pounds."

"I hope you two aren't going to get into that conversation again," Amy said, glancing over her coffee.

"No. I will not let the conversation go in that direction." Francine's eyes narrowed with her eyebrows shooting up. "Richie is a big boy. He can eat what he wants."

Amy pushed her mug to the center of the table. "Time to get back to the original reason why we are here. It sure as hell isn't for the coffee."

"Not at all. For some reason the coffee tastes burned today," Francine snapped. "I'm going to ask for another cup of coffee."

"This happened the last time we came here," Amy said. "Except the last time you announced to the whole diner that the coffee smelled like dirty feet."

"No, you didn't," Richie said, sipping away at his coffee.

"I did. I wound up drinking water that day with my turkey sandwich. Even the tomatoes tasted sandy."

"You two are out of control. When Francine and I are alone, this never happens."

"That's because I don't want to embarrass you," Francine said, biting her bottom lip.

Richie put his arms around her, kissing the top of her head. "You are too much. I don't even want to know what you do when you two are here alone."

"Are the three of you finished with your comedy skit yet?" Jason asked clenching his lips tightly shut. "We don't have much time before you have to leave for the stadium."

"Boy, are you being serious," Francine said.

"Yes, I am. Richie is going on the road Sunday night after the game. I want to discuss some preliminaries so I can start working on the new blueprints. Once they are complete, I can get permits and file them with the city."

97

Francine glanced over to Amy and busted out laughing. She held up her hand. "I'm sorry. It's just hard seeing you so serious. You have a mean look on your face."

Amy touched Jason's cheek. "I think his look is sexy."

"Now that's an interesting scenario. I haven't heard you call anyone sexy in a very long time."

Amy giggled. "Yeah, I know."

"We are going off track again," Jason said.

"Jason, you officially have the floor," Richie said. "Can you two try to restrain yourself from interrupting Jason?" He glanced at his watch. "He's right. Time is limited."

The waitress brought their dishes over and replenished their coffee mugs. "When you get a chance, the boy over there would like to meet you, Jason. He just got here."

"Not a problem. I will stop by his table in a bit. Put their bill on my tab."

"And he's generous too," Amy said.

Richie glanced at his watch. "Let's get down to business. I have to leave in a half hour."

Jason looked at Francine and Amy held her finger over Jason's lips. Francine knew exactly what he meant. She reached for her fork and started eating to distract her from making any other comments.

"I'm going to work on the blueprints today and come up with a preliminary plan. I called Con Edison. We should have lights on by tomorrow morning."

"Good job." Richie and Jason bumped knuckles.

"I think we can leave the kitchen as is. From what we saw the other day, all the counters and appliances are stainless steel. I'd like Francine to come with me to take a look at the restaurant, see what we can salvage and what needs to be tossed. Most importantly, where we can put the bar and set up the televisions."

Richie tapped Francine on the shoulder. "The decorating is your department."

"Okay. I think before we do any decorating, we need to know how we are going to set up the dining room."

"That's why I'm going to work on tentative plans from the original blueprints of the restaurant. Once I survey the place, I will be able to better plan things out."

"Cool," Richie said, moving his cup as the waitress placed their food on the table.

"I'm going to stop by there when we leave. I still have the generator in the truck. I want to get another look, so I can try my best to make my sketches as accurate as possible."

"How much property is there behind the restaurant?" Francine dipped a strawberry into the yogurt and popped it into her mouth.

"Looks like the property goes back over a hundred feet. Why?" Jason asked.

"I think putting an outside garden would be beneficial in the summer," Francine nonchalantly said.

"She's right. I think that's a great idea," Richie said. "The hottest thing is having music playing outside."

"I can see a Tiki Bar setup," Francine added.

"I agree." Jason flipped open a pad, making notes. "To start, I think we should concentrate on the inside, getting it up and running. I'll have something put together for tomorrow."

Richie finished his coffee and stood. "Come to the house tomorrow morning with Amy. This way we can lay the blueprints out on the kitchen table and discuss things."

"Perfect plan," Jason said.

"Can you drop us off at work?" Francine asked. "I have a few appointments later."

"While you take care of the ladies Richie, I'm going to sit with the boy and his family for a bit. I'll see you in the morning."

Toni wore a short black skirt, complemented by a white linen button-down shirt. When she opened the door, she smiled to see Eric in dress pants with a blue button-down shirt, along with a blue and black striped tie. Any thoughts of her being overdressed were put to rest.

"Beautiful." Eric grinned.

Toni felt her cheeks heat up. "Thank you."

"Go ahead, turn around, let me see."

She twirled around twice. "I'm happy I picked out this outfit."

"So am I." He leaned his head down toward his shoulder.

"You sure you like it?"

"Yes. It's perfect." He walked toward the door. "If you're ready, I have tickets for a show at the Saint George Theater. I know the owner."

Toni shut the door, locking it and followed Eric out to the car. He opened the door to a brand new black Cadillac with beige seats. She slid in. As she put on her seat belt, he closed her door and walked around the back of the car to get in at the driver's side.

Now the next question would be what they would talk about. She hated first dates. She always messed up. Either she revealed too much about herself or she didn't say enough. Tonight, she would let Eric lead. He seemed like the kind of man who liked to have control of the situation. But the silence was killing her. Why wasn't he saying anything to her? Just as she was about to ask him what kind of music he liked, he pulled over to the curb.

"I'll be right back."

He left the car running and walked into the corner bodega. The silence in the car had been deafening. You'd think he'd have some questions to ask her. She wanted to click on the radio, to break up the silence, but decided turning it on wouldn't be such a good idea.

The driver's door opened, and she jumped. She hadn't seen him come out of the store. He got into the car and handed her a dozen red roses.

"I wanted to start our date right."

Toni lifted the roses up to her nose. "They are beautiful, thank you. What a wonderful surprise."

"I thought the same thing. I always hate first dates."

"So do I," Toni admitted. "They are always awkward. I never know what to say. You never know what offends some people."

"I hear you. See, we have something in common already." He pulled away from the curb and continued down Hylan Boulevard. "Are you seeing anybody?"

"No, I am not." Toni crossed her legs. "How about you?"

"Nope."

"Are you married, divorced or a lifelong bachelor?"

"Divorced for many years."

"Now that's a relief. I am so tired of meeting men who are married. All they are looking for is a booty call."

"Have you ever been married?"

"I was married right out of high school. Got divorced when my husband announced to me he was gay. I've been on my own since then."

"Must get lonely."

"Never. I am so involved with my job, or shall I say business, that I don't have much free time."

"You have a business?"

"Yes. I am partners with two of my friends at the Rag, Mills and Bell real estate."

"Nice. Do you mind if I have a cigarette?" he asked as he lit one.

Toni didn't bother to answer. She just shook her head no when she caught him glancing over at her. Pulling down his sun visor, he opened the lighted mirror, and ran his fingers through his thinning hair. Again, there was silence in the car. She readjusted the roses, placing them on the left side of her seat as he pulled into the parking lot. When he opened his door, she took the lead and got out too.

"I was coming to open the door for you." He placed his hand under her elbow, leading her into the theater.

"Vito." Eric dropped his hand from her elbow. He approached Vito and hugged him. "How are you doing? It's been awhile?"

"Yes, it has." Eric turned to Toni. "Vito, this is Toni."

Vito hugged her. "Nice to meet you. Your table is ready, if you follow me."

Vito led them to a table in front of the stage. He held out her chair for her.

"Thank you," Toni said.

"What can I get you to drink?" he asked.

"I'll have an apple martini."

"Rum and coke?" Vito asked Eric.

"I wouldn't have anything else."

Eric leaned against the table when Vito left. "What do you think?"

"I can't believe we have a table up front."

"That's the perks of knowing the owner."

"I've been here so many times and sat up there," Toni said, pointing to the balcony.

"As long as you're with me, you'll never sit up there again," he said. "Vito and I have been friends for a long time."

Vito returned with their drinks. "Enjoy the show."

"Thank you." Toni played with the stem of her glass, trying to think of a conversation to start.

"Why do you look so nervous?"

"I'm not...well yeah I am. I'm horrible at first dates."

"There's no need to be. I don't bite." Eric laughed. "Let's start with the basics. Where did you go to high school?"

"I went to the old New Dorp high school. How about you?"

"I went to Curtis."

"That's where I wanted to go. I even made the AP class, but my mom didn't want me to go there. She was afraid that instead of going to school, I would be jumping on the ferry going into Manhattan everyday."

"Would you have?"

"Absolutely."

Eric sat back in his chair and smiled. "You're going to love the show. I've seen Mark Davis perform before. He's hilarious."

"I'm not familiar with him."

"He's a great comedian. Some of his humor is on the dark side, but believe me you'll be laughing all night."

Toni didn't know what to think about Eric. In a lot of ways, he seemed rough around the edges, but there was something charismatic about him, which made her want to get to know him more.

"Do you like sports?" she asked trying to get the conversation going.

"No. I couldn't care less." His eyes narrowed. "Why you do?"

"Yes. Baseball and football."

"You can keep both of them. If I watch any sport, it's boxing. That's real men playing a real sport."

Toni ran her tongue over her teeth. What was with this guy? If he weren't so good looking, she would have walked out of the theater. When she looked up, their eyes met.

"I didn't mean to offend you. I remember you saying your friend's husband played for the Pelicans. I'm just not into sports."

"That's okay. No need to explain yourself."

Eric lifted his glass off the table, taking a sip. "When I was a kid, my mother and father forced me to play baseball and football. To this day, I am still turned off by the official American pastime."

"That's understandable. Sports aren't a huge issue. I'm also a huge music lover."

"So am I. Nothing is like some good old rock and roll music."

Toni grinned. "I agree with you on that. I also love dance music. Back in the day, I always went out dancing."

"Looks like that's strike two. I like dance music, but I don't dance at all."

"Not even to a slow song?"

"Nope. My shoes never touch the dance floor. I just sit back and admire." Eric stood. "Would you mind if I go out for a cigarette?"

"No, not at all. I'll check my email while you puff away."

Before she even finished talking, he was walking out the door. Now she felt uncomfortable. She hoped he didn't take off on her because they weren't in sync on two major date makers. There had to be something that both of them like doing. Turning around, she spotted Eric standing by the curb smoking. *Yuk.* She hated cigarette smoking. Already this was not going well at all. All she needed to do was get through the next hour, and then she would be home relaxing.

Eric returned just as the show began. Before sitting, he moved his chair next to Toni's and wrapped his arm around her shoulder. The show was awesome despite the decapitation jokes. Instead of running out after the show, they stayed to finish their drinks. Tony finally found something in common with Eric, their love of watching movies. What surprised Toni the most was that Eric liked watching romance movies too.

"There we go. Now we have found something we both enjoy doing. I love my Hallmark movies," Toni said.

They also both agreed they hated politics and reading the daily newspaper.

"I am so happy you are a movie junkie like me. I can sit all night in front of the television eating Chinese food out of the containers, while enjoying a thriller."

Eric went to stand, but changed his mind. Looking at his pale yellow fingernails, Toni knew he was a heavy smoker. Her father's nails looked the same way.

"How do you feel about books being made into movies?" he asked, finishing his rum and coke.

"I'm not a big fan of it. If I read the book first, I'm usually disappointed because the movie never captures the same effect as the book."

"I don't have the patience to read a book. I would rather watch it on television."

Toni tilted her glass toward his. "Something else we have in common."

"I bet we have even more things in common."

While Toni took the last sip of her drink, something above Eric's left wrist caught her eye. She didn't want to stare, but each time he raised his hand, black lines from some sort of tattoo were revealed. Eric signaled the waiter for the check.

"I thought we would go downstairs where there's music and karaoke."

"I'd like that. I didn't know they had a downstairs. I don't hear anything."

"That's because Vito soundproofed the room upstairs. When he first started the music, people complained it was so loud they couldn't enjoy the show. So he made an entrance outside or you can also use the elevator in the back by the restrooms."

"I can't stay too late. I have work tomorrow."

"You work on Saturdays?"

"Yes. Sometimes even on Sundays," Toni explained.

"I hear you. Same on my end. A lot of doctors are open on Saturdays and Sundays. Tomorrow I have four appointments with doctors. I have to get up by seven o'clock."

"That sucks." After she said it, she covered her mouth with her hand. All night she tried to be ladylike, leaving the curse and swear words out of her vocabulary. "Sorry," she whispered when she removed her hand.

"Sorry for what? You didn't say anything wrong." Eric stood.

"You're right, I didn't."

Eric led her to the back of the theater to the elevator. The elevator doors opened to the sound of classic disco. With his hand resting on her hip, Eric led her to a small round table in the center of the room, by the dance floor.

"I'm going to put my name on the karaoke list," Eric yelled above the music into her ear. "Do you want me to include your name too?"

Toni shook her head no. Singing wasn't her thing. She'd sit back and listen to everyone else make fools of themselves.

"Where's Anthony M?" the DJ asked.

Eric returned with two glasses, placing them down on the table before maneuvering his chair next to hers. No words were exchanged between the two of them. Talking was impossible with the music being so loud. Taking a sip, she listened to Anthony M sing. She was impressed. He sounded like Elvis. When he finished the crowd went wild. Taking a break from karaoke, the DJ played a cluster of dance music.

"Eric Summers, come on up," the DJ announced.

Eric got up without saying a word to Toni. From where she sat, she watched Eric talking to the DJ. After a few minutes, the disco music went off. The music started and Eric's voice echoed throughout the room. After the first verse, her body cringed. He was so off-key that people sitting behind her were laughing. *Lovely.* Now she would have to lie to him about his horrendous performance. Hopefully that would be the only song he sang.

Four songs and two hours later, they were walking to the car. The music had been so loud that she didn't have to mention anything about his singing performance.

"Would you mind if I had a cigarette before I get into the car?"

"No, not at all."

"Great. I don't like the smell of cigarette smoke lingering in my car." Eric lit a cigarette taking a long drag. "Would it be all right if I gave you a call tomorrow? Maybe we could go out and get a cup of coffee before you have to leave for the ball game."

Toni hesitated. Something told her to say no. but she found him charismatic and the exact opposite of who she usually dated. She smiled. "I'd like that."

"Consider it our second date."

"Okay. That sounds nice."

"Speaking of sounds, what did you think of my singing?"

Shit. I hate lying. "You sounded good."

Eric reached the cigarette to his lips. "There's another place that's better on the other side of the Island. Maybe we can do that next Saturday."

"I'd like that."

Before Eric opened the car door, he kissed Toni. The whole way home, he had the radio so loud in the car that no conversation took place between them until the car came to a halt in front of her house.

Toni reached down and picked her handbag off the floor. "Goodnight, Eric."

He leaned over giving her a quick peck on the lips. "I'll talk to you in the morning."

Chapter Eight

The scent of freshly brewed coffee and bacon filled the house. Francine pulled the blankets over her head, but the scent of coffee beckoned her to get out of bed. The sound of Richie's voice and his mom's echoed up the stairs. When she heard his mom say she was going to take a shower, she slid out of bed in her red heart fleece pajamas, sliding her feet into her fluffy white slippers.

She walked down the stairs, into the kitchen, kissing Richie. "Good morning, sexy."

"Now that's a good morning."

Francine poured a cup of coffee and sat down. "I guess your mind is in motion as you're looking at the blueprints of the store."

"I have so many ideas."

"Tell me." Francine placed a bran muffin in her dish.

"Look at this place on the left of the building," he pointed with his fork. "This is all dead property. I guess the previous owner didn't see any use for it, but for us, it would be perfect. More parking spaces."

"Do you think we would need them?"

"Yes. Jason is using his architectural skills to come up with plans."

Francine took a bite of the muffin. "What are you thinking?"

"Sports bar restaurant. Maybe after nine, we can have a DJ come in, even have a karaoke night."

"That sounds awesome. I don't remember seeing a bar in there."

"There wasn't one. Jason is working on getting the electricity turned back on so we can get a better look at what's inside, without having to take the wood off the windows."

"Nice. Let me know what I can do to help."

"There's really not much you can do. Your responsibility is to your company."

Francine pushed her seat back and stood. "About that." She walked over to the counter and leaned against it, facing Richie.

"You seem to have something on your mind."

"I do. This has been something I've been thinking about for quite sometime." Francine sat back down, taking Richie's hand in hers. "All these years, I have put my business first during the baseball season. I hate the fact I missed so many games, even when you weren't pitching. This is our time now, to do something together. You are the love of my life. I don't ever want to be led off that path."

"What are you talking about?" Richie slid his chair closer to her. "We've been through this from the beginning. You are never going to lose me."

"I know that. What I am saying is, they are two different kinds of businesses. I really want to be a part of this venture with you."

"How are you going to handle working two businesses?"

"I was thinking of turning the real estate agency over to the girls."

Richie's eyes narrowed. "Really?"

"I have no doubt they can handle it. I've been away plenty of times before, leaving them in charge."

"Just think about this before you make the decision. If things don't pan out with the restaurant, at least you'll have something to fall back on."

"You're right. I'll work something out with the girls. A special compensation for them running the business."

"That would be a wise decision."

"What would be a wise decision?" Richie's mother asked, walking into the kitchen.

"We're just talking about our new business venture, Mom."

"This is the first I'm hearing of this," his mother said. "And what's that?" she pointed at the blueprints.

"Francine was left this property. When we went to investigate, it turned out to be an abandoned restaurant."

"Why were you left property? Was it from a relative?"

"No Mom, it wasn't. The property was left from a couple I had helped many years ago," Francine explained not wanting to elaborate on things to cause Richie's mother to ask loads of questions.

"That was nice of them. So this is the place?"

"Yes. We're not sure on the shape of the place because we couldn't see much. But we were thinking about making it into a sports bar restaurant," Francine answered.

Richie's mom's eyes shot wide open along with a huge smile. "That's wonderful. I can help out by doing some of the baking, especially Grandma's recipes. You remember how Grams made homemade bread. And how about at Christmas, her famous struffoli. We can be different, having struffoli on hand all year long. I'm sure the bakers I hire will love me." She laughed.

Richie sat back in his chair holding his coffee mug. "Mom, this isn't a bakery."

"Oh yeah, that's right. I can make Grandma's famous apple, peach and blueberry pies, her apple crumb, homemade cannoli, cream puffs…"

"Mom." Richie held his hand up.

"I know, I know. Write everything down. Let me go get my notebook."

Before either one of them could stop her, she had already taken off.

"We're in deep trouble. You have to tell your mother that we're opening up a sports bar, not a dessert bar."

Richie shook his head. "I hate to break her heart, bring her down, especially when she is this excited."

Francine's mind shot in all directions. The thought of working with his mother everyday didn't sit well with her. Richie's mom was a good person. She didn't have the heart to tell her. But what if…

"Wait a second. I just came up with an idea."

"Tell me before my mom comes back."

"I think everything she said could work out perfectly for us."

"What do you see?"

"We can have dessert specials every night. Maybe once a week, if we're doing karaoke and keeping the bar open late, we can do a dessert menu. Or," she lifted her hand, "during the summer months, if we're doing music outside, we can do cappuccino, espresso, latte and dessert."

"I think you have something here."

"I got everything." Richie's mom walked over to the kitchen table and placed a photo box and notebook on the table. "I found all your grandmother's recipes, and a notebook to write down what I need to make. "

Francine couldn't believe how excited his mom became. Angelina was your typical Italian mom, always in the middle of everything. For a woman in her late sixties, she had the

111

spunk of a thirty-year-old. Richie's mom would be an asset to the restaurant. She would give it the family feel, something that had long vanished in other establishments over the years.

"Wow, Mom," Francine said when she opened the box. "You have a lot of recipes in there."

"My mom used to bake something different everyday. Back in the day, my parents didn't have money. She made her own bread, too. We never ordered out."

"The foster homes I was in, there was rarely a home cooked meal on the table. Most times I was on my own for food. I lived most of my life eating fast food and cereal, until I met Richie."

Angelina put her arm on Francine's shoulder. "You are part of our family now. I look at you as a daughter."

"I feel the same. I am so happy to be part of such a loving family." Francine pointed to the box. "What kind of recipes do you have in there?"

"Everything from desserts to full entrees."

"We can use some of her recipes for the menu."

"I agree," Richie said. "However, I do want to have hamburgers and French fries on the menu. The younger guys would rather eat that versus a dish of lasagna, while watching a football game."

"I agree, but if we separate the restaurant, one side bar restaurant, the other side a full dining room, we can also utilize the pizza ovens too," Francine added.

"Besides, this will keep me busy and away from your father. Please," she rolled her eyes, "you will know exactly what I'm talking about when you're home all day."

"Mom! Dad works. What are you talking about?"

She winked at Francine. "We'll reopen this conversation in twenty years. Men will always be men."

"Mom…"

Saved by the doorbell. "I'll get it." Francine walked to the front door and opened it. Jason and Amy stepped into the hallway.

"Good morning." Jason shifted the posterboard he was carrying to his other arm as he kissed her.

Francine poked the board. "What's that?"

"I stood up all night working on the restaurant, putting my architectural degree into use. Is Richie in the kitchen?"

"Yes. Go on in. He's talking with his mom. I'll be there in a few," Francine said standing on the first step.

Jason rolled his eyes. "Problems?"

"Not at all. Everything is good."

"Thank God." Jason wiped the back of his forehead with his hand. "Do you have coffee up?"

"On the stove."

Jason walked with his posterboard into the kitchen. When Francine heard all three of them talking in the kitchen, she sat on the upstairs steps.

"What's going on? Is everything okay?" Amy asked.

"I was about to ask you the same thing."

Amy sat down next to her. "Things couldn't be better. Jason is awesome. I guess the timing was right for me to meet him. I still can't figure out how I missed him at your house all these years."

"That's because you weren't looking for him."

"I feel as if I'm living in a dream. Jason is everything I've dreamed of." She grinned. "I'm sure his flaws will come out once he gets comfortable with me."

"Hopefully you will be lucky like me. Sure Richie has flaws, but they are minimal. My biggest complaint is he rolls his dirty socks in a ball before throwing them into the laundry basket. If I don't check for them, when they come out of the dryer the only part of the sock dry is the outside."

They both giggled. The last time they giggled like this had been when they were teenagers. Seeing Amy happy made Francine feel content. Amy had had her share of bad luck when it came to men. Every time she met someone decent, they turned out to be fools, mamalukes.

Amy squeezed Francine's hand. "Say a prayer for me that things will work out."

"I have been every night. I love seeing you smile like this. I'm sure everything will work out. Like I said, Jason is a great guy. He too has had his share of bad luck in the love department too."

"Francine, are you two coming?" Richie called out.

Francine stood, followed by Amy. When they reached the kitchen, Francine couldn't help but laugh. Jason had set up the posterboard with props in front of it.

"What did you do, go to the craft store?" Francine asked.

"Yes, I did. I needed to make the board three-dimensional. The girls' department had a wonderful selection of furniture. The other furniture, I made. I will give you all my presentation over a cup of coffee."

"Isn't this awesome?" Richie said.

"I'll put up a fresh pot," Angelina said.

Francine rested her arms around Richie's neck. "I can't believe how much work you put into this, Jason."

"I love it," Angelina said. "He was thinking along the same line as me." Pointing to the posterboard, she announced, "That glass counter is for the desserts I'll be making."

"Was that a coincidence or were you conspiring with Jason last night?" Richie asked his mom.

"Oh, please. Would I do something like that?"

Both Francine and Richie replied, "Yes."

"I can assure you this was all my idea, with some help from my girl, of course." Jason took Amy's hand and sat her down on his lap.

"Your girl? You met someone. Who?" Angelina asked.

Jason chuckled. "Amy."

"Amy?" Angelina tapped her right foot up and down on the navy ceramic tiled floor. "Does your mother know you're dating Jason?"

"Not yet. We just started dating."

114

Francine felt the tension immediately fill the room. She knew exactly where mom was going with this. Time to get her off this delicate subject. She squeezed Richie's shoulder.

"Mom, what the hell are you talking about? What difference does it make if she told her mom or not? She's an adult," Richie lashed out.

"It's the repercussions that will come out of this relationship. When I was growing up…"

Richie slid Francine off his lap and stood. "Mom. Things are different now. I'd appreciate it if you kept your remarks to yourself. You're making everyone feel uncomfortable."

Angelina's cheeks turned red. Francine knew Richie had embarrassed her. But in all honesty, she deserved to be stopped. The last thing Francine wanted was for Jason and Amy to not come over while she stayed with them.

"I'm going upstairs to clean. I'll be going out to eat with Dad later, so make sure you eat something before you come home from the ballpark. Everyone have a good day."

Angelina stomped her feet going up the stairs, right before the door to the bathroom slammed shut. Silence lingered over the four of them for a few minutes as Francine's nerves came to a boil.

"How could you?" Francine leaned against the counter resting her hands on her hips.

"How could I what?"

"Talk to your mom like that. You embarrassed her."

"She deserved to be. She had no right to say anything to Jason and Amy. They are both adults, responsible for their own actions."

Francine rested her hands on her waist. "I agree with you that she shouldn't have said something in front of everybody."

"My parents were raised racist. They believe you don't date, let alone marry out of your race or religion. My mom's parents came from Sicily and my dad's from Naples. My father's parents saw my mother's family as coming from a poor part of Italy."

Francine threw her hands up. "Why are we even discussing this? Our two best friends have found each other. This is a happy time for all of us."

Jason touched Amy's face. "Sweetheart, I don't know about your family, but mine are going to be stunned to see me bringing home a white girl."

"And mine will be shocked to see you. But the bottom line is I don't see you as another color. I see you as a loving, compassionate man who is kind and has captured my heart. What other people think is their own problem."

"I agree. I don't care what anyone has to say." Jason sat back down. I want Richie to see this before he leaves for the ballpark."

"Wait till you see this," Amy said.

"Before I begin, I want all three of you to know these are only suggestions. The property belongs to Francine, so whatever you don't want or like, I will respect your decision."

"Wow, how professional." Amy giggled.

Jason chuckled. "I didn't forget how to give a presentation. Those architectural degree I took in college sharpened my skills with the ruler and pencil eraser."

"I'm loving this already," Francine said.

"In the back of the restaurant is the kitchen, pizza ovens and walk-in refrigerators. I thought on the right side, we'd place a long wooden bar. Over here," he pointed above the picture of the bar, "we can put six televisions. I think we should put a wall up at the end of the bar blocking off the back area. Then we could add a TV there too."

"So far I like what you're saying." Richie took a sip of coffee. "I think separating the room is a great idea. But what if we want to utilize the space behind the building like we discussed?"

"Not a problem. On the other side of the kitchen is another door across from the bathrooms. We can use that door as access to the back."

"I didn't even know there was a backdoor," Francine said.

"I took another ride out there to walk around the building. It's hard to figure out how much property there is from looking at a blueprint. Believe me when I say you have a lot of room to play with out back and on the side."

"Do you have the house?" Amy asked him.

"No. Let me run out to the car. Wait till you see the second part of my presentation."

Francine stood. "Can I get you anything?" she asked them.

"No thanks," Richie said.

"I'll help myself when I'm ready," Amy said.

A few minutes later, her front door closed and Jason appeared with a painted wooden house. "Babe, can you move the furniture in front of the posterboard."

Amy rose, pushing the dollhouse furniture to the side of the table. Jason placed the wooden house down in the center of the table.

"This is the restaurant, what I think the front looks like."

Jason lifted the roof off the wooden box. Inside, Jason had made the three sections, which they had talked about. Francine watched as he placed the pieces of dollhouse furniture into the box.

"Now imagine all these tables and chairs throughout the dining room. Here," he pointed to the back, "is where the bathrooms are and the backdoor leading to the rear of the building.

"Hey, man. What a job you did. This is crazy the way you constructed this."

"I have plenty of time on my hands in the off-season." He chuckled. "My mom will be proud to know I learned something in college."

This time they all laughed.

"Not to go into a long and drawn out explanation, I think the model speaks for itself," Jason said.

Francine took a closer look into the box. Jason had gone as far as painting the floor. She glanced at Richie who sat grinning, but wondered if they were making a big mistake opening a business when other establishments were going through a recession. On the flip side, the restaurant would keep Richie busy. He needed to be around people, continue to be on a routine. Even with the restaurant, he could continue to do his charity work.

"I think you did a wonderful job," Francine said. "The detail is amazing. Too bad you couldn't find a miniature bar."

"They didn't have it in the dollhouse aisle. I would have gone to a train store. I looked up the train stores this morning, but unfortunately all the stores we once had on Staten Island are gone."

"That's because no one plays with trains anymore," Amy added.

"The big thing is video games." Francine drank the last of her coffee. "I bet the young kids couldn't even put train tracks together."

Richie stood. "I'm sorry, guys, but I have to get going. I want to sit in the whirlpool for a bit and loosen my arm."

"Maybe you shouldn't pitch tomorrow," Francine suggested.

Richie's eyebrows narrowed, with his cheeks turning red. "I am not going to sit out tomorrow night's game. This is my last season. I plan on it being the best. I think I can withstand some soreness here and there."

"I know, baby, but I hate to see you in pain."

"That's why I go in the whirlpool and have the trainer rub down my shoulder. I will be okay just as long as we stay on the five-man rotation. That will give me enough time to rest. You have to trust me on this."

118

"I want to but…"

"He'll be all right," Jason said. "I'm going to get the ball rolling. I'm hoping to have the electricity on within the next couple of days. I also have to see what permits I'm going to need. But nothing for you to worry about."

The men banged knuckles.

"I'll walk out with you." Jason closed the posterboard and covered the wooden house. "Do you want me to drop you ladies off at work?"

"You can drop me off." Amy looked at Francine. "How about you?"

"I'll meet you there in an hour. I have something I need to take care of."

Richie kissed her. "Love you, baby. Don't worry, I'll be okay."

"Love you too."

After saying her goodbyes, she walked them to the door, closing the door behind them. Now she needed to do her usual damage control. She hated when Richie yelled at his mother, embarrassing her. Angelina did tend to baby him, but her comment about Jason and Amy was totally out of line.

"Mom," she called up the stairs.

When she didn't answer, she walked upstairs and down the hall to the bathroom where she stood washing the towels with a scrub brush.

"Mom, what are you doing? I washed the towels the beginning of last week."

"I need to keep busy," she said, not turning around to face her.

"Please, stop. You could have used the washing machine. Let's go down and have a cup of coffee."

Angelina stopped cleaning and sat on the toilet seat. "I didn't mean to make everyone feel uncomfortable. I was just surprised to see Amy with Jason. In my day that was unacceptable."

"I understand. But in today's society, it doesn't matter. The important thing is happiness, which is hard to find. I was the lucky one when I met Richie. I finally had a family to call my own."

"I see you as a daughter. You are the peacekeeper of the family. For that I am grateful." Angelina stood, opening her arms. "I appreciate you staying behind to talk to me."

Francine hugged her. "I love you. You're the mom I never had. I will always have your back."

"Thank you."

"Now let's go downstairs. I'll show you what Jason made. You're going to love doing the baking there."

Angelina put the scrub brush under the sink. "I can't wait to see the plans."

"You're going to love it."

Chapter Nine

Francine woke up to her favorite scent. Coffee. She had felt bad for Angelina, spending most of the afternoon telling her the story how she was left the property. Taking it a step further, she went over the blueprints, posterboard and wooden house Jason had constructed. She had to admit, they had a really nice afternoon.

Even though Angelina was her mother-in-law, Francine felt a strong bond with her. Though not strong enough to have her living with them, but for a couple of days she could deal with Richie's mom. The problem was every time his mom was around, she could count on putting on five pounds. She had to admit Angelina did make the best cakes and cookies. And the breakfast scones and muffins she made from scratch, you couldn't stop at just one.

Turning on her left side, she glanced at Richie, who was still asleep. She quietly slid out of bed, rushing down the stairs to the scent of blueberry.

"Good morning, Mom."

"Morning, sweetie. Did you sleep okay last night?"

"I slept so good that I didn't hear Richie come in."

"Neither did I." Angelina poured two mugs of coffee, handing her one. "I hate going to sleep upset."

"I feel the same way. I tried waiting up for Richie, but I couldn't keep my eyes open."

"You two didn't argue, over me. Did you?" she asked placing a piping hot scone in a dish in front of her.

"Not at all."

"I want to thank you for yesterday."

"I didn't do anything."

"I appreciate you staying home, spending time with me."

"I didn't mind at all. I wanted to bring you up to speed on the restaurant. But between you and me, I am nervous about his shoulder," Francine whispered over her coffee mug. "I believe he should tell the trainer he's having some pain in his shoulder. But you know Richie, he's thick and doesn't listen to us."

"You continue to be by his side, his support. That's why I'm certain my Richie will be fine. He loves you so much." Angelina sat down next to Francine. "Are you going to the game tonight?"

"Yes. Would you like to come with me?"

"Thanks so much for the invite. It's still a trifle bit too cold out there for me. I don't need my arthritis to start flaring up. I'll take a rain check."

"I'm going to hold you to it." Francine broke the scone in half and took a bite. "Mmm. Do I taste a hint of apple and nutmeg?"

"You are good."

"But I don't see pieces of apple in here," Francine said ripping a piece apart.

"You're not going to find one either. I grated an apple so it all mixes together and there aren't any chunks."

"Mom, these are great. My favorite are the prune scones. I don't know how you make them, but one thing's for sure, they are definitely on the menu at the restaurant."

Angelina's eyes watered. "You mean that?"

"Of course I do. I'm not sure exactly what we're going to do or what kind of menu we will create, but one thing's for sure, your baked goods will be placed in one of the menus."

"What are you thinking?"

"A lot of people don't like going out to eat dinner, but would love to go out, have a cup of coffee and dessert, something they can't buy in a supermarket."

"Whatever you decide to do, I am in."

Francine looked up when she heard the backdoor opening. In came Richie with two bouquets of flowers. He handed her two-dozen red and white roses and his mom a bouquet of purple orchids.

"How did you do this? You were just sleeping, snoring, not moving in bed."

"I bought them last night as a peacemaker for my rash behavior yesterday. But when I got home, both of you were sleeping. So I left them outside because I wanted to personally give them to you."

Francine stood, wrapping her arms around his neck. "I love you." She kissed him. "Come sit down, have breakfast with us."

"I can't. I want to get to the ballpark early so I can sit in the whirlpool and have the doctor massage my shoulder before I start preparing for tonight's game."

"Okay. I'll be there around six."

Richie walked over to his mom and kissed the top of her head. "Love you, Mom."

"Should I leave you something on the stove for later?"

"What do you think?" he asked Francine. "Do you want to go out and grab something to eat with everyone?"

"I'm indifferent."

"You know what, Mom, why don't you leave us something. If we don't have it tonight, you won't have to cook tomorrow."

Richie grabbed his keys off the key holder. Before closing the door, he blew Francine a kiss and mouthed, "I love you."

"Looks like it's just you and me." Angelina took the coffeepot off the stove and refilled their mugs.

"I got an idea. After coffee, I'll take you out to see the restaurant so you can see what we've been talking about."

Angelina relaxed her shoulders and leaned her elbows against the table. "You will?"

Francine smiled, nodding her head. "Of course. I'm excited about you being a part of this. For some reason, I feel this restaurant is more than a pure coincidence. I think this is something to bring our family together."

"I agree with you." Angelina sat down across from her. "Your life hasn't been a bowl of cherries."

"Bowl of cherries?"

"That was an expression my grandmother always used. But the point being, you had all the luxuries, and less than a part-time husband. I am sure through the years this was hard for you."

Francine stood, leaning against the counter. "It has been very hard, Mom, but I don't regret it at all, except..." Francine crossed her arms and lowered her head.

"Maybe things will change, now with Richie home all the time. It will give you more time to concentrate on the two of you, hopefully leading into the two of you fulfilling your dreams."

"I don't know how to answer that. I've come to the realization that if God wanted us to be parents, he would have given us the chance years ago."

Angelina stood, walking over to her. "You two are still young. Some people get pregnant right away, and some it takes more practice on a regular basis, if you get my drift."

124

Francine giggled as she felt the heat build in her cheeks. Even after all these years, with Angelina being a mother figure to her, she still got embarrassed when it came to talking about her sex life.

Angelina touched her face. "It's okay, Francine. I'm a woman too, with the same needs as you. Things always have a way of working out."

"Thanks, Mom."

"You can always come to me. Boys will be boys. I know Richie is a lot like his father. Sometimes he doesn't think correctly. You know men, they are all alike." This time Angelina snickered.

"At one time, I envied all my friends because of their relationship with their mothers. I never had that luxury, until I met you."

"Thank you." Angelina hugged her. "I know I haven't always been nice to you when it came to Richie. He is my only son."

Francine waved her away. "That's all past history."

Angelina placed her coffee mug in the dishwasher. "I'm going to get changed. When do you want to leave?"

"As soon as you're ready."

"Give me a half hour to wash up."

"Perfect."

Francine drove past the property. She made a U-turn in the middle of Page Avenue, and then another U-turn in front of the property behind Jason's truck. Once she took another look, she realized why she passed the property. All the weeds and garbage were removed from the front of the building. Over to the left of the building, three young male workers worked on the land next to the building. Francine got out of the car and walked over to where the guys had removed some of the debris, to see that what they originally thought was land, was indeed a parking lot filled with litter.

"Wow." Angelina walked around, her head turning from side to side. "This is a huge piece of property."

"Tell me about it. I didn't realize just how big, until all the junk was taken out."

"What was here?"

"There were overgrown bushes and trees, along with appliances and bags of garbage." Francine walked over to the big dumpster, which was already three quarters of the way full. "Take a look in there."

"I'm too short and too old to climb up on this, but I can see the crap piled up in the corner."

"I have to say Jason is right on the ball. We could never have gotten this much done."

"Jason has always been a hustler, as well as a dear friend. One thing I can attest to, he is a good man and a good friend to Richie."

"Yes, he is. I am just praying he will get through to Richie about pitching with his shoulder hurting." Francine kicked a few pebbles out into the street. "I would hate to see his career come to an end because of a shoulder injury. He would never be satisfied with that."

"You know my son. No matter what we say to him, he does exactly what he wants to do. But I'm sure he'll make the right decision."

"What I'm afraid of is the decision being made for him."

Sirens sped down Page Avenue right past them. Cars were backed up for two blocks waiting for the red light. This was an excellent sign. With the right advertising and menu, they could have a successful business. Richie and Jason were right, especially Jason. A sports bar restaurant, would be the most efficient way to be successful."

"Are you ready to go in?" Francine asked.

"Yes. I am really excited to see my son's new business adventure." Angelina touched her arm. "This time, I'm not saying a word. If Richie listened to me twenty years ago and went to college for his degree, chances are his life would be totally different. He made the right decision then, and I'm sure he'll make the right decision now."

"Richie is smarter than we think. Knowing him, he has everything already mapped out in his mind." She touched her head.

Francine opened the heavy glass door covered with plywood. Stepping in, she was surprised to see the lights on. Leave it to Jason to get things in motion.

"Jason," Francine called out.

Within seconds Jason appeared from the back of the restaurant. When he saw Angelina with her, he rolled his eyes. Francine gave him the thumbs up and quick nod of her head before Angelina caught her.

"Hi Angelina. Nice to see you. So glad you stopped by," Jason said.

"Francine insisted I come by with her today," Angelina bragged.

Francine immediately changed the subject. "I can't believe you got the electricity on already."

"That's the strange part. When I called the electric company, they said the service is suspended until further notice. So after pulling a few strings, they turned the lights on."

"Did you ask whose name the service is in?"

"Leon Vance."

"Who the hell is Leon Vance?"

"I have no idea."

"I'll have Toni look into it."

"Ladies, follow me. I taped copies of the plans for each section on the wall." Jason led them to the far corner of the room. "This is where I would like to see the bar. Let this be the focal point of this room."

"You're right."

"Jason, about yesterday, I want to apologize if I made you feel uncomfortable. I was out of line," Angelina said.

"No need to apologize. All is forgotten. I'm just happy you stopped by."

"I'd love to see my baking area."

"Straight back and to your left through the metal doors. I don't know about the actual baking ovens."

"That doesn't matter. I can always bake at home."

"While you ladies check out the kitchen, I want to check on the workers outside. I thought we would start by clearing out the front, side and back lot so we can see what we're dealing with."

"Thanks, Jason," Francine said, pushing the door open.

"This is gorgeous. I wish I had a kitchen this size in my house," Angelina said, roaming around the room. "These look brand spanking new." Angelina bent down, tilting her head to the side. "If you look at the top at the right angle, you can see the counter tops were never used either."

"How do you know that, Mom?"

"Because there are no knife cuts on the surface."

Francine squatted down, looking at both countertops. "You're right." On further inspection, she found packing slips still taped underneath. Reaching up, she took a few pots down. "Look at these. Brand new. No way were they cooked in at all."

"Check out the cabinets."

Francine went into the walk-in closet. The closet shelves were empty. Running her fingers along a few of the shelves, all she came up with was balls of dust. If the cabinets were being used, there would be some sort of residue from the spices, or something left behind.

"Not only does this look abandoned, but it looks as if no supplies ever hit these shelves either. Even when we moved in our house, I still had to clean out the cabinets after the cleaning service. I found papers and crumbs stuck in the corners of the shelves."

"There's one last place I want to look at."

Angelina opened the door to the walk-in freezer. Inside there wasn't a single thing left behind. Not even a speck of blood from a steak. Francine reached up to run her finger over the hooks. They too were unused.

Francine took her cell phone out of her back pocket. She tapped on the screen before holding the phone up to her ear. "Hey, Toni. What's going on?"

"Not much. I'm just doing that research for you."

"I need you to see what information you can find on a Leon Vance."

"I'll get right on it. Where are you now?"

"I'm at the restaurant with Richie's mom," she said, walking back into the soon-to-be bar area.

"I have some information for you on the background of the restaurant. But one thing's for sure, Leon Vance wasn't the person whose name I see on the lease."

"Interesting. See what you can come up with. I should be back to the office within the hour. Do you want anything?"

"Yeah, a new pair of thongs from Katie Lingerie."

"Ha. That will have to wait until tomorrow. Are you forgetting that Richie is pitching tonight? We have to leave for the ballpark by four to beat the traffic."

"Not a problem. I'll see you in a bit."

Francine pressed end and slipped her phone back into her pocket. Turning around, she spotted Angelina talking to Jason with her hands moving in all directions. She couldn't help but laugh. No one can believe Angelina was in her late sixties. She was sharp and always made sure she looked her very best.

Francine bit her bottom lip. "Jason, I feel something isn't right here."

"Why do you say that?"

"Don't you think it's weird that everything in this place has never been used? There isn't even a morsel of a crumb in the walk-in pantry."

"I wouldn't worry about it. It doesn't matter who rented this place before us. The bottom line is this place belongs to you. Your name is on the deed."

"I guess you're right. I always think too much, which means it's time for me to go. Are you about ready?" she asked Angelina.

"If you don't mind, I'm going to stay here for a bit with Jason."

"I'll give her a lift home. But before you leave, I want to show you the property in the back."

Francine followed Jason to the opposite side of the restaurant. He pushed the metal backdoor. The door had been painted navy on the inside, and the outside the black paint was rusted and chipped.

"Dear God." Francine covered her mouth, shocked at the size. She didn't expect any more than just a small path, which led to two dumpsters in the corner. Jason already had the back cleared out.

"I expected the exact reaction." Jason pushed an irregular piece of cement with his foot in front of the door to keep it open. "This isn't the whole thing either. The property goes way beyond those trees."

Francine twirled around. "You're kidding me. How do you know?"

"My neighbor is a contractor," Jason explained. "I measured according to the blueprint. You have a lot of room to do things."

"We don't even have to take down those trees."

"I'd love to plant flowers back here. Make a small botanical garden," Angelina suggested.

Francine glanced over at Jason. She was sure Angelina would drive him crazy once she left. It seemed everyone was so excited about this project except for her. Sure she wanted to do this with Richie as a family venture, but something told her they were getting in way over their heads. Her great grandfather had a bakery. She remembered her grandmother telling her she never saw her father. He left the house at three in the morning to bake the bread and cakes.

"That sounds wonderful, Mom. Jason will put your idea on our list."

"A wonderful idea too," Jason added. "Giving the restaurant an old school feel is a great suggestion."

"While you two talk about this, I'm going to head out. I want to stop by the office to see what information Toni pulled up about this place."

"I'll see you tonight after the game." Angelina gave her a kiss goodbye.

"And I'll meet you at the game with Amy."

Francine saluted him goodbye with her right index finger. The trip back to the office took her less than twenty minutes with that being a first. She couldn't believe she didn't hit any traffic but was surprised she didn't have to park two blocks away at a parking meter.

"Damn." Francine walked to the office and poured a cup of coffee. "There wasn't a spot to be had out there."

"There must be some sort of fair down at the school."

"I didn't pay attention." Slipping her sweater off, she placed it behind her chair and then proceeded to lower the heat.

"I know." Toni shook her head. "But this morning, it was freezing in here."

"I believe you. I just can't wait for the weather to get warmer. I know we are going to be freezing tonight at the ballpark."

"I already have my gloves and the pullover Pelicans sweatshirt Richie gave me."

"Don't worry about it. People will just think you're a thirty something groupie."

Toni burst out laughing. "Wouldn't that be funny trying to compete with the teenagers? Not that I don't feel like one."

"I know what you mean. I still don't know where all the years have gone." Francine lifted her paper cup out of the cardboard holder and took a sip. "Before we start going down the road of reminiscing, I want to hear everything you found out about the property."

"Oh this is a good one. But before I tell you what I found out, I want to assure you the property is legally yours."

"I don't know if I should be happy or concerned with that statement." Francine twisted her wrist back and forth. "From your tone, I know you found out a lot."

"A lot is the understatement. I have the full story on the property." Toni tapped on the keyboard before turning the computer around so Francine could see it. "This is the original blueprint of the property. Marvin Peacock was the owner. The store belonged to his grandfather. While the Peacock family operated the store, it was a hardware store. Back in the day, they used the side property in the summer to sell plants and the winter to sell Christmas trees and wreaths."

"I remember Marvin telling me the one thing he missed about the holidays was not being around people, and sharing the Christmas spirit."

"About ten years ago, he leased it out to Ralph Wilson, who kept the business going." Toni pointed to the computer screen. "Four years ago, Ralph had a massive heart attack. The store remained closed until Marvin leased it out to Leon Vance and Doug Sussman eighteen months ago."

"Okay."

Toni tapped away at the computer screen. "Leon Vance applied for permits a few weeks after he leased the property. He cleared out the counters, racks and remaining merchandise, and placed it in a storage facility on the west shore."

"That makes sense. West Shore Storage is only a few miles down the road."

"The complication is that they weren't supposed to change the store. In the original lease they signed, they were to keep the hardware store intact."

Francine leaned back in her chair. "They knew Marvin would never find out. He lost his wife and was in the nursing home with Alzheimer's. No one would have known the difference."

"Exactly. I also investigated the will. Marvin updated the will over twenty years ago, when he was of sound mind."

"What I don't understand is why they abandoned the restaurant. Why would anyone gut out an old hardware store, put a dining room and kitchen, submit new blueprints and then take off?"

"The good news is everything's in place. They even have a liquor license."

"That's a huge plus. I just think something isn't right. Where are these two clowns?"

"I don't know. I tried looking them up, but there's no record of them. What I can tell you is that Doug Sussman has a long rap sheet. He has spent time in prison for fraud, possession of a weapon and marijuana."

"You're kidding me?"

"Nope. After putting all the work into the building, passing an electric and plumbing inspection, they disappeared. The lease on the property is up. The restaurant never opened."

"I could have told you that. On further inspection in the kitchen, I can confirm that none of the pots were ever used. Even in the pantry, there was no trace of any food being there. All I could find were dust balls. It just doesn't make sense."

"I know. I have a few calls out there to see if anyone has any information on Leon and Doug. Hopefully we'll have some answers soon."

"That's good." Francine sipped her coffee. I would assume we would have to transfer the liquor license to our name."

"You also have to come up with a name for the restaurant. The last known name of the place was Peacock's Hardware store."

"I'd like to come up with something really unique, different. A name that will outshine the others."

"I'm sure you'll come up with something. I just hope these two idiots don't show up and give us a hard time."

"I doubt they'll show up. They probably ran out of money. Who even knows if they were paying Marvin the rent?"

"There isn't anyway for me to check into that but don't think we have anything to worry about."

Francine crossed her arms and crinkled her lips. "I still feel weird about the whole thing. Those two men invested a lot of money into their business. What if they come back wanting their money?"

"They have no supporting arguments. Like I told you, their lease was up months ago. Just give me a moment." Toni went through the pile of papers in the folder under her keyboard. She pulled a multiple page, stapled document out of the folder, handing it to Francine. "This is the lease. It expired four months ago. So legally, they have no claim to the property again."

Francine flipped through the papers. Toni was one hundred percent right. Vance and Sussman had no claims at all to the property. Chances are they were long gone, owing Marvin back rent. She wasn't going to obsess with this.

"I'm stopping home to change." Francine stood, sliding her sweater on.

"Sounds like a plan. Let me close everything up. I'll meet you at your house in fifteen minutes."

"See you there."

Chapter Ten

A few hours later, Francine and Toni sat at the ballpark watching batting practice. The stadium was fairly empty. Not many people got there early to watch batting practice except for the young girls and groupies. Richie warmed up in the bullpen. Francine thought about walking down toward the bullpen, but changed her mind. From their seats, next to the first base line, she could hear the young girls screaming his name.

Francine rested her coffee cup on the holder in front of her. "Remember the day we fought with the usher because he didn't believe I was Richie's wife."

"How can I forget? You caused such a commotion that Gary Thompson had to go into the locker room to get Richie." Toni giggled. "You wearing Richie's shirt made you look like a groupie."

"But the shirt was authentic. The real thing. Richie had pitched his first major league game in it before they changed the uniform colors."

"Here he comes, here he comes," a girl's voice screeched from behind Francine.

Francine looked over her shoulder at the girls running down the steps a few sections over from them with the ushers shouting after them. The young girls leaned over the railing with pieces of papers and baseballs in search of Richie's autograph. Richie obliged by stopping and signing for all the young girls screaming out his name. The usher yelled if they didn't get up to their seats, he would have them removed from the stadium.

"Memories," Toni said.

Richie walked toward the dugout, stopping in front of Francine.

"How's your shoulder feeling?" she whispered.

"So far, so good. I feel strong."

"Promise me if you feel any pain you will tell the trainer."

Richie drew a cross on his chest and tapped on his nose. "Cross my heart. I promise. I don't want to put myself into anymore danger of having to get surgery."

"I don't blame you. I don't want that either. I want to start our new life at the restaurant at the end of the season."

"Speaking of which, start thinking of a name. Something catchy."

"I will. I was thinking of The Perfect Pitch Sports Bar and Restaurant."

"I'm thinking that's a great name." Richie leaned into her, giving her a soft kiss on her lips. "Love you."

Francine twirled around, wearing the very jersey that had gotten her in trouble all those years ago. "Love you too," she whispered.

While Richie jogged into the dugout, Francine sat back down next to Toni.

"I'm hoping I have that with Eric."

"Oh yeah." Francine called the waitress over and ordered two beers. "I'm sorry. With all the excitement of the restaurant, I never got around to asking you about your date."

"Eric is a nice guy. I think he's sexy. The best part, he wasn't looking for sex after taking me out for dinner. And you know my track record. That for me is a first."

"I know. I hate these men. They think because they take you out for an expensive dinner that entitles them for free dessert at the end of the evening."

"I found him to be respectable. When he dropped me home last night, he asked if he could take me out again next week. He even asked if it were all right if he called me today."

"Now, that's a very good sign. I hope this time you really find true happiness."

"It's hard meeting anybody normal."

"Toni, you're at my house all the time when we have parties, which are filled with many single athletes."

"I know. But I don't want to get involved in that kind of life where my husband is away for eight months during the season and nine if they're in the playoffs and World Series."

"I think if anything, the time Richie and I are apart really brought us closer together. Sure he's a pain in the ass, but what man isn't once you get to know them and they get comfortable."

"You make it sound so easy."

"For me it is."

"Lo Maro, Lo Maro," the girls chanted when Vinny ran in from the outfield.

Vinny Lo Maro was the Pelicans relief pitcher. If anyone besides Vinny came in, Francine would cringe. The hardest thing was sitting there watching him pitch, especially when he doesn't have his groove on.

"Hey ladies." Vinny gave Francine and Toni a kiss on the cheek. "Glad to see you out here. When you yell out here for Richie, the guys in the dugout go hysterical. I personally think they are jealous because their wives aren't out here." Vinny flipped the ball he was holding into the stands. The girls screamed. "Let me go and sign some autographs. I love seeing the girls smile. Catch you after the game."

Once Vinny was out of ears reach, Francine turned to Toni. "I just don't know why you don't go out with him. He's a great guy with so much to offer. The best part being, he has no excess baggage."

Toni's face lit up. "He's a great guy but not my type. If only…"

"Toni…" someone called out.

They both turned around. Francine didn't recognize the man, but by the look on Toni's face, she did. Her eyes were sparkling and her smile seemed to go on forever. He made his way down to them and gave Toni a kiss.

"Francine, this is Eric," Toni said.

"Hi, Eric." Francine extended her hand to shake his. "Nice to meet you."

"Yep." Turning his back to Francine, he spoke to Toni. "I don't like sports but decided to give baseball a shot." He reached into his jacket pocket and pulled out two tickets. "I got us seats somewhere down there," he pointed to the outfield.

"Come sit." Francine tapped on the chair next to her. "Thee seats are reserved for family and friends."

"Thanks, but I got it," Eric said.

Toni's mouth dropped open. "Don't be ridiculous. These are the best seats in the house."

Francine swiped the tickets out of Eric's hand. She dropped her gaze to them and immediately shook her head no. "My God, these seats are all the way out in right field."

"I couldn't put you out like that," Eric said.

"Never. No one passes up the best seats in the house." Francine giggled. "Don't worry, I won't interfere with your date."

"Our official second date," Toni added.

"I promise not to interrupt or throw in any unnecessary remarks."

"Not to worry. You just made it better." Eric sat down next to Toni. "Sitting here, I'll learn more about the game, than sitting in the outfield with the fans with black, white and yellow lines painted all over their faces.

"I'm a good teacher," Toni said while zipping her Pelican's sweatshirt.

"So am I." Eric winked.

Francine bit her bottom lip as she turned her attention back to the baseball diamond. Eric seemed to be okay but couldn't see Toni with him. Toni was so carefree, while Eric came across as being stuffy. From what she had observed so far, Toni glowed sitting next to him.

"Hi, Mrs. Raggalio."

Francine looked over to her left where a young woman sat. "Hi. It's Francine."

"Hi Francine. I'm Kristin Richards, Ernie, the second baseman's wife."

"Nice to meet you."

"I'm the new one this year. My husband was traded here from Atlanta during the off-season. I really don't know many people here or where to go shopping. I tried reaching out to some of the younger wives during spring training, but the women weren't too receptive."

"I'm sorry to hear that. I've lived in Staten Island my whole life. I was born and raised here. Where are you living?"

"We found an apartment right near the stadium. But Ernie and I agree we'd rather buy a house. I just hope he doesn't get traded again."

"You can't think in those terms. You have to go with the flow. Each time Richie's contract comes up for renewal, I always fear he could be traded. But the point is you can't think like that. As long as you don't travel during the rush hour, it's a half-hour drive."

"Do you come to every game?"

"No. I try not to miss a game Richie is pitching. But attending every game is way too much."

"I notice some of the other wives and girlfriends are at all the games."

"Let me give you a word of advice. People come and go. When you see them, acknowledge them by saying hi. Don't worry, you'll be a part of the crowd in no time."

"What about you?"

"I do my own thing. After the game, I'm out of here. I have my own business. If you decide you'd like to look at houses in Staten Island, give me a call. I'll show you around." Francine opened her handbag and handed her a card.

"I will tell Ernie. Hopefully we'll come on out to Staten Island."

"Look around at the different boroughs. You'll know when you find the right place."

Kristen played with her long, braided, dirty blonde hair. "Do you know anywhere I can get my haircut?"

"I get my hair done in Staten Island."

"Maybe I can come out there while the guys are on the road to get a haircut."

"That sounds great. We can make it a day. I can give you a brief tour of the Island and then go get something to eat."

"Really?" Her blue eyes shot wide open.

"Yes." Francine touched her hand. "Don't worry, Kristen. Things will be okay. You're just the new gal on the block. Everyone will warm up to you. Just give it time. Look," Francine pointed to herself, "you made your first friend. I will introduce you to the ladies when they come."

"What ladies?" Amy asked.

"Hey." Francine stood hugging Amy, and then Jason. "This is Kristin Richards. She's new to the team. This is my friend Amy and her boyfriend Jason."

"Nice to meet you." Kristin shook both their hands.

"Hi, Toni." Amy yelled over Francine.

Toni stood to hug Amy and Jason. She stepped aside. "This is Eric."

"Hi Eric," they said together.

"This is Amy and Jason," Francine said.

"Nice to meet both of you." Eric shook both their hands. "I'm happy to have finally met your two best friends. I totally approve," he said to Toni.

"I'm so happy." Toni giggled.

Francine turned to Amy and mouth, "Duh." What did his approval have to do with anything? They had been the three musketeers since they were teens. She'd be damned if she'd let some stuffy nosed idiot with no knowledge of the game of baseball come between them.

Toni and Eric stood. "We'll be right back. Eric wants to buy me a souvenir."

Francine covered her mouth with her fingers, not letting Toni and Eric see her giggling. When they walked up the stairs, Francine turned to Amy. "I hope he doesn't distract her from her job. Because," Francine took a sip of her beer, "I don't know about you, but this whole restaurant thing has been a distraction for me."

Richie stuck his head out of the dugout. "Hey, Jason."

"I'll be right back," Jason said to them. "I'm going to say hello."

When Jason was out of earshot, Francine turned to Amy. "Something's not right with the restaurant."

"What do you mean?"

"Why would someone put money into opening a restaurant, buy top of the line pots and appliances, and just abandon everything?"

"Maybe the previous owner went bankrupt."

"No way. Marvin owned the property. He leased it out to those men. Toni found out very little about them."

"I wouldn't give it much thought. Maybe they changed their minds, took their losses in stride and filed for bankruptcy."

"Maybe you're right. I'm looking for something that isn't there," Francine concluded.

"Yes, you are." Jason stood in the aisle with his arms crossed. "Forget about it, Francine. The bottom line is the property is legally yours? Who cares what the two clowns who leased the building were doing or thinking. We will have an establishment unlike any other on the Island."

"You're right. What do you think about the name *The Perfect Pitch?*"

"I love it." Jason lifted the phone. "I'm ordering a beer. Do you want anything?"

"Yes, another lite beer," Francine said.

"Me too. Want to share a pretzel?" Amy asked Francine.

"Sounds good to me. That will be enough to hold me over until later."

"Good afternoon, ladies and gentlemen. Welcome to the New York Pelicans ballpark. We'd like you to all rise for the singing of the National Anthem sung by the boys' choir."

The young boys were lined up at home plate. As they sang, the stadium went silent except for the fans that sang along. A line before the end of the song, everyone started cheering. While the boys were ushered off the field, the Pelicans came out of the dugout, causing the stadium to go into a cheering roar.

Francine leaped out of her seat, cheering along with the rest of the fans. Coming out to the ballpark never got old for her. She loved interacting with the fans.

She stamped her feet while chanting. "Let's go Pelicans, yeah, yeah, yeah."

Richie gave her the thumbs up after taking his warm-up pitches. The smile on his face quickly faded. He walked

142

around the mound, kicking the pitching rubber before meeting Chad Hartman, his catcher. They stood with their backs to home plate, until the batter from the opposing team came out and stood inside the batting circle. Both returned to their positions.

"Play ball," the home plate umpire announced.

Richie rotated the ball in his hand, moving his fingers all around the stitching. Francine knew his routine. He loved playing with the ball to throw the batters off. His split finger fastball had been his ace. The batter never saw it coming.

Richie stood with his back to her on the mound. Chad Hartman gave Richie the signal before punching his glove in his left hand. Richie went into his windup. He released the ball, the batter swung and she heard the ball hitting the catcher's mitt.

"Strike," the umpire hollered.

The next pitch was a pop-up behind the plate. Chad leaped out of his position, looking up, following the ball until it slammed into his glove. The next two were groundouts to the shortstop and first baseman. As Richie jogged off the mound, he gave Francine the thumbs up. She sighed in relief. His signal meant his arm wasn't throbbing, an excellent sign.

The next six innings flew by. They were ahead by five runs. Each time Richie took the mound, Francine could see the pain in his face. The team had a nice enough lead for Richie to take it easy. When the Pelicans were in the dugout, Francine wondered if he would tell the coach about his shoulder.

Richie pitched a decent game. Not one of his best. He usually had double figure strikeouts in every game he pitched. Today, he only had five, with most of the outs coming from pop-ups and groundouts. Francine always kept track of his pitches during the innings, something she had always done when she attended the games he pitched. Today, he hadn't thrown as many pitches, but the look in his eyes each time he came off the mound showed his pain. She knew he pushed himself to the limit. What she hoped was he admitted this to himself, and then relayed his pain to the pitching coach.

The infielders took a few extra minutes to come out of the dugout. The home plate umpire went over and circled his arm. Within seconds, the team took the field with Richie taking his position on the mound.

The two pitches were balls, way out of the strike zone. The next pitch, the batter swung and missed. Then the next six pitches Richie threw, the batter fouled off into left field before grounding out to the third baseman. Richie wiped the back of his hand along his forehead. He turned to look out at the outfield. Taking a deep breath, he dug his foot into the pitching rubber before calling a timeout.

Manager, George Parsons walked out to the mound with Chad joining them. They spoke for a few minutes before George pointed to his right arm. The bullpen doors opened and Vinny LoMaro jogged to the infield. Richie handed him the ball, smiled and walked off the mound. Everyone was on their feet cheering. Before walking down the dugout stairs, he lifted his hat, which made the fans scream even louder.

Amy squeezed Francine's forearm. "Don't worry, everything will be okay."

"I hope so. I know damn well his shoulder is on fire. He has this thing about having complete games."

"Ladies, you don't understand," Jason said. "Richie coming out of the game is killing him inside. Even if you're having the worst game of your career, you continue to its completion. It's a man thing."

"I understand," Francine said, talking over Amy sitting in the middle. "I saw the pain in his eyes the last game he pitched. He might not want to admit it, but I watched him throughout his whole career, and so has Amy." Francine felt her eyes starting to water. "I feel for Richie."

"Just be there for him, offering your support. It's better he takes it easy now so his arm is well rested if they make it into the playoffs."

"I know, but this isn't the way he wanted to end his career. He wanted to retire on a high note."

"And he will. Richie is an icon. He has broken records and really made them way out of reach for others. He is respected by the whole baseball community."

Vinny wrapped up the game with the Pelicans winning five to nothing. It would be at least an hour before the players came out. Jason suggested they go to the players' lounge as they always did and grab a drink. He tapped on his cell phone and after getting a response, he returned his phone back into his pocket.

"Richie will meet us at the lounge when he's done. He said he is getting physical therapy on his shoulder before coming over."

"Francine."

Francine turned around when she heard her name called. There standing at the top of the stairs stood Toni and Eric. They walked up the stairs to meet them and walked over to the VIP elevator.

"What happened to you two?" Francine asked.

"After Eric bought me the fourteen karat gold diamond earrings, we sat in the picnic area talking. Look." Toni lifted the hair over her ear to show off her new earrings. "We appreciated the offer to sit with you. We started talking and lost track of the time." Toni put her hair down. "You're not mad, are you?"

"No. Never."

"I missed our seats. It's so hard paying attention to the game from there." Toni whined in a whisper.

"But we were able to be with each other," Eric announced to both of them. "How are we going to get to know each other if we are sitting here with your friends and you're gabbing with them during the whole entire game?"

145

Francine bit her tongue, trying her best not to lash out at Eric. Toni loved baseball. At times Francine believed Toni loved it more than she did. Her gut feeling was Eric purposely kept Toni away from them. She hoped her instincts were wrong this time.

Eric did seem a little strange coming dressed to the ballpark draped in an overabundance of gold jewelry, designer sweatshirt, wearing black snakeskin boots. She wouldn't say anything, only because she really didn't know him. This just might be his way of showing off.

"We're going to the players' lounge for a drink. Would you like to join us?" Amy asked when the doors to the elevator opened.

Toni said yes, but Eric said no.

"I have to get up early for work tomorrow morning. We ate at the game. We'll take a rain check, thank you."

"Okay. Enjoy your night. I'll talk to you tomorrow," Francine called after them as Eric had already started walking away with Toni.

During the trip home, Richie and Francine didn't speak. Usually on the ride home from the ballpark they were laughing and singing. When the Brooklyn Queens Expressway turned into the Gowanus, Francine broke the silence.

"What's wrong, Richie? Please talk to me."

Francine caught him glancing over at her, but his lips still remained locked. He reached over, squeezed her hand, before returning it back to the steering wheel.

Francine looked out the window as they drove over the Verrazano Bridge. He got off at the South Beach exit, driving into the beach parking lot.

They sat quietly for a few minutes before Richie broke the silence. "I put on my big boy bloomers, like you always tell me, and spoke to the pitching coach."

"Is that why he took you out of the game?"

"No." Richie shook his head. "I took myself out of the game. I couldn't take the pain anymore."

"And what did he say?"

Richie's eyes filled with tears, which was a rarity. Francine placed her cup in the holder, unbuckled her seat belt and sat sideways in her seat. Reaching into her handbag, she took out a tissue to wipe his eyes.

Richie took a deep breath, slowly exhaling. "Things aren't looking too good."

Francine reached her hand out, resting it on his knee. "Do you feel like talking about it?"

"Yes, because I need to tell someone the truth behind what's going on with my shoulder," he mumbled.

"Oh Richie, I'm not liking the sound of your voice. I want to help you in anyway I can."

"That's why I don't discuss this at home. I don't need my mother breathing down my back with everything I do. She can really be a pain in the ass."

"I know."

"But my injury, I don't want her to know the extent of it."

Extent of his injury? She didn't like the sound of this. "How bad?"

"Pretty bad." He tilted his head down resting it on the steering wheel. "I really don't have a lot of choices here. I can do physical therapy for a couple of weeks and hope my shoulder will miraculously heal, or not waste any time and go for the surgery."

"Did the trainer put you on the disabled list?"

"The moment I asked to be taken out of the game."

"I'm sorry, Richie."

"The thing is, I need to do physical therapy for three to four weeks. If the therapy doesn't help, which the trainer believes it won't, then I'll have to have the surgery."

"What's the recovery?"

"Depends on the amount of damage." Richie turned his head toward her. "The trainer said I should be up and running in six to eight weeks depending on my therapy."

"What does he suggest?"

"Surgery."

"What do you want to do?"

"What I want to do and what I can do are two different things. I think the way to go is have the surgery. This way I might be back by the end of the season."

Francine touched his face. "I am so sorry. If I could take the injury for you, I would."

"I know you would. But this is just a part of life. I had a good run with the Pelicans. I am one of the lucky ones who grew up here and played my whole career in New York. My career has given us the best of everything, giving me the chance to help my parents and sisters. I have you, who stood beside me through the good and bad. I couldn't ask for anything more."

"Honestly, how is the pain?"

"Unbearable." He reached over to Francine, running his fingers from the middle of her neck, down her shoulder into her shoulder blade. "The pain is ridiculous. It feels like a burning knife is being jabbed there."

"Is there anything I can do to make it better. Maybe a hot oil massage?" She smirked.

"Babe, if you even touch that area, I'll jump right out of the car."

"What are you going to tell your parents? They're going to find out when the Pelicans make the announcement."

"As usual, you're right. I'm going have to tell them, I'm just not going to let on how serious the surgery is. No need to have them worry for no reason."

Francine rocked her head up and down. "Does that mean you're going on the road tomorrow?"

"Yes. I made the decision to have the surgery. I want to get back to pitching as quickly as possible. The trainer wants me to come, so he can keep my arm loose. He'll make all the arrangements. The day before the surgery, we'll fly back into New York together."

"You have nothing to worry about."

This time Francine's eyes watered. The thought of him being in so much pain with nothing she could do to help him made her sick to her stomach. She felt helpless, but knew she had to be there for him after the surgery.

"Hey, why are you crying? It's me who's going under the knife, not you."

"I hate feeling helpless, not being able to help you."

"Well…" Richie reached for her face, pulled her close to him, kissing her lips. "I said I had pain in my arm, not that I'm helpless." He winked.

"Oh I know that look." Francine licked her lips. "I can slide into your favorite purple nighty."

Richie started the truck, stepping on the gas. "Oh baby, don't tease me. I'll have us home in a flash."

Chapter Eleven

Over the course of the next week, Richie's parents moved back into their home. Richie called Francine every day, sometimes two to three times a day while on the road, making sure she was all right. She'd play along with him, however, his tone frightened her. She heard the pain in his voice and it saddened her. No doubt Richie was suffering. Her biggest challenge would be keeping her emotions to herself, not letting on how nervous she was.

The ride down Hylan Boulevard to work was out of control. She couldn't remember the last time she had seen so much traffic. Even the traffic on the back roads crawled. Her cell phone rang, and she pressed the button on the steering wheel.

"Hey, babe," Richie's voice echoed through the car. "What are you up to?"

"I'm sitting in traffic on my way to work. How are you feeling?"

"Not sure…"

Francine rolled down her window. "Asshole. What the hell do you think you're doing?"

"Babe, what happened?"

"The car next to me cut me right off. If I weren't paying attention I would have hit him. There must be a full moon out there today. So what's going on?"

"I'll be arriving home around nine o'clock."

"Surgery?"

"Tomorrow. I took an hour-long MRI. The trainer and the team doctor determined that I need the surgery ASAP. Yesterday I did the pre-op testing."

"Damn. I'm going to have to start making arrangements. I have a lot of things to do."

"Babe, slow down. You make it sound like you're making funeral arrangements. What you can pick up for me is a bottle of Sambuca. I'm going to need something to dull the pain."

"Sambuca? Since when do you drink?"

"I was being funny. Ha, ha."

"You're not funny."

"I'm trying to make you laugh. I know you are worried. I can hear it in your voice. You never yell out the window at drivers. You always reprimand me when I do."

Francine heard Richie continuously clearing his throat on the other end of the phone, meaning he was nervous. Now she needed to shut down her emotions. He needed her to be strong, there was no denying that. She had to keep her voice upbeat.

"If you give me your flight number, I will make sure I'm there to pick you up."

"No need to. Vic is flying in with me. We'll have a car waiting for us."

"Who's doing the surgery?"

"The team's doctor, Dr. Weston."

"I'm surprised Vic isn't doing the surgery."

151

"He'll be assisting in the operating room. Orthopedic surgery isn't his specialty. Doctor Weston is one of the top orthopedic surgeons in the country. The Pelicans are lucky to have him on staff."

Francine beeped her horn. "Richie, let me get going. I have to concentrate on the road. A car just crossed the double yellow lines and drove down the wrong side of the street to make a left-hand turn."

"I have to get going, too. Vic wants me to get into the whirlpool before we leave."

"Okay. I'll wait up for you. Safe trip home."

"And you watch the road."

"Love you."

"Me too."

Twenty-five minutes later she pulled up in front of her office. She grabbed her handbag off the passenger seat and walked to the door. Pulling on the handle, the door didn't budge. Francine reached into her handbag and took out her office keys to unlock the door.

"Amy, Toni," she called out.

"I'm in the bathroom, Francine," Amy called out.

Francine slipped her sweater off, throwing it over the back of her chair. Opening her appointment book, she didn't have anything set up for the day. A little at a time she was passing the appointments over to Amy, giving her more responsibility.

Amy walked into the office zipping her pants. "You're here early. I didn't expect you until after lunch, especially with all the traffic."

"Tell me about it. A ten-minute ride down the hill took me over a half hour."

"Supposedly there's a multicar accident on the Gowanas. Traffic is jammed up on the whole Island, and over the Goethals Bridge."

"Jammed isn't the word." Francine leaned against her credenza. "Where's Toni?"

"She's running late. Overslept. How's Richie?"

Francine slid into her chair. "He's on his way home. Tomorrow is his surgery."

"Oh man. Don't worry about things here. I'll make sure everything runs smoothly."

"I know you will. The problem is I'm going to need more than a day away from the office. If it's all right with you, I'd like to take the next two weeks off. I know you can handle it."

"Without a doubt. But I hope Toni is onboard. She seems to be infatuated with Eric. He calls her at work all the time. If she misses his call, he'll call her back ten minutes later. I'm only hearing one side of a conversation, but from what I'm hearing, I get the distinct feeling he wants to know everything she is doing."

"Have you questioned her?"

"Yes. She insists there is nothing to worry about. He keeps telling her that he really likes and respects her."

"I'll talk to her later when we get back from the store."

"Who's we?" Amy asked, reaching for her jacket.

"You and me." Francine grinned. "I need to pick up a few things before tonight. I don't want to run out and leave Richie home alone."

"When are we going?"

"Now. I checked the book. We have nothing planned for this afternoon."

"Cool. This will give us a chance to talk. I don't like to say too much in front of Toni. She is so involved with Eric, that he is occupying her whole life."

Francine stood. "She hasn't had a boyfriend in over two years. I'm thrilled to see she has met someone."

"You know Toni. She gets attached way too fast. I think we'll have to keep an eye on her. We don't want her to go into another depression."

"Absolutely not. I can't remember the last time I saw her this happy." Francine reached for the notepad on her desk, writing a quick note to Toni, letting her know they would be back in a bit. "Are you ready?"

"Let me grab my handbag."

Francine held the keys in her hand. She held the door open for Amy, locking it behind them.

"I hope the traffic is gone by now. I don't feel like sitting in bumper to bumper traffic all the way to the store," Amy said while buckling her seat belt.

"Don't worry, I'm not getting on the highway." Francine said pulling away from the curb. "What's going on with you?"

"What isn't? I feel like I died and went to heaven."

Francine glanced at Amy who sat with a huge smile on her face. "Jason."

"Yes. He is everything I've looked for in a man and more."

"Hmm." Francine tapped her fingers on the steering wheel.

"No, I didn't."

"I didn't ask you anything."

"But I know what you were thinking." Amy giggled. "With Jason, things are different. Sure I want to wrap my legs around his waist, but I want to wait. When I'm with him, things feel so right. I'm falling for him."

"No way. That's great." Francine took her eyes off the road for a few seconds and looked back just in time to jam on her brakes. "What's wrong with these people today? They come to a complete stop, jam the lane, and then make an illegal U-turn with no blinker or warning."

"Please concentrate. Keep your eyes on the road. I hate when you start looking around without paying attention to the road."

"I'm having a hard time concentrating today. I'll pay closer attention. These people are out there driving like animals. I thought they gave tickets for talking on your cell phone while driving."

Francine turned into the mall parking lot, finding a spot right in the front. Shopping in the morning was the best time of the day. Any later, the teenagers lined the mall. She pulled an index card out of her jean pocket with the list of things she needed to buy.

"Where are we going first?"

"I need to get a few packages of white tank tops along with button-down shirts to make it easier for him to dress and undress while his arm's in a sling. You know Richie, he's going to want to do everything by himself."

"There isn't a man in the world that doesn't act like a baby when they have any kind of injury."

"Tell me about it."

They walked into Macy's and headed over to the men's underwear section. Francine found the tank tops. Sifting through the rack, she found two packages of white extra large. Now she had to find them in black. Squatting down, she dug away at the tightly packed packages. Glancing over her shoulder, she didn't see anyone around, giving her the thumbs up to pull the whole bottom shelf apart. All she kept finding were small and XX-large. *What the hell?*

Francine dropped to her knees and made her way along the six-foot wooden display. "Yes." She clenched her fist in victory when she found one package of black. Moving along on her knees, she dug through the shelf, until she found another package of gray. "Perfect," she said out loud.

"Perfect? Oh my God, Francine. You made a mess all around you."

Francine looked down next to her. There were packages of tank tops surrounding her. She handed Amy the packages. "Here. Hold these for me while I put the packages back on the shelf. Thank God nobody saw us."

"That's where you are wrong," a stern voice said from behind her.

Francine turned around on her knees, trying her best not to start laughing. The mess she made was horrific.

155

"I'm sorry. I have every intention of straightening up."

"What I don't understand is why you didn't ask for help. I'm standing right over there," the elderly salesman pointed to the cash register.

Francine lowered her head. "I didn't see you. But don't worry." She picked up a few packages and placed them back on the shelf. I had no intention of leaving this for you to clean up."

From behind her, she could hear Amy snickering. Biting down on her bottom lip, to stop herself from laughing, she mumbled, "Sorry."

"Stand up," he ordered. "I'm not going to have you crawling on your hands and knees fixing my display. If you had asked, I would have pointed you to the display next to this," he pointed, "which is filled with extra-large to XXX-large."

Francine held on to the shelf, giving herself support to get up on her feet. She had to look up to come face to face with Mr. Lipton, Manager.

"Is there anything else I can help you with?"

"I also need boxers and button-down cotton shirts."

"Do you need extra large in the boxers?" he asked.

Francine giggled. Boy, did he need extra large in the boxers. When her eyes met Mr. Lipton's, he didn't seem amused at all.

"Size, please."

"Medium boxers." Francine turned, looking for Amy who was nowhere to be found. She left her with this nut job that wasn't going to leave her alone for a minute in his department.

"These are the mediums."

Francine lifted the package. "My husband isn't going to be happy with these. Do you have anything more upscale?"

Mr. Lipton looked down at her. He didn't have to say anything, for Francine knew exactly what he was thinking. She stood dressed in moccasins and jeans with rips in the thighs and knees. They weren't worn. They were the latest style. She wore Richie's Pelicans T-shirt and had no makeup on, with her hair in a ponytail. Not the clientele you would expect to be buying expensive merchandise.

"Come this way." He led her to the back wall where all the designer boxers hung, not packaged on the shelves. "This is where the mediums are."

"Thank you."

Francine flipped through the rack. Every once in a while she would glance up to see Mr. Lipton standing against the wall with his arms crossed. She picked out six pairs on velvet hangers and handed them to him.

Mr. Lipton walked them over to the counter placing them down next to the tank tops. Again she looked around. Where the hell was Amy? Out of the corner of her eye, she spotted her sifting through the tie display. From where she stood, the perfectly spiral display didn't look perfect anymore. Francine giggled.

Not amused, he remained expressionless. "What else can I help you with?"

"Cotton, you know like T-shirt material button-down shirts. I think I'd like to look at them in an extra large, since they always shrink when you wash them."

Mr. Lipton's eyes narrowed. "I'm sure you didn't purchase them from here."

"Of course I did. I'm just not a hand wash, hang to dry kind of gal. I throw everything in the washer and dryer."

"Figures," he mumbled loud enough for her to hear.

Francine followed him across the store.

"Are these what you are talking about?"

"Yes!"

"What size are you looking for?"

"I'd say extra-large. My husband is tall and has wide shoulders. I want it big enough so he doesn't have to struggle. He's having shoulder surgery tomorrow. I want to get him shirts to make him comfortable."

"We don't have a big selection." He lifted a few hangers off the rack. "These really aren't a big seller. This is all we have."

Francine looked at the navy, charcoal gray, beige, light gray and red shirts he held in his hands. "I'll take them all."

"These are very expensive."

"Nothing I can't handle."

"Is there anything else I can help you with?" he asked before pivoting on the heels of his loafers toward the register.

"No thanks. I just need to find my friend." Francine looked around. "Amy," she called out loud.

"I'm coming," she called back. "I was looking for something for Jason but didn't see anything appropriate. I was going to get him a tie…"

Francine kicked her, but it was too late.

Mr. Lipton looked over to the ties. "Oh dear. My tie display too?" He walked over to the register, mumbling under his breath and quickly rang her up. "That will be eleven hundred, thirty-nine dollars and twenty-two cents."

"Oh?" Francine turned to Amy and laughed. "I didn't realize how much I spent."

Mr. Lipton leaned his hands against the counter. "Is this a problem?"

"Of course not." Francine placed her oversized handbag on the counter. "Now where the hell is my wallet?" Glancing up at Mr. Lipton, Francine saw his right eye twitching.

"I told you to get rid of those big handbags of yours. You're always losing things in there."

Mr. Lipton cleared his throat. "Ladies, I don't have all day. I have a few displays to fix."

Francine used her cell phone as a flashlight. "Here it is. I knew it was in here." She opened her wallet searching for her Macy's charge card. "Now where the hell did I put my card?"

The longer it took Francine to find the card, the more Mr. Lipton lost his patience. Francine could hear him tapping his foot on the other side of the counter. Finally, Francine found her card. "Here you go."

Mr. Lipton took the card, looked from the card to her, shaking his head. "I need to see your driver's license."

Francine looked him right in the eyes. She knew the routine. "Why?"

"Store policy."

Opening her wallet, she handed it to him displaying her driver's license.

His mouth dropped wide open. This time Amy kicked her, giggling.

"I'm so sorry Mrs. Raggalio. I thought you were some...were trying to..."

"It's okay. I get this all the time."

"My deepest apologies."

Francine took the shopping bag and smiled. Reaching into her pocket, she took out a fifty-dollar bill and slid it into his suit jacket. "Thank you for all your help. Again, sorry about the displays."

An hour later they walked into the office with three lattes. Toni sat at Francine's desk talking with a client.

"These are the ladies I just told you about. Francine, Amy this is Marion Roberts. She owns the property at 1111 Saint Johns Avenue. The property is below Bay Street and is the equivalent of six lots."

Holy shit. That property must be worth close to five million dollars. "Nice to meet you Mrs. Roberts," Francine said.

"Please, call me Marion. When you say Mrs. Roberts, I think of my mother-in-law."

"Me too."

"I was just telling Toni that I don't want to break up the property. I want to sell it just as is. My husband and I envisioned building a luxury apartment building. But when my husband died, so did all our plans. I held on to the property for another two years, but decided now is the time to let it go."

"That won't be a problem, Marion. I'm sure we will be able to accommodate you anyway you need."

Marion stood. "Thank you. That's why I am here." She turned on her high-heeled, black Louboutin. "Let me know when you have any bites."

"We will," Toni said.

Francine and Amy both said, "Nice meeting you."

When she walked out and crossed the street, all three of them yelled. This would be one of the biggest deals they would ever handle. Maybe now wasn't the time for Francine to step away from the business. This deal she wanted to see through.

Amy handed out the lattes. "I know it's a little too early to be drinking, so let's make a toast with our lattes."

All three of them held up their lattes, tipping the white plastic tops together.

"To a big score."

Toni double locked the office door. Shortly after Marion left, so did Francine and Amy. She didn't mind being left alone. After completing the paperwork on Marion's property, she went online to purchase a few new outfits.

During the week when she had gone out for dinner with Eric, he had passed a few remarks about the way she dressed. She had always worn short skirts and low shirts supported by a pushup bra. He thought she dressed too provocative, causing people to stare at her. When she got home that night, she took a good look at herself in the full-length mirror on her bedroom door. Eric was right. She bought jeans and button-down shirts. Eric would be so surprised when he picked her up tonight.

By the time she got home, and freshened up, she heard a car horn blowing outside. Shutting the light in the bathroom, she peeked through the blinds to see Eric sitting outside in his car. This was the third time he has done this to her. He tells her one time, comes a half hour earlier, and then complains that she kept him waiting.

Why didn't she tell him to go to hell? Why, because she was lonely and didn't want to be alone. Both her friends were involved in their own personal lives. Francine would be helping Richie recover from his surgery, so she didn't plan on seeing much of her. And since Amy had met Jason, she had been spending a lot of time with him.

Toni opened her front door, waving to him. She grabbed her handbag off the doorknob and locked the door behind her. Once in the car, Eric leaned over to give her a kiss hello. He surprised her by not complaining about her keeping him waiting for five minutes. But the tone in his voice and the way he tapped his fingers on the steering wheel, she knew he'd be bringing it up later on.

During the ride to The Finn there was no conversation. Eric had the radio on in the car so loud that she already had a headache. He pulled up in front of the restaurant, slid out of the car and walked around to her side to open her door.

She reached for his hand. "Thank you."

"Not a problem." He released her hand. "Sorry, I don't like public display of affection."

"You're kidding me," she mumbled under her breath.

She had always been the romantic type. Holding hands and snuggling while walking down the street on a cold winter night in the snow had always been her dream. With Eric that wasn't the case. But on the plus side, he always took her out to expensive restaurants and lavished her with expensive gifts. She had never owned a bottle of ninety-dollar perfume or even owned a designer bag. This lifestyle she would just have to adjust to, ignoring his imperfections the way her foster parents did through the years.

As usual, they sat at the same table. Eric always sat in the chair against the wall facing the front of the restaurant, insisting she sit across from him with her back to the door.

Another strange request, but one she could live with. Eric really seemed to like her. Maybe with Eric she would have the family life she didn't have when growing up. Her foster parents never treated her like they did their own kids. Hopefully Eric would make her feel the love she had always desired.

Eric shut his menu placing it on the edge of the table. "I thought we could share an order of baked clams and fried calamari."

Even though she wasn't a big fan of either one of them, she agreed. What they had as an appetizer really didn't matter. Taking one last look at the entrees, she closed her menu. "I'm going to have the skirt steak dinner with the red bliss potatoes and broccoli."

"That's a lot of food for a little woman."

Toni smiled and waved him off. "Not a problem. I can handle it."

"We'll see about that." Eric raised his hand and snapped his fingers to get the attention of the waitress.

"Good evening," the waitress acknowledged the both of them. "Can I start you off with a drink?"

"Two diet cokes with lemon," Eric ordered for them.

"I'd really like a raspberry margarita," Toni said.

Toni watched the waitress's eyes go from her to Eric who just nodded in agreement. *What the hell?* She was a big girl and could order her own drink of choice for the night. Why did Eric always have a say in everything she did?

When the waitress walked away, Eric leaned toward her. "Just one. I don't want to walk out of here with you hanging onto me because you drank too much."

Toni wanted to leave, even if it meant her walking home. In her oversized handbag, she always brought a pair of slip-on sneakers along with a metro card. She needed to make a quick decision. First, she decided to question him on his last statement.

"Why would you say that? I never drink that much. I'm always in control. I know my limit."

"I'm just telling you. The last woman I dated had an alcohol and prescription drug problem. I don't want to get myself into that kind of a situation again."

"Eric, I'm not your ex-girlfriend. I don't do drugs. I only drink while socializing. I don't have any liquor in my house."

"And why's that?"

"Because I don't drink," she snapped loud enough for the people around them to look.

Catching Eric's glance, he showed no emotion on his face. She would bet that he realized he had spoken out of line. She didn't want to get involved in a relationship where Eric controlled her.

"Here you go." Eric buttered a piece of bread, placing it in her dish.

"Thank you."

Toni lifted the bread, took a bite and placed it back down in her dish, acting as if nothing had just happened. Maybe she was reading into something that wasn't there.

The waitress placed a glass of diet soda in front of each of them, and the margarita in front of Toni. "Are you ready to order?"

Eric ordered the appetizers, along with their dinner. Toni sipped on her margarita, looking around the crowded room. The sound of laughter coming from the patrons made her smile.

"Everyone seems exceptionally happy today. Maybe one night we could double date with my friend Amy and Jason."

"Maybe we can. I'll let you know."

"That would be awesome."

Just as they started talking, a man's voice came over the microphone. "Good evening. Welcome to our first night here. I am DJ Wired, and I will be your host tonight." The music started playing and that was the end of any conversation at all until they pulled up in front of her apartment.

"Thank you for such a wonderful dinner," Toni said.

"Aren't you going to invite me in?"

"Not tonight, Eric."

"I don't understand. Why?"

"I want to get to know you better before we take our relationship to the next level."

Eric shook his head. "Sweetheart, I have already taken you out for dinner over a dozen times since we've been together. Get over your fears. I'm a man, I have needs."

At times, he confused her. He could be sweet one minute and then say something stupid the next. Her brain warned her to be cautious, but her heart told her to go with her feelings. Eric had just been busy with work, not getting his quota of accounts. Maybe next time they went out she'd talk to him about these things that bothered her.

"I will keep your needs in mind." She leaned over the armrest, softly kissing his lips. "Goodnight, Eric."

Chapter Twelve

Toni rocked on her sofa with her knees held close to her chest, dumbfounded at what had just transpired a little while ago. The tone in Eric's voice left a lot to be desired. What kind of woman did he think she was? She didn't sleep around, let alone sleep with a man after going out with him for a few weeks.

One thing that bothered her was the way he turned from hot to cold in less than thirty seconds. She liked him, yet was wary of him. She couldn't understand why he would be so insistent of rushing her into having sex with him. If he really liked her, he would give her the time she needed. She wanted to be sure that what she felt in her heart was love, not lust.

Sure she wanted to run her fingers through his hair, feel his warm breath on her neck, and his thin lips showering her body with kisses. Before she got out of the car, she saw his swollen groin saluting. Yes, she felt bad leaving him like that, but hell, all she did was kiss him. She would never do anything to purposely arouse a man without following through.

Toni stood. Turning on the gas under the teakettle, she took the tea bag of decaffeinated green tea, placed it in her cup, then proceeded to spoon in three teaspoons of sugar. She needed to make a decision on what to do about Eric. He could have just had a bad day at work, but his abrupt shift in personality cautioned her.

Maybe she needed to reassess this relationship. Then again, after the way they'd left things, he might not call her again.

The teakettle whistled just as her cell phone whistled. She turned the gas off and picked up her phone. Eric.

"Hi."

"Hey, Toni, what are you up to?"

"I was in the process of making myself a cup of tea." Toni poured the boiling water into her mug. "What are you doing?"

"I'm in bed. I couldn't fall asleep knowing I left you upset."

"I wasn't upset."

"I saw the look on your face when you got out of the car. Usually, you'd turn around, wave goodbye to me and wait for me to pull away from the curb to close your door. I watched you walk into the house and slam the door shut."

Toni lifted her mug and took a sip, not knowing how to answer him. "I was disappointed that you insinuated because you took me out for dinner, it entitled you to take me to bed."

"I didn't mean it to sound that way." Eric cleared his throat. "You got me so aroused. I'm sorry. I don't want to ruin what we have going here."

"Neither do I," Toni whispered. *Did he tell me he's in bed?* Toni glanced at the clock on the cable box. It was barely nine-thirty. "Why are you in bed so early?"

Toni heard Eric chuckling on the other end of the phone. What did she say that was so damn funny?

"Sweetheart, I had to take care of the mess you left me in when you got out of the car. Besides I get up at five-fifteen every morning. I need to stop at the warehouse to pick up the samples for the day."

"Do you have a busy day tomorrow?"

"Yes, a long, drawn out day. Every time I go into the doctors' offices, I have the receptionists all going crazy over me. Must be my charm."

"Yes, it has to be." Toni put her mug down on the counter. Eric reminded her so much of her foster father, who was so into himself, but had a heart of gold. "You have nothing to worry about, Eric. I'm not mad at you. You can put your head down on the pillow and go off into a deep sleep with dreams about me."

"That's exactly what I was going to say. Morning comes around real fast."

"Yes, it does."

"What are you doing tomorrow?"

"Richie is having shoulder surgery tomorrow morning. I want to be at the hospital for Francine. She's going to need support."

"For?"

"She's scared. We've been together since high school. We're always there for each other."

"What are you two dating?" he asked, his tone sarcastic.

"No," she snapped. "Why do you always say things like that for?"

"I'm teasing you. Can't you take a joke?"

"I'm a little sensitive these days. I haven't been in a relationship in a long time. Please just bear with me. I need to take things one step at a time. Okay?"

"You're making my head spin, sweetheart. Why don't we do lunch tomorrow around two?"

"Call me first. I don't want to leave Francine until I know Richie is out of surgery. I don't mean to put my friends first, but this is important."

"Fair enough. I'll catch you sometime tomorrow. Goodnight."

"Night."

Toni pressed end. Now that was a wacky conversation. He started the conversation in an apologetic way and ended the call with the same tone he did when she got out of the car earlier. What was it with this guy? Was she thinking too much into things, or should she count her blessings and run? But there was something about him she truly liked. She'd go out on one more date and see what happened. If their date ended the way it had the past few times, then she would pack it in, sending him on his merry way.

"Babe, I'm home."

Francine double-checked herself in the mirror. Richie would go crazy when he saw her in the red see-through lace outfit he had bought her so many years ago. The black stiletto thigh-high boots completed the outfit. She wanted everything to be perfect. Tonight would more than likely be the last time they would be able to make love for quite some time.

"I'll be right down," she hollered down the stairs.

Picking up the perfume bottle, she sprayed his favorite scent from head to toe. She knew this would drive him totally crazy. As she walked down the stairs, she ran her fingers through her hair, a nervous habit of hers.

"Where are you, sweetie?" she asked in a low seductive tone.

"I'm in the dining room. But..."

Francine walked into the room. Vic sat at the table with Richie, grinning.

"Oh my God!" Francine covered her breasts with her hands, and then shifted them to between her legs.

"Calm down. I'll take care of things." Richie took his jacket off the back of the chair, and held it out for her. Francine slid her arms through the sleeves and Richie zipped it closed.

"I'm sorry. I had no idea Vic was down here."

"Hey, not a problem." Vic chuckled, standing. "I'm going home to tell my wife. Maybe she'll come up with some creative ideas too."

Francine felt the heat rise in her face. "I am so sorry, Vic. I thought Richie was alone."

"Not a problem. I wasn't staying. The cab is outside waiting." He hugged Francine. "Everything will be fine tomorrow. Doctor Weston is tops in his field. I will be right there with him. I will keep you posted the whole time."

Francine sighed. "I think I'm more nervous than Richie."

Vic banged knuckles with Richie. "He will be fine. He's in good hands. You two go enjoy your evening."

Richie walked Vic to the door. When she heard the front door shut, she stood, walking over to the counter.

"What are you doing, sweetheart?"

"Getting your dinner."

Richie walked over to her, covering her lips with his. Francine wrapped her hands around his neck. "I'm sorry if I embarrassed you tonight."

"Me, no. I think you're the one. You were redder than an apple."

"I bet. Now about dinner."

"I'd like to start with the dessert if you don't mind. Doctor said no dessert for a couple of weeks."

"Maybe for me. But for you, well I think I can keep you nice and satisfied."

"That's one thing I can count on." Richie leaned over, lifted her and cradled her in his arms. "How about I take you upstairs for dessert?"

"You can take me anywhere you want."

"How about we skip out of town? We can go to Hawaii for a couple of weeks."

"Hmm. That sounds like a wonderful idea."

"Owww." Richie gently placed her feet down on the floor. "I'm sorry, sweetheart. I wanted to carry you up the stairs, but the pain in my shoulder is unbearable."

"I'm sorry. I didn't mean to hurt you."

"You didn't. As soon as my shoulder heals, I'll be carrying you all over this house."

"I remember the day you carried me into this house."

"Yeah, so do I. I shocked the hell out of you."

Francine reached her hands to his face. "The day we got married was the best day of my life. I still feel the same love in my heart as I did back then. I can never imagine my life without you." She raised her lips to meet his. When she felt his groin rising, she took a step back. "It scares me knowing you are in pain and there's absolutely nothing I can do to help you."

"As long as I go to sleep with you at my side, with you being the last person and the first one I see when I wake up, I know I can make it through the surgery without a problem."

"I will be there for you the whole time. I will never leave your side."

Richie took her hand, leading her upstairs. His eyes bulged wide open. "Tonight, the candles give the room an erotic feel, smell."

"I know how much you love lit candles. I want tonight to be perfect. Because after the surgery…"

"I don't want to talk about my surgery anymore. I want to talk about us." Richie unzipped the jacket she wore, slowly slipping it off her shoulders. He turned her around. "Let me see my girl." A big grin appeared on his lips. "I'm going to sit down on the edge of the bed. You can make me very happy if you dance for me."

Francine stood with her hands resting on her hips. "Dance with no music?"

"I'll take care of that right now."

Richie reached into his pocket and took out his cell phone. He played around with the screen, and within a minute music blared. "How's that?"

"I like it." Francine ran her fingers through her hair as she swayed her hips. Her hands rested behind her head, and then extended out while her body rocked side to side. "Do you like?" she asked.

"Oh yeah."

Francine continued dancing, keeping her eyes on him, seeing the look of contentment shining in his green eyes. Her tongue circled around her lips. "I want you," she pointed. "I want you so bad. I want to rock your world," she sang, lifting her foot up onto the bed next to him.

He placed his hands on her waist. "I love when you play." He lifted her up, placing her down on the bed next to him. "I also love making love to you."

Holding his face between her fingers, she lowered his head until their lips met. The softness of his kisses pulsed through her, causing her body to shiver. When his hands dropped to her breasts, her nipples hardened, brushing against the lace of her bustier.

"Oh Richie," she moaned. "If you don't make love to me right now, it's going to be over before it begins."

"Don't worry, sweetheart. I'm going to be making love to you all night long."

When the alarm went off the next morning, Francine rolled over, reaching her hand out to shut it off. She yawned. Turning to her right, she stretched her arm out to only touch an empty place next to her. On the nightstand, Richie's wallet, crucifix and chain, watch and wedding band lay on the white daisy doily Angelina had made for her many years ago. This made the reality of the surgery hit her heart.

Why had she sat on the Internet earlier looking up the side effects and cautions of the anesthesia? Even though it's rare, the thought of Richie going into a coma still haunted her. Before going downstairs, she jumped into the shower. The hot water felt good beating on her face, blending with her tears. She wanted to get all her tears out of her system before Richie saw the fear in her eyes.

171

With her hair pulled back into a ponytail, along with minimal makeup, she walked down the stairs. She searched through the first floor of their house, wondering where Richie went. Returning to the kitchen, she poured a mug of coffee. She smiled. Even though Richie couldn't drink or eat, he still made certain her coffee waited for her when she came down.

Francine heard the key in the front door. Thank God, he came home. In the back of her mind, before she went to sleep last night, she thought about Richie just taking off to avoid the surgery. He was scared, no doubt in her mind. Even as they made love the night before, Richie seemed a million miles away. She needed to be the strong one, reassure him that everything would be okay.

"Sweetheart," Richie called out.

"I'm in the kitchen. Thanks for making me coffee."

"You're welcome."

Richie appeared in the doorway with a bouquet of roses. "Just a little something to thank you for everything you've done for me."

"You don't need to thank me. What I do is out of my love for you." Francine took the roses from him, giving him a kiss on the lips. "We've been through so much. This is just another bump in the road."

"You're right," Richie agreed. "Down to the sleazy motel you met me at when I was on the road playing AA ball." He chuckled. "I can still remember the day you walked into the science lab and made the announcement you were not dissecting a frog."

"I got sent down to the principal's office. When they sent me back to class, I was partnered with you. You told me, 'don't worry. I got your back.' And to this day you still do."

"Come here." He reached his arms out.

Francine put her flowers down on the counter and collapsed into his arms, holding him tight. His warm breath on her neck made her feel secure. He kissed the top of her head repeatedly, before taking a step back.

"Are you ready?" Richie asked her.

"No, not really. But the sooner you get the surgery done, the sooner you will be on the field pitching."

"You know it's going to be a long road."

"Yes, I do. And I'm going to be with you throughout the whole thing."

On the ride to the hospital, they reminisced about their teen years. Mostly talking about how she sat in the stands for all his practices and games he pitched and how she always had positive things to say after a bad game.

"Is there anything pending I need to take care of?" Francine asked.

"Nothing. Jason is taking care of the restaurant. And my mom said she would bring dinner over every night."

"She doesn't have to do that."

"You know Mom. I'm sure she'll show up at the hospital too."

As soon as they arrived at the hospital, Francine spotted the paparazzi and two of the major news channels. Francine rode a block down, made a U-turn and drove to the back of the hospital, pulling into one of the employee parking lots.

"Sweetheart, how are you going to get out of the lot? You don't have a card key."

"Don't worry. I'll figure it out. What's important is I get you into the hospital without the flashes of cameras and microphones being shoved into your face."

Richie laughed. "That's what I love about you. You think of everything."

"Yes, I do." Reaching her right arm to the floor of the car behind his seat, she pulled out a black tote bag. She took out an oversized pair of sunglasses.

"Are you kidding me? I'm going to look like a fool."

"No, you're not."

Francine got out of the car, meeting Richie standing on the walkway. He took her hand in his, squeezed it before walking into the employee entrance. Once inside, the staff ushered them through the glass bridge and a set of stairs before leading them to the elevators in the lobby, to be met by Vic.

"How did you guys get in here without being bombarded by the press?"

"You know Francine, so don't even ask."

The elevator door closed, bringing them up to the second floor.

"I don't even want to know." Vic tapped Richie on the shoulder. "While Francine checks you in, I want to check your vitals and get you prepared for surgery."

"Oh no," her voice cracked. "Am I going to be able to see him before surgery?"

"Yes. Ask the girl at the desk. She'll come get me. You can stay with Richie for a bit."

"Thank you."

Francine watched them disappear through the doors. This made the whole thing feel surreal. The outcome of this surgery would determine if Richie could pitch by the end of the season. She would hate to see him go into retirement like this.

Francine brought the paperwork Richie had completed at home. The staff at the hospital had accommodated them, making certain no one from the press entered the lobby.

Francine returned to the second floor. She didn't even have to ask the receptionist. Nurse Kay, her nametag read, had been waiting for her by the wooden door.

"Good morning, Mrs. Raggalio."

"Please, call me Francine."

"I will." She nodded. "I will be taking care of your husband before and after the surgery. Don't worry, Francine, he is in good hands. Doctor Weston is the top in his field. Each year he makes the top one hundred doctors in the country. This year he's in the top twenty-five."

Francine rubbed the palm of her hand along her forehead. "Dr. Weston is known throughout the sports community. I'm just nervous."

Nurse Kay led her around the nurses' station, opening the glass door to Richie. "You can stay with him until he is taken to the operating room."

"Thank you."

Francine closed her eyes. The sight of Richie lying in bed hooked up to monitors sent shivers through her. Opening his eyes, Richie grinned. "Hey, don't look so jealous."

"Jealous? What are you talking about?"

"My designer nightgown and paper hat."

Francine sat down on the side of the hospital bed. "You are crazy."

"Crazy in love with you. And don't ever forget it."

"I won't. My love for you grows increasingly every day we're together. You're my rock, my reason for being the woman I am today. Our life together has been a fairy tale." A tear escaped from her eye, rolling down her cheek. "I keep thinking one day I'm going to wake up and it will be over."

"Our love will never be over. We have only just begun to live our life together. We have grown together while never losing sight of who we are."

"I love you too."

Francine leaned down to kiss him. He held her face between his hands, softly kissing her lips. After a few minutes, he dropped his hand to her chin.

"We're going to have to part, before my groin grows to full length. I don't think the nurse will appreciate a patient with a pup tent."

They both giggled.

"Sorry to break this up, but it's time," Vic said, entering the room dressed in scrubs. "Dr. Weston is getting ready."

Francine's eyes watered.

"Sweetheart, don't cry." Richie wiped the tears with his fingers. "Everything is going to be okay. I'm in good hands."

"I know you are."

Chapter Thirteen

Francine paced back and forth in the waiting room. Each time she pivoted in her sneakers, the sound of squeaking rubber echoed through the small room. Amy and Jason sat on the orange leather sofa, while Toni stood in the corner whispering on her cell phone.

"You are making me nervous," Angelina whispered. "Please sit down."

"I can't, Mom."

Angelina put her arm around her shoulder. "Our futures are already laid out. Whatever is meant to be will happen."

"I know, Mom. But you know how much Richie loves the game."

"Yes, however, Richie already made the decision to retire." Angelina dropped her hand from Francine's shoulder and reached into her pants pocket to take out a set of rosary beads. "Hold these rosary beads and say a prayer. God will lead the way. Right Vincenzo?"

Richie's father just shook his head. Francine knew he hated when Angelina went off on the prayer tantrum.

"Francine, everything will be fine. This is a routine surgery for pitchers. Doctor Weston is one of the best in the country," Vincenzo said.

Francine hugged him. "Thanks, Dad."

"Don't let her drive you crazy. You know Angelina. She worries too much," he whispered.

"We're both scared." Francine leaned on the windowsill overlooking the beach. "I've never been this scared in my life," she mumbled, starting to pace the room again.

A hand touched her shoulder. "Come on, sit down with us," Jason's husky voice said. "This isn't doing you any good walking around the room. You're making me dizzy. I just came back with scalding hot lattes for us."

"What's going on? Why is the surgery taking so long?" Francine cried.

"I'm sure they started later than they had originally anticipated. It happens all the time."

"I hate not knowing what's going on. That's my husband in there. This is driving me absolutely crazy."

"And my son."

"Come on, Angelina. Let's go take a walk." Vincenzo smiled at Francine. "We'll be back in a few minutes.

Jason put his arm around Francine leading her over to the orange armchair. "Sit here." He handed her a latte. "Instead of you walking around, let's talk about what the future holds while your in-laws aren't here."

"What do you mean?" Francine asked, her eyes flooding with tears.

"Don't cry." Amy handed her a tissue. "We have a lot to look forward to."

"She's right," Jason said. "I still can't believe he went on all this time dodging the surgery. Don't worry, Richie is going to be up and pitching within a few months, especially with his determination."

Francine forced a smile. "You're right. I bet he'll be driving me nuts after a week."

"A week. I'd say after two days," Toni chimed in walking toward them. "Remember when he broke his thumb."

"How could I ever? He walked around the house with a baseball in his hand for two days before he started pitching into the net in the back yard." Francine lifted her latte off the table, taking a sip. "Once the cast came off, he started physical therapy immediately. He was back on the mound in less than two weeks."

Jason crossed his arms. "See what I mean."

"Yes. But you have to remember this year is the most important one in his career. He wants to go into retirement on a high. If he has to retire because of this injury, he'll be devastated."

"Never going to happen. And you know that," Jason pointed to Francine. "Richie will do everything in his power to get himself back into form. He's a professional, a fighter. He knows what he wants. Unfortunately, he'll need to be babied for a couple of days."

"Don't start crying again." This time Amy wiped the tears streaming down her cheeks.

"Everything will be fine."

"She's right. Do you think Richie will let me take over all the renovations at the restaurant without him?" Jason asked.

Francine sniffed. "I don't know."

"We spoke this morning. Do you know what he worries about the most?" Jason asked.

"No."

"You. He's worried about you. He asked me to keep an eye on you, making sure you don't get so wrapped up in him that you put your own health at risk."

"That's Richie for you."

Jason sat on the wooden table facing Francine. "He also wants me to go over the plans with you to see if you would like any changes, especially since it's your property. He felt bad we took over, and didn't bother asking you what you wanted to do."

"I didn't even give it a thought. Whatever's mine is Richie's. That's the way it's been since we were kids."

"I will take care of the office with Toni. Since she's good on the phone and the computer, I will leave that to her. I will host the open houses and try my best to recruit new clients," Amy assured her.

"Don't make yourselves crazy recruiting clients. Did you forget we just got the listing for the six-lot property from Marion Roberts?" Toni asked.

"That's right, I forgot," Amy said, sitting down next to Jason.

"I've already been calling contractors about the property. So far I've gotten five appointments set up. On investigating the property, the lots have no restrictions on them."

"Nice. Were they interested in all six lots?"

"Two of them wanted all six lots to build a condominium community on them. Two of them wanted to put single family houses, and the last contractor was willing to take three lots."

"That's a start. Truthfully, I can care less what they build on the property. I just want to get rid of the property to the highest bidder."

"Before I forget to tell you, I've been digging for more information regarding your property," Toni said.

"Did you find anything out?" Amy asked.

"No." Toni walked over to the window ledge and leaned against it. "I can't seem to find much information on Leon Vance or Doug Sussman." Toni opened her handbag, taking out a small notebook.

"You're nice and organized." Jason laughed.

"She always had a bit of obsessive compulsive disorder in her," Amy said.

"Ha. I'm not even going to address your comments." Toni flipped open the pad. "The liquor license is in Doug's name, along with the food handler's certificate. Leon, I couldn't find anything in his name. I would say he was the silent partner."

"A silent partner with his name on the lease as co-renter? Something doesn't sound right," Francine said.

Jason stood. "I agree. But none of this is any of our problem. The place is yours."

"You're right," Francine said. "I loved your presentation, the way you set everything up. My suggestion is while I'm nursing Richie back to health, go ahead with the plans you presented to us."

Jason grinned.

"Look at him," Amy pointed. "He has been waiting for you to tell him to move forward."

Francine saw Jason's eyebrows shoot open looking right at Amy. He probably never expected Amy to rat him out. But in Francine's eyes, she didn't. Now she knew how much Jason was committed to the project, not that she ever doubted it.

"I place the whole project in your hands. Richie is so looking forward to getting our business venture started. But now with the surgery, he's going to be limited on what he can do for the first couple of months. I can assure you he will drive me crazy. He hates being confined to resting all day."

"He's going to have to if he wants to heal a hundred percent. If you need anything, you call me or Amy and we'll be right over."

"Francine has us too," Angelina said standing in the doorway with Vincenzo. "I can come stay with you if you'd like."

"Thanks Mom, Dad. But I'll be fine. I do appreciate your offer. While Richie's sleeping, I can do some work, make phone calls and prepare our meals."

"You concentrate on Richie," Toni said. "We," she pointed to herself and Amy, "will take care of the office. I know Richie. He isn't going to want you doing work."

"I agree with her," Jason said. "Our boy is going to need a hundred percent attention. I really don't trust him to just lie in bed, not doing anything. He's going to try his best to get himself up."

"I purchased quite a few books on my Kindle. I'm going to use this time to relax and gear up for when he starts his physical therapy."

"Mrs. Raggalio."

Francine turned toward the door where Vic and Dr. Weston stood in blue scrubs with matching paper shoes. Angelina joined her, taking Francine's hand in hers. They both said, "Yes," at the same time.

"Everything went well," Dr. Weston said. "The surgery wasn't as serious as I originally thought, but serious enough. His recovery will be a lot quicker but he's going to be in excruciating pain. He needs to rest for the first week. I'll leave a prescription for painkillers. It's going to be your job to make him as comfortable as possible without giving him any extra medicine."

"I'll make sure of that. I don't want him to get addicted to painkillers."

"That's why I'm going to give you a prescription for ibuprofen to give him between pills."

"Will he be able to pitch again?" Francine asked, crossing her arms against her chest.

"If he follows my instructions, he should be ready to pitch by mid-September," Dr. Weston said.

"I'll be stopping by everyday to check in on him when the team is playing at home," Vic added, tapping his right foot on the high gloss polished floor.

"What do you mean when you say to keep my husband as comfortable as possible?"

"Honestly, Francine, the worst of it will be the first two weeks. I'll need you to apply ice packs on his shoulder at twenty minute intervals for an hour three times a day. You'll need to do that for the first week. The good news is I'll be around for the next eight days before going on the road to California. During that time, you will bring Richie in to see Dr. Weston."

"Okay." Francine still felt out of sorts, her nerves still getting the better of her. Even though both doctors said Richie's surgery had been successful, she needed to see Richie herself, to make sure he was okay.

Dr. Weston reached his hand out. Francine shook it.

"Is there anything I can do to help?" Angelina asked, reaching her hand out to Dr. Weston.

"The best medicine you ladies can give Richie is your love and support when he starts doubting himself," Vic said.

"I will be there for my son no matter what."

"Richie is going to be fine. He's in good hands with Vic."

"Thank you so much."

"Now if you would excuse me, I have some paperwork to do before going home."

Francine forced a smile. "Again, thank you."

Dr. Weston nodded before heading out the door. Francine crossed her arms, turned to stare out the window.

"Hey, what's wrong?" Vic asked, placing his hand on her shoulder.

"Can I see Richie now?"

"Yes, in a few minutes. You can sit in the recovery room with him. He should wake up in a bit."

Jason joined them by the window. "Is there anything I can do to help?"

"You can help by making sure Richie stays put and doesn't go anywhere near the restaurant."

"How did you know about that?" Jason asked.

"Richie told me about it as we prepped him for surgery. He can't lift anything, including a paintbrush for the next six weeks. By the time he's ready for physical therapy, I'll be home with the team. In the meantime, Richie needs to see Dr. Weston next week," Vic said. Besides, Dr. Weston was the lead surgeon. He can give you a better understanding of the injury."

Francine nodded her head. "Can I go see Richie now?" she asked again.

"Yes."

"What about us?" Angelina asked pointing to herself and Vincenzo.

"You can see him when the nurse wheels him out in the wheelchair to go home."

"Come on, Vic. You've know us for years," Jason said.

"This doesn't have anything to do with our friendship. Rules are only one person at a time in the room."

"Don't worry," Francine squeezed Angelina's hand, "you're going to be the one I call to relieve me when he drives me crazy."

"Are you ready to go in?" Vic asked.

"Yes…"

Amy hugged her. "We'll be out here waiting for you."

"Why don't you all go get yourselves coffee in the cafeteria? Richie should be in recovery for at least two hours."

"Do you want anything, Francine?" Toni asked.

"No thank you. I'm fine."

"Let me bring Francine into recovery. I'll be right back with his prescriptions. Angelina can get them filled at the pharmacy across the street. This way Richie will have them when he leaves."

Richie's parents, Jason, Amy and Toni all shook their heads in agreement.

"Come follow me," Vic said.

Vic held the heavy wooden door open for her. "Tell me the truth, Vic. Are you sure Richie is going to be okay?"

"Yes." Vic slid his hand under her elbow, leading her down the hall. "Richie is still sleeping. When he wakes up, he will be very groggy. More than likely he'll be out of it for the rest of the night when you get home. When he gets up, give him one painkiller. Then for the first few days, if he's sleeping, wake him up every six hours to give him a pill."

"Okay. That shouldn't be a problem."

Vic stopped walking. "Don't make it be."

"What do you mean?"

"Richie is going to be in so much pain, he will be begging you to give him a painkiller. You're going to feel bad, but don't. I've given him the highest dosage possible. Things are going to be tough the first couple of days. I'm a phone call away."

"Thank you, Vic."

Francine held onto Vic as he pushed open the glass door. Richie lay motionless on the bed hooked up to multiple monitors. Her eyes dropped down to his chest, beneath the thin hospital blanket. She watched as the blanket slightly moved up and down. At least she saw him breathing. Taking a step back, she felt lightheaded, leaning on Vic for support.

"Everything is going to be okay. He hasn't totally woken up from the anesthesia yet."

"The machines," she mumbled.

"They are monitoring his blood pressure, heart rate and administering him oxygen. He'll be fine."

"Can you bring the chair up to the head of the bed for me? I need to be close, hold his hand, let him see me there when he wakes up."

Vic slid the chair to the side of the bed. Francine pushed the chair closer with her foot before plopping down on it.

Vic rested his hand on her shoulder. "Are you going to be all right?"

"Now I will. I'll feel better once he opens his eyes."

"I will check in on you in a bit. Everything is going to be okay. The worst is over. More importantly, the extent of the damage wasn't as bad as I originally anticipated. I am confident Richie is going to make a full recovery sooner than anticipated, pending he keeps to his strict physical therapy schedule."

"Thank you, Vic."

Once she heard the glass doors close, she pulled her chair even closer to the bed. Francine ran her fingers through his light brown hair, resting her hand over his and her head on the edge of the pillow on her chair.

Just as Francine started to doze off, she felt Richie's hand twitching under hers. Her eyes shot open and gazed into his, a small wrinkle of a smile twitched from his right lip.

"Told you I'd be all right," he whispered.

"Yeah, after giving me the scare of a lifetime."

Leaning over him, she planted a soft kiss on his lips. "How do you feel?"

"I'm feeling high as a kite." Richie coughed. "Remember that day?"

"How could I forget? It turned out to be the first and last time we smoked pot. I had never been so sick in my whole entire life. We swore if we got through that night we would never do drugs again."

"And we never did. That had been the turning point in our relationship."

"We've been together ever since." Francine touched his lips. "We have a long road ahead of us. And I'm going to be right there by your side until you are walking back onto the pitching mound."

After an hour, Dr. Weston walked into the room, with a nurse following with a wheelchair behind.

"Good news. You are free to go home. I gave your mom paperwork. It is imperative you follow the instructions." Dr. Weston opened his iPad. "I'll see you a week from today at eight thirty in the morning at my office in Manhattan. If you have questions, you can call Vic or myself."

"Okay, Mr. Raggalio. I need for you to stand, slide into the wheelchair."

"I can walk out."

The nurse waved her finger at him. "On my shift, every patient who leaves the hospital is given the royal treatment. Once you get outside, you're on your own."

Francine took hold of the wheelchair, wheeling him out into the hall toward the waiting room. Behind her, she could hear the nurses snickering and drooling over Richie. She had become mute to this through the years. All these years later, the flirting from the women didn't bother her.

"Look who's here," Francine called into the waiting room.

"Oh thank God, my baby is okay," Angelina cried. Walking right to him she put her hand on his cheek. "I was so worried.

"Dear Lord, Angelina. Why must you be so dramatic?" Vincenzo asked. "He's a grown man."

Angelina rolled her eyes and mumbled words in Italian under her breath, before lifting her handbag off the sofa. "Sorry, I didn't mean to get so carried away."

"Let's go home, Angelina."

"You're right. I need to cook dinner." Angelina waved goodbye. "I'll see you later sweetie. Bye guys. Thanks for coming."

"See you two later," Francine said.

After they left, Jason stood. "How are you feeling?" he asked bumping knuckles with Richie.

"Like I'm floating on a cloud in the sky, making endless love to my wife," he said looking up at Francine.

"Oh stop it." Francine kissed the top of his head. That's on the list of no-nos for a couple of weeks."

"Let me run ahead. I'll pull the car up to the front. I'll take you and Richie home. Amy will drive your car," Jason said.

Rummaging through her handbag, she handed Amy her keys. "Just a heads-up. I parked in the employee parking lot. I'm not sure how you're going to get out."

Amy laughed. "With you, Francine, I wouldn't see it any other way."

Jason pulled his car through the thick black metal gates into the circular driveway in front of his house. He put the car in park. Amy watched him through the rearview mirror as he pushed the metal gates closed, before getting back into the car. Slowly he drove around the circular driveway, stopping in front of his two-story stone house.

"Welcome to my home."

"Your house is gorgeous. Nothing like I expected. In all the years I drove around looking for house For Sale signs, I would have never found your house buried away behind the shrubbery. Jason opened her car door. "I am big on privacy." Jason opened the door. "My great-grandparents owned this property."

Amy turned to face him. "Really? I thought you grew up in Chicago."

"I did. My father's grandparents lived in Staten Island. My parents met while my dad was in the military stationed in Illinois."

Amy warmly smiled. "I love hearing stories like this. Makes me believe in love."

"Yes, you're right. My great-great-grandfather was Native American. Without going into my full family tree at this time, this land has been passed down from one generation to another, until it landed in my hands."

"Wow. Are you telling me this is a custom-built house?"

"You're the expert. You can give me your evaluation after the official tour."

Jason slid his hand through hers, leading her into the center hall.

Amy pivoted in her two-inch heels on the ivory marble floor, turning around, looking at the spectacular entrance hall.

"Gorgeous. I can't imagine coming in here without shoes."

Jason chuckled. "Leave it to you to think of something like that. The cleaning company had been in earlier to clean the floors. Usually I have a circular oriental carpet when you walk in because I know exactly what you're saying. After taking a few falls, I called in the interior designer to find me a unique carpet. The round table over there," he pointed to the corner, "is usually in the center on the carpet. I'm having the carpet cleaned. It should be back here in a few days."

Jason took both her hands, pulling her up against him, softly kissing her lips. "I have a lot more to show you, but not all tonight."

"I'd like that."

He smiled.

Amy melted.

Whenever he smiled, his dimples became more pronounced. Reaching her hand up, she ran her fingers along his mocha cheek. Gazing into his hazel eyes, she knew tonight they were going to bring their relationship to the next level. Her libido screamed to feel his body crushed against hers, and her heart told her to go for it.

Amy stepped back. "I'm ready to see your special room."

Jason brought her down the hall, up a set of spiral stairs, stopping in front of two French doors covered in white curtains.

"This is my pride and joy."

Jason opened the doors, which led into a sport's room. The room was filled with trophies, picture frames, sport's medals and team jerseys.

"Wow, this is amazing. Who did those jerseys belong to?"

"They are all mine. My mom saved them all from peewee football through my professional career. The first Super Bowl I played in, my mom and dad came here and put this room together. If you walk around, you can see she had saved pictures of me from my freshman year of high school."

Amy strolled through the room, looking at all the mementos. She wanted to stall, not rush, savoring every moment of the night. The more time she spent with Jason, the more she felt the love in her heart expanding.

"This is awesome. I can't believe your mother saved all these things."

"Neither can I. Through the years my dad always yelled at my mom for being a hoarder, saving every little thing, but in the long run, this was the reason why."

"Your mom sounds like a lovely woman."

"She is. I can't wait for you to meet her. I know she'll love you."

"I don't see your Super Bowl rings."

"I have them upstairs in my jewelry box."

Amy turned to face him, leaning against the waist high bookcases that lined the room. "How come you don't wear one of them?"

"I tend to be on the humble side. I don't like to bring attention to myself. But," Jason reached out taking her back in his arms, "I'm going to give you two choices."

"Hmm. Tell me."

"We can go back down to the kitchen, order ourselves some dinner, or I can bring you upstairs to show you my Super Bowl rings."

Butterflies flew around in Amy's belly. If she went upstairs, there would be no turning back. "I'm thinking that insomuch as I am starving, I'd like to see your rings. How many are there?"

Jason leaned down. With his tattooed forearms, he swept her into his arms. He carried her down the hall into another room.

Gently he placed her on the bed. When he tried to stand, Amy took his hand. "Where are you going?"

"I thought you wanted to see my rings."

Amy lowered her eyes, embarrassed. How could she have gotten the wrong impression? "I do."

"Good. Because there is one ring in particular I want you to see."

Jason walked over to his hutch and opened the doors. From the bed, she could hear him snickering. She knew that snicker by now. He was definitely up to no good. In a few moments, she could see him turning around with a box of condoms in his hands. When he turned to walk toward the bed, she didn't see anything in his hand.

Sitting on the bed next to her, he opened his left hand and held a thick gold chain with one of his Super Bowl rings dangling from the end.

"This is my very first ring. I can remember the day my team won the game with me making the final run from the forty-five-yard line of the opposing team. I made that play with only thirty-seven seconds left on the clock."

"I remember that game. Francine had a Super Bowl party at her house that year."

"Think back to when you were in high school. Do you remember what the boys gave their girls?"

Amy frowned. "No. I wasn't allowed to date until I was eighteen. I was the product of a mom who got pregnant at sixteen. The only good that came out of things is my parents are still together and as much in love as they were back in high school."

"Then this makes things much easier for me. In my day, when you went steady with a girl, you gave her your school ring." Jason lifted the chain, leaned forward and placed it around Amy's neck.

"Oh no. I can't accept this." Amy went to take the chain off, but Jason stopped her.

"This ring represents my commitment to you." Jason placed his arm around her neck, gently placing her head down on his pillow.

"Commitment?"

"Yes. I love you." He laughed. "I never thought I would say those three words to anyone. However, from our first date, I knew we were meant to be together."

"Oh Jason." Amy raised her hands, placing both on his cheeks, gazing into his eyes. "I love how your dimples shine, when you're smiling. I love how you respected me enough to wait for me to be ready. I love you."

Jason leaned up, pulling his shirt over his head. His chest was solid, his muscles covered with tribal print tattoos. He kissed her softly down her neck, as his thick fingers unbuttoned her shirt, massaging her skin.

"You are beautiful. Definitely worth the wait." He slid his tongue from her lips, as he unhooked the front of her bra. "Your skin is so soft."

"You're driving me crazy."

Jason kissed her lips. "This is our night. I want to take things nice and slow, savoring this moment. I want this to be a night you will remember for the rest of your life."

"Knowing that you share the same love in your heart, it's going to be a memorable night."

Chapter Fourteen

The next few weeks were tough on Francine. Richie was in so much pain that he lay in bed all day, calling out to her. Vic was her godsend. He stopped by everyday to check in on Richie, giving her a chance to respite herself.

Her heart went out to Richie. She could see the pain in his eyes, deep into his soul. For the first time in their marriage, they didn't make love. Not that they didn't try. That's when she knew Richie's pain had taken him over.

Those earlier weeks were now behind her. After Richie got over his pity party, he opened his eyes to the reality of the situation. His recovery would be up to him. That's when he asked Francine for her help.

She stopped treating him like a baby, leaving him to fend for himself. In the beginning, he went ballistic, telling her she didn't care about him, but once he got the hang of getting dressed, and doing simple hygiene, she knew he was on the road to recovery.

Today was Richie's second week of physical therapy. The previous week, he had done wonderfully. The doctor insisted he keep his hand in a sling, which he did, but spent all his free time squeezing the blue exercise ball.

The night before, Francine took the balls out of his hands and placed his hands under her shirt, on her breasts. This time, he lifted her shirt over her head, raising his arms all the way up before he removed his own. Richie didn't hesitate at all. If he felt any pain, he didn't let on.

His soft lips slid down the side of her neck. She let out a moan as her body electrified from his touch. When Francine rested her hands on his chest, he took her hands in his holding them above her head. He moaned out in pain. He was feeling better, but still on his way to recovery.

Francine shook her head, bringing herself back to the present. She pulled up in front of her office after dropping Richie off at therapy, happy to be back to the office. Through all of this, Amy had been her lifeline. She stopped by the house every night to make sure Francine was all right. Toni, on the other hand, had become wrapped up in her relationship with Eric, which turned out to be a good thing. The last time she stopped by with him, Toni shined, totally out of her depression. It seemed like Eric had been the perfect medicine.

Francine pushed the door open. "Amy, I'm finally back home."

Amy met her in the small vestibule by the outgoing mail basket. "Thank God. I'm so tired of talking to myself all day long."

"You have Toni."

"Toni?" Amy sighed. "All she talks about is Eric this, Eric that. I'm so tired of hearing it."

"Toni deserves to be happy after all the bad luck she has had with men."

"I have to agree with you on that."

Francine reached her hand out to touch the Super Bowl ring dangling perfectly on the thick gold chain around Amy's neck. "I love this." Reaching into her shirt, Francine pulled out her thick gold chain. "I still wear Richie's World Series ring around my neck. Whenever I think about that night, I still get goose bumps."

"Oh yeah. You jumped right onto the field."

"Yep. And Vic stood there holding a World Series Championship T-shirt and baseball cap for you. Those were the early years of Richie's career," Francine reminisced. "It's hard to imagine where all those years have gone."

Francine glanced at Amy's left ring finger. Empty. Jason had shown her the very large diamond engagement ring he had purchased for her the day before. When she didn't hear from Amy, she figured he hadn't proposed yet. Amy would be so surprised to get a ring, since they hadn't been going out for that long.

"What's going on in that mind of yours?" Amy asked.

"Just thinking about things. I've been preoccupied with getting Richie back on his feet. I hate to see him being forced into retirement."

"Stop it," Amy shook her. "Think positive. What's wrong with you? You always tell me 'be positive' all the time. Now it's time to take your own advice."

"You're right." Francine walked into the office. "Let's go sit down. I need to be brought up to speed on what's going on here."

"Nothing to be up to speed on. No, wait." Amy picked up two folders from her desk. "This morning I got a call from these two contractors making an offer."

Francine sat behind her desk, opening the files. "Looks like both contractors' prices are close. What do you think?"

"I say go with the best price. Unless you want to sell according to what the contractor wants to build on the land."

"Let me take a look." Francine read through the files. "Looks like one wants to build a community of condominiums." She placed the folder open on the left side of her desk. "And, the other one wants to build three high rise apartment buildings."

"What do you think?"

"Honestly, I think keeping the total community in mind, we should go with the lower bid, the contractor who wants to build the condominiums."

"Gotcha. I'll contact him in a bit." Amy held out her hand. "Let me see the file."

Francine handed the file to her.

"Okay. Simon Abbots Builders. Simon can be reached anytime after two. I'll catch him later on."

"Speaking of later, what's on your agenda with Jason?"

"Jason is down at the restaurant. You can't believe the difference in the place. He is working so hard at getting the place up and running by the time Richie is able to go there."

"What has he done so far?" Francine asked, twirling in her chair to face Amy. "I haven't had a chance to see anything, as you know."

"He built the bar."

"Are you kidding me?"

"Nope." Amy grinned brightly. "You can't believe the job he has done. I'm so proud of him."

"Maybe over the weekend Jason can take Richie down there to show him how the place is coming together, giving me a few moments to myself," Francine's eyes pleaded.

"Wouldn't that be nice?"

"Don't even go there in the complaining department."

Amy laughed. "Don't worry, I won't. I couldn't ask for my life to go in any other direction. Being with Jason has totally changed me. I love him so much."

"I have always told you when the time comes, you would meet your soul mate."

"I waited long enough. Just as I've been waiting for Toni to get back from a simple errand down to City Hall to pick up the blueprints on a property, which I think was built on top of a creek. Before I sign the client, I want to check to make certain I'm thinking of the wrong area."

"Excellent. I'd rather pass on the property then sell to a client knowing there will be a potential problem for them soon," Francine said.

"You're too honest for your own good." Amy pointed at her.

"We have a successful business here because of our honesty. I would never compromise my reputation for a sale."

"I agree with you. I think the six-plot property is going to be our ace in the hole. We should be good to go."

"I need to change the subject here from work. Let's go out when Toni comes back. We need a girls' liquid lunch," Amy said.

"Oh yes, we do. But I can't do a liquid lunch today. I must pick up Richie from therapy in an hour. He's complaining that he's tired of sitting in the house all day long. He wants to stop at the store to pick up a few things."

"Why don't you take him down to the restaurant. Jason is there, doing some work."

"That may not be such a bad idea. Why don't you come with me?"

"I'd love to but I think Toni might get annoyed. I've been leaving her here a lot while running out doing errands."

"She can come with us. What's the difference?" Francine opened the appointment screen on the computer. "There's nothing pending for today. If someone really needs to get in touch with us they will call our cell phone."

Amy leaped up, sending the chair flying on its wheels. "Works for me. How could I ever pass up an opportunity to see my man."

"Wow. I love seeing this side of you again. You are so alive."

Amy giggled. "And satisfied."

Francine held up her hand. "I don't want to hear it."

The front door to the office opened with Toni walking in waving blueprints in her hands. She swung her handbag over the back of her chair. She placed the papers on her desk, took off her jacket and tossed it onto the floor before taking a deep breath and turning to them.

"Sorry. Let me catch my breath. I ran here from down the block. There isn't a spot to be had outside."

"You shouldn't have run here," Amy said.

"I know. But I have gotten so much information down at City Hall. I couldn't wait to get back here to show you."

"The property?" Francine asked.

"The property on Reid Avenue is fine. The houses on the bottom of the street were not built on the creek. You were thinking about the houses on Quintard Street."

"That's great news. I have four people interested in that property."

"Leave the call for tomorrow," Francine said. "Come on, Toni. We're going down to see the restaurant."

"Before we go, I need to show you something." Toni picked the blueprint off her desk.

"You don't have to show us the blueprint of Reid Avenue."

"It's not Reid Avenue. This is the original blueprint of the hardware store."

"The hardware store?" Francine asked, rubbing her forehead.

Toni knelt on the floor in front of their desks. Carefully, she unfolded the blueprint. "Yes. I think this is something you should see."

"You sound quite serious." Francine sank down on the floor next to her.

"I'm not sure if what I'm reading is right or not, but I think it's something the two of you should look at."

"What are we looking for?" Amy asked, joining them.

"This is the original blueprint of the property you were left. I went crazy looking through the books for this. So much dust." Toni sneezed. "I'm still sneezing."

"I don't understand. What made you look for this?" Francine asked.

"While I was down there, I decided to surprise you with the blueprint. I thought how cool it would be to frame it."

Amy's eyebrows flew up. "Damn, that's a great idea."

"I thought so too, until I saw this." Toni pointed to the tiny print in the lower right hand corner of the paper.

"What does that say?" Francine leaned over squinting.

"Updated July first. I can't make out the last two digits of the year."

"Did you inquire?" Francine asked.

"No, didn't think of it."

"Typical Toni. But I still don't understand."

"Take a good look at the structure. Here is all the land." Toni circled her finger around the building.

"Okay. I don't see anything out of the ordinary," Francine said.

Reaching to her desk, she took off another set of blueprints. "The copy is a little hard to read, because it dates back to nineteen forty-four." Toni opened the other paper. "Now look at the original."

Francine looked at the papers in front of her. This copy showed an additional structure under the building. "What is this?"

"That is the basement."

"The basement?" Both Francine and Amy said at the same time.

"Yes. I have a gut feeling there is a basement under the restaurant that was either filled in or closed off. From what I'm seeing here," she pointed, "there used to be cellar doors at the back of the building."

"Impossible. You can't make a basement disappear," Francine said.

"Yes, you can." Amy stood. "Do you remember Garbers in the plaza when we were kids?"

"Of course. That was the place to shop. Downstairs in the basement…"

"Exactly. After Garbers left, Lionel Kiddie City Toy Store moved in there. They closed the hole in the floor, and used the freight elevator in the back of the store for layaway at Christmas. I remember picking up a carload of toys for Richie's sister." Francine lifted the blueprint off the floor, placing it on her desk.

"I went along with you for the ride." Amy laughed. "We struggled for over a half hour trying to fit all the toys into the back of Richie's truck."

"But when Kiddie City closed, and the new toy store took over, all of a sudden the basement disappeared. They swore there wasn't one and we didn't know what we were talking about."

"Hylan Plaza all has basements," Toni added. "That's what I'm trying to tell you. Something is going on over there. We have to find the old entrance to the basement. There had to be some indication in the concrete that the building was updated along the way."

"There isn't anyone to even ask. Marvin has no living relatives."

Amy grabbed her coat off her chair. "I say we go check things out."

"I can't go anywhere until Richie's done with therapy."

"Would you mind if Toni and I take a ride out there?"

"No. You two go. I'll meet you there with Richie. This way while he bullshits with Jason, I can join you two out back."

"Let's go, Toni. It's your turn to drive."

Toni puckered her lips, throwing kisses in Amy's direction. "Not a problem. I have a few errands to run anyway down on the south shore."

They both turned to wave goodbye to Francine. Francine walked to the door, locking it. Returning to her desk, she grabbed the two sets of blueprints placing them down on the floor again. She loved Toni to death, but a lot of times Toni savored the drama of an adventure. Maybe she had found something. Before kneeling, she grabbed a pen and ruler off her desk. Upon examining the blueprints, she concluded if these were the original ones, then Toni had been right.

Francine tried to read the fine writing in the lower right hand corner of the sheet. The writing had been so faint. Maybe when Marvin bought the property the basement had been already filled in. Francine picked up the papers, placing them back on her desk. She made a note on her calendar to go down to City Hall to see if there was another updated version in between the original, dated nineteen forty-four, and the one in two thousand something. Chances are there was another updated blueprint.

On the way out to the truck, her cell phone went off playing *Anything at All* by These Machines. Reaching into her handbag, Francine grabbed her cell phone.

"Hey, babe. I just got into the truck. I should be there in ten minutes."

"Be careful. Love you."

"Love you too."

Francine placed her cell phone in the cup holder next to her.

Richie would be surprised when she told him she had a special afternoon planned for him. This would be the first time since his surgery that they went out gallivanting. Their usual schedule started with the doctors, then physical therapy, before heading back home with Richie spending the rest of the day lying down in front of the television.

When they saw Dr. Weston last week, he agreed with Francine that Richie should start getting back to his regular routine. There was no reason for him to be sitting around all day. He could start doing some walking around the track up at the college to keep in shape.

She slid in the spot in front of the therapist's office when she spotted Richie talking to another man. He waved goodbye before opening the door and sliding in to the passenger seat.

"Can I drive?"

"Nope. I have the wheel today. I have a surprise for you."

"Oh yeah." Francine removed her cell phone from the cup holder, tossing the phone back into her handbag.

"I have a surprise for you too."

"Really?"

"Yep. And if you're a good boy, I may let you drive home."

"This is why I love you so much." Richie chuckled.

Surprisingly there wasn't any traffic as they rode down Hylan Boulevard. At Page Avenue, Francine made a right.

"I know where you are taking me."

"You do?" Francine asked, glancing over at him.

"But first, I need you to make a stop at your friend's lingerie store."

"What did you do?"

"You'll see when we get there."

Francine pulled in a spot right in front of the store. He got out first and went around to open the door for her. He held out his left hand for her to grab with a huge smile spread on his lips. They walked into the store hand in hand.

"Hey you two." Katie got off the stool behind the counter, coming over to greet them both with a hug. "I can't believe I have Richie Raggalio standing right here in my store."

Francine waved her finger. "I don't believe either one of you. I know you two are up to no good."

Katie and Richie both burst out laughing.

"Okay, you got me," Richie said. "I spoke to Katie after I called you. I figured if we were out this way, we could stop by the restaurant. So I had her make up a package for you."

"Oh really." Francine shook her head. "Wait until you hear what my surprise is. You could have saved yourself a lot of money."

"Hey. Are you two using me?" Katie laughed.

"My surprise was to bring you out to the restaurant. And of course, I was going to make a stop here. Every woman can use a new matching bra and thong." Francine grinned.

"That's right," Katie said.

Richie slid his wallet out of his back pocket. "Let me settle my bill with Katie."

"Oh no," Francine shook her head. "Since I'm here, I want to look around and see what else is here."

"What are you looking for? I bought you a whole bag of goodies!"

Francine pivoted on her boots. "I'm sure you didn't buy this." She held up a package of edible underwear, "or this."

"What's that?" Richie asked walking over to her.

"This, my darling, is chocolate body paint. And this is a soy massage candle."

"We have plenty of candles."

"Not this one," Francine sang.

"This candle," Katie said in a seductive voice, "turns into massage oil. Want to smell?" she asked placing the candle under his nose.

Richie bit his lips but couldn't hold back a smile. "You're killing me."

"That's not my intent." Francine dropped them into the navy bag. "I can't get enough of my husband."

"So I see. He's so hot and sexy." Katie winked.

"Okay. I see this women thing going on over here." Richie handed Katie his credit card. "Please add the other things on my tab."

"Baby, the other things are on me."

"No, don't be silly," Richie said.

"Honey, I'm not done shopping yet. I want to show you something."

"I don't like the sound of this." Richie shuffled his feet over to Francine. "What do you have in your hand?"

Slowly, Francine opened her hand to show him a tan dice.

"A dice?"

"Take a look at the dice."

Richie took the dice from Francine. She watched the color in his cheeks go from rosy to red. He walked back to the counter and dropped the dice into her bag.

"Games on," he said batting his eyebrows. "Do you want to skip stopping by the restaurant?"

"Absolutely not. We can have a quickie in the dressing room."

"See what I mean," he said to Katie. "She's always wearing me out."

"Hmm." Katie rested her chin on her hand. "I got the perfect solution."

"And what's that?" Richie asked.

"Why don't you roll the dice to see what sexual position you get?" Katie suggested.

Francine bit her bottom lip before bursting out laughing. She laughed so hard tears appeared in her eyes.

"That's it with you two. I'm going to wait in the car." Richie extended his hand. "Keys please."

Francine unhooked the key ring off her jean's belt loop and handed it to him. "You can drive."

"Geez, thanks. I can drive a thousand feet down the road." Richie air blew Katie a kiss. "I'll see you soon."

When the door closed behind Richie, they both giggled.

"You are too much, Katie."

"I couldn't help it. The look on his face was well worth the comment." Katie ran the credit card through the machine before handing it back to Francine. "You guys are so funny. I love the way you react to each other."

"I consider myself extremely lucky. Not many people can say they still love their high school sweetheart all these years later."

"You're right."

Francine signed Richie's name on the receipt. "Damn, he spent a lot of money," she said, looking at the four hundred and seventy-three-dollar receipt.

"Don't worry. You will be very happy with what he bought you.

"Thanks, Katie."

"You're welcome." Katie walked from behind her counter with Francine's bag and hugged her. "I can't wait for you guys to open up down the block. I'll get to see you more."

"Oh absolutely." Francine took the bag and walked to the door. "Love ya."

"Love ya too."

Chapter Fifteen

"Wow," Francine and Richie said at the same time.

"I can't believe what Jason did to the front of this place. He told me he cleaned it out, but I never expected the property to be this big in the front and side."

"The side lot would be perfect for valet parking on the weekend. I think the front lot could be used as a drop-off on weekends and parking during the week."

Richie walked over to the side lot. "I can't believe Jason already got pavers put down. He told me he was working hard to get things moving along, but I never expected him to get this much done."

"He wants to get a lot of things done before training camp begins. Amy told me he comes here everyday."

Richie took Francine's hand. "Baby, this is all happening because of the huge heart you have. Even as a teenager, you went out of your way for others. I'm sure Marvin is looking down and is so proud of you."

Francine leaned her body against his, standing on her tippy toes to reach his lips. "This is going to be our future, right here."

"You're right. But I'm scared. My life has always revolved around baseball."

"And it still will. This is our baby," Francine pointed to the building. "I like the idea of a restaurant, sports bar. We can even do a karaoke night during the week."

"I will do anything as long as we are happy. The moment there is any tension between us because of this business venture, we are going to sell."

"Let's seal that deal with a kiss." Francine pressed her lips against his.

"Hey are you two going to stand out there making out, or are you going to come in to see what I've done while you were sitting on your ass watching television and sleeping all day?"

"Oh shut up." Richie laughed, putting his arm around Francine's shoulder. "You're just jealous I get to spend all day with my girl."

"I'm not even going to go there."

Jason held the door open for them. When they walked in, they both gasped. Francine couldn't speak. The old dinky counter had been replaced with a long red mahogany bar. Walking over to it, Francine ran her fingers along the shiny top.

"Damn, Jason. Where did you get this?"

"I told you. I have expert craftsmanship hands." He held out his hands. "Not only can I catch a football, but I can build a bar."

"That's my bro." Richie bumped knuckles with Jason.

"I put the last coat of varnish on last week. I can't believe how high gloss the top of the bar looks."

"I can see. You did an awesome job Jason," Francine said. It wasn't until she noticed the shiny brass rail along the bottom that she realized Jason had also pulled up the rugs, replacing them with wood floors. "I love the floor."

"The floor too?" Richie asked, walking behind the bar.

"Yes. I guess you weren't paying attention to the model I showed you at your house."

"I wasn't. I don't remember looking at all the details," Richie admitted. "I guess I was more concerned with this damn shoulder."

"Hey man, at least you don't have your arm in a sling anymore."

"You're right. I do have more mobility back."

"Before you two guys start talking shop, do you know where the girls are?" Francine asked.

"They're out back. They were talking about making some sort of flower bed along the back of the building." Jason laughed. "You girls are funny. This is supposed to be a sports bar, not a sports garden."

Francine went along with the laugh. No way would she try to explain to them what they were up to. As far as Francine was concerned, they were just appeasing Toni. If the basement had been closed, then there would have been another blueprint in the book. Or maybe Marvin closed it up and never bothered to change the blueprints, so he didn't have to hire an architect and file permits. He might have said screw it in order to save money.

Francine walked out the backdoor and there was Amy along with Toni on their hands and knees, pushing grass with their hands off the concrete.

"Well if it isn't the Nancy Drew dream team." Francine laughed, resting her hands on her hips.

"Are you going to help us or are you going to stand there watching?" Toni asked.

"I'm going to help you. But I think before we go crazy, we take another trip down to City Hall to see if there is another blueprint beside the two of them."

"Just keep looking," Toni snapped. "I went through the book twice."

"Okay, I believe you," Francine said. "I didn't mean to agitate you."

"I think the opening has to be over here somewhere," Amy said, pointing to the metal tape measure. "I've followed the dimensions on the blueprint to a 'T.' If I calculated right, the opening should be right around here."

Francine dropped to her knees. She joined Amy and Toni in pulling the overgrown weeds and grass off the back of the building, exposing the concrete foundation.

"We're going to have to dig some of the dirt away from the building," Amy concluded.

"I think we should take another look at this." Francine stood, shaking her right leg that had become stiff. "I'm going to grab the shovels. Using my hands isn't cutting it."

"I agree with her." Amy stood. "I'm thinking something is here. A basement just doesn't disappear."

Francine handed Amy and Toni a shovel. Immediately, Francine and Amy began, while Toni tapped her shovel around the area. As she shoveled, Francine kept her eyes on Toni who seemed to be on a mission of her own.

"What's she up to?" Francine asked, nudging Amy.

"I don't know. She didn't say a word to me."

"I'm going to keep digging." After digging a foot down and six feet wide, Francine finally was able to see the difference in the concrete. The smooth concrete had turned into unleveled bricks held together sloppily by cement.

"Hey, I found something here," Francine called out.

"Where?" Amy asked.

"So have I," Toni said.

Francine leaned her shovel against the side of the building. "What did you find?" she asked walking with Amy toward her.

"I'm not sure if it's anything. But listen." Toni banged the shovel two feet behind her to the dirt and then three feet in front of her. "I hear an echo. Do you?"

"Do it again," Amy ordered.

Toni tapped her shovel again in front of her and behind her. The sound was different. But how could it be? Francine thought.

Toni lifted her shovel. "Let's dig over here."

All three women started digging. After a few minutes, they hit something hard. They dropped to their knees and used their hands to move the dirt, to reveal a metal plate with a big thick round metal handle.

"I knew there was something fishy about those blueprints," Toni gloated.

"What should we do now?" Amy asked standing.

"Open it, see what is under the door," Francine said.

Toni pulled on the handle while clinching her teeth. "It won't budge."

"Let me see." Francine leaned over the silver square. She reached for the thick ring and pulled hard. "Shit!" she yelled. "I don't think we're going to get this door open."

"Please you two," Amy waved her hand. "That's what you get for not going to the gym."

"You and that damn gym," Francine snapped. "If you're so strong, go ahead, open it yourself."

Amy walked between Francine and Toni. While she leaned over, holding the ring in her hand, Amy pulled as hard as she could.

"I feel it lifting, but I can't get a good enough grip on it," Amy cried.

"I got an idea. While you lift, I'll try to slide the shovel in the space."

"I'll get mine too," Toni lifted her shovel off the ground. "This way we'll work together."

"Okay, on three," Amy said. "One, two, three…"

Amy lifted and Francine and Toni slid their shovels in the space. They all reached out, grabbed the circle and pulled. The metal door flew open as the girls fell on their butts.

"Wow. I can't believe we got the door open," Amy commented standing.

"Teamwork." Francine looked down the hole. "There are stairs."

"Who's going to go down there?" Toni grinded her teeth.

"The three of us," Francine walked back to the building and picked up her flashlight. "I'll lead the way."

Francine turned her back to the hole. Slowly, she walked down the wooden stairs, with each step creaking and moving under her feet.

Looking over her shoulder, she counted four more steps before hitting flat ground. She glanced up. Both Amy and Toni looked down, shining their flashlights, directing the way for her.

"What do you see?" Amy asked, poking Toni.

Francine shined her flashlight in front of her. "There's a cave leading somewhere."

"Don't move. We're coming," Amy said.

Amy came down the rickety steps with Toni following behind. Once they were together, Francine shined her light ahead. They walked about twenty feet before hitting a thick wooden door.

"What do you see?" Amy asked poking Francine.

"I don't like where this is going."

"Are you kidding me?" Francine shined the flashlight in Toni's face. "You're the one who started this mission. We're in this together. We have to find out what this is all about."

"Okay, okay. Open the door."

At times Toni got on Francine's nerves. She never followed through with projects she started. Since she met Eric, it only had gotten worse.

Francine turned the doorknob. When the door opened, the light automatically turned on. Quickly she shut the door and the light went back off.

"Well, I'll be damned. The light is hooked up to the door," Francine said. "Are you ready?"

Amy and Toni shook their heads. This time Francine pushed open the door and gasped.

"Oh my God, what is this?" Amy asked, her eyes popping wide open.

"I don't like what I'm seeing."

Both Francine and Amy snapped, "Shut up," at the same time.

Francine walked in first. The scent of mildew and marijuana slapped her in the face. To the left sat tables full of dust free knockoff designer handbags and shoes. On the right side were the bags of marijuana and blue pills.

"What the hell?" Francine lifted a pair of stilettos. "These are nice. I wonder if they have my size."

"Are you crazy?" Amy asked.

Francine lifted a few pairs, searching for a size seven. "Look at these. I love them."

Amy swiped the shoes out of her hand. "Focus. We have to figure out what's going on here."

"Nothing like basement shopping," Toni joked.

"Francine, Toni, snap out of it. This is serious. You have illegal shit in your basement." Amy poked Francine. "This isn't normal."

"You're right." Francine took a deep breath before walking across the room, stopping when she spotted another set of stairs in the far corner. "Come look over here. I wonder where these stairs lead."

"Let's go see."

Amy walked up the stairs with Francine and Toni following. Francine wondered what the hell she had gotten herself involved in. Amy pushed on the wall and pushed it open.

"Dear God, we're in the pantry closet," Amy said, walking inside, stepping aside for Francine to walk in.

"This isn't good. We need to backtrack and shut all the doors. We don't want anyone to know we found this secret room."

"I'll backtrack to close the door along with the trap door outside. I'll meet you inside," Toni said, tightening her blonde hair in the ponytail.

"Good idea. But before you leave, we have to make a pact not to breathe a word of this to anyone, not even the guys." Francine scratched her head. "I have to figure out what to do."

"I agree. Let me get started before the owner of this illegal stuff catches us."

"Thanks." Francine closed the door of shelves and sighed. "This is a nightmare. What the hell are we suppose to do?"

"Not tell the guys until we figure out what's going on," Amy said.

"I hear you on that. This is so weird," Amy agreed.

"What's weird?" Jason asked. "And how did you get in here past us?"

"You two were so busy talking, you didn't see us." Amy sat up on the counter.

Francine slid her hand into Richie's left hand. "How are you feeling?"

"Getting hungry."

"Hey, guys, if you don't mind, I'm going to head on home." Toni walked into the kitchen. "I have a date tonight with Eric. He is a stickler when it comes to being on time. I like to be ready before he comes to pick me up."

"That's one thing I can agree with him on. You're never on time," Amy nodded.

"Don't we know. Why don't you ask him if he'd like to triple date with us?" Francine laughed.

"You want to have a ménage a trois?" Richie asked.

Francine pointed at the two of them, waving her index finger back and forth. "You two can only wish."

They walked back into the restaurant with Francine shutting off the closet light behind them.

Jason's eyebrows shot up. "Hey, you can't condemn a man for trying."

"Listen, you guys, I'm going to get going."

"Where are you going?" Richie asked. "Why don't you join us for dinner?"

"I'll take a rain check," Toni said grabbing her handbag off the bar.

"Any time," Jason said. "If you change your mind, we'll be at The Finn."

"Okay. Thanks. I'll see you girls in the morning."

"Have a good time," Francine said.

"Don't do anything I wouldn't do," Amy added.

When the door closed behind Toni, Richie returned to his post behind the bar. "I can see myself back here."

"Yeah, so can I."

"However, before we do anything," he pointed to Jason, who joined him behind the bar, "we want to know what the hell the three of you were doing outside with a tape measure pulling weeds."

Francine exchanged looks with Amy. How would she be able to explain this crazy story to them? She waited several seconds, hoping Amy would come to her rescue, but when she stood there with a blank look on her face, Francine had to tell a little white lie.

"We were playing around with the idea of putting paver blocks down to make a dance area and Tiki bar during the summer," Francine lied, hoping Richie didn't see through her.

"I think it's a great idea. A lot of restaurants are doing the same thing." Jason slid his hands in his back pockets. "We can serve frozen drinks, appetizers and desserts."

"That's right up my mother's alley. She'll be thrilled to be baking away."

"Before you go any further," Jason extended his arms around the room, "tell me what you think."

"I love it. I can't believe what you have done with this place." Francine turned to Richie. "Wait until your parents see this. Your mom is going to go crazy."

Jason chuckled. "Been there, done that. Your mother-in-law makes it a point to stop by to see how everything is coming along."

"Are you kidding me?" Richie and Francine said at the same time.

"No way. Go check out the kitchen. She has already been stocking the bakery shelves."

"What bakery shelves?" Francine asked, not taking notice when they came through the magic door.

"Go look."

"Did you look already, Richie?"

"Jason gave me the grand tour."

"Amy?"

"I'll come with you."

"What has my mother-in-law done now?"

"She's a gem." Amy laughed. "She has been coming here almost everyday to set up the kitchen." Amy stood in front of the swinging doors. "Before you go inside, I want you to know Angelina has really helped out Jason, researching companies to get baking and cooking supplies. Your father-in-law also helped Jason with the floor."

"Really? Angelina had just complained to me the other day about how lazy he has become."

"Yeah, to throw you off. Go ahead," Amy motioned with her head, "go take a look."

Francine pushed open the door and gasped. Her mother-in-law had transformed the cooking area into a kitchen. Different colored cooking and baking utensils hung on one of two blue and white hanging holders from the ceiling.

215

Walking over to the walk-in pantry, she opened the doors. This time she covered her mouth with her hands. The pantry was completely filled.

"I can't believe I didn't see any of this when we came through the door. When did this all happen?"

"Angelina has been placing orders for the kitchen. She's been a big help to Jason."

"She never told me she's been coming here."

"I know. She didn't want you to think she was trying to undermine you." Amy opened the cabinet below one of the stations and took out a chef's hat. "But I tell you one thing, she is really excited about coming here to do her baking."

Richie walked into the kitchen. "Who's excited about what?"

"Did you know your mom has been coming here helping Jason?"

"Not at all. She doesn't tell me anything."

"Nice hat." Jason walked over to Amy, taking the hat off her head and placing it on his own. "I don't know about you guys, but I am starving."

"So am I," Francine said.

Richie held out his hand, looking at Francine with puckered lips. She knew what he wanted, the keys to the truck. He had been dying to drive for the past week. She assumed the drive from Katie's to here just didn't do it. Reaching into her pant's pocket, she returned the car keys back to him.

"I'm ready," Richie said dangling the keys.

"We'll meet you at The Finn at five-thirty," Jason said. "That will give me enough time to go home to shower."

Francine gave them the thumbs up. "Perfect."

Toni slid her bare feet into the black stilettos Eric loved. Eric was a hard guy to crack. Just when she thought she had had enough of him, he would do something nice for her, causing her to sway her mind.

He hadn't been that bad. At times he reacted to situations much differently than she would have. He always portrayed the tough guy persona. However, when they were alone, he acted totally different. He spoke in a soft tone, cuddled her and reassured Toni how much he needed her.

Toni smiled. Eric had been the first man in a very long time to treat her so well. Most men were looking for dinner, and then sex. But Eric had been patient with her. He respected her decision to wait to consummate their relationship. She had to be sure he wanted to be with her because he cared about her, not because he loved her blonde hair and blue eyes.

After checking her eyes in the small round mirror in the hallway, she grabbed her mascara out of her handbag to add another layer. She added another thin layer of lip gloss and smiled in satisfaction.

A car horn outside meant Eric had just pulled up. Toni pulled a black crocheted shawl over her black and gold shirt. Eric always loved when she got dressed up. By their third date, he had brought her to Macy's and bought her a whole new wardrobe. She loved everything he had picked out for her. For a man, he had exquisite taste in women's clothing.

Toni locked the front door behind her and made her way down the short front walk. Eric smiled when she slid into the car.

"I love how the shirt looks on you. Nice and sexy."

"Thanks. I just hope my skirt isn't too short," she said pulling the front of her skirt down to mid-thigh.

"You look perfect." He leaned over to kiss her. "Everyone's eyes will be on you as you sit by my side all night long."

"You surely know how to boost a woman's confidence."

"Only if she deserves the compliments."

Toni didn't answer. There was nothing left to say. That's what happened a lot when she went out with Eric. So many times the conversation went dead because basically they didn't have much in common. He hated sports, except for rugby, didn't like going to the beach or pool, choosing to spend most of his time in his apartment watching movies.

Every subject she brought up, he didn't seem to know anything about. He told her upfront he didn't like complications. He just wanted to live a quiet life with someone who would be by his side.

"Would you like to go out to dinner at The Finn?" he asked.

Immediately she wanted to say yes. But when they walked in and he saw Francine and Amy, he could freak out on her. He'd accuse her of setting up the whole charade, even though he suggested the restaurant.

"You might want to go someplace else?"

"Why?" he asked, glancing at her.

"My friends are going to be there. But if you don't mind, they did invite us to join them."

"Are you talking about your friends with the sports guys?"

"Yes."

Eric lifted his hand off the steering wheel. "I'll pass. I have nothing in common with them. I always feel awkward when I see them. I have nothing to say. I don't know anything about baseball or football. The only common denominator is men throwing a ball around the field."

Toni couldn't help but giggle. Her understanding of sports compared to Eric's knowledge of movies. He was a stay at home guy, while she loved being outside at a sporting event. Maybe this relationship had lethal implications because of lack of compatibility.

"How about we go to Jade Island for Chinese?"

Definitely far enough away with no chance of running into her friends, she thought. "That sounds great. I love the food in there. It's the only place where you can still get a Pu Pu Platter on a wooden lazy Susan, and Mai Tais in real coconut shells."

"Huh. Mai Tais. I'll make sure I keep them coming. Maybe I'll get lucky tonight."

"Hey, you never know."

And that's where the conversation ended for the rest of the way to the restaurant. Immediately he turned the volume of the radio up, staring straight ahead.

He pulled in a spot in front of the restaurant. This time, he got out and lit a cigarette instead of coming around to open the car door for her. If this were any indication of what the rest of the night would be like, then she would take the bus home. His mood swings sometimes left a lot to be desired. But then he smiled at her, reaching his hand out to take hers.

"Let's have a good time. Leave our work problems outside."

"I couldn't agree more."

Eric held the door open for her as she walked in. Something had to give. She couldn't spend the rest of the night with little talking.

They were seated in one of the booths on the left side of the restaurant. Within minutes, a dish of wide noodles with duck sauce was placed in the center of the table. The young Chinese waitress smiled at them.

"Can I get you anything from the bar?" she asked.

"I'll have seltzer with a twist of orange along with a shot of tequila and a Mai Tai for the lady and we'll start with a Pu Pu Platter."

"Thank you." She bowed her head. "I'll be back with your drinks and menus."

"She can't bring me my shot of tequila quick enough. Boy, did I have a horrible day."

"Sorry to hear that. I know we said no work talk, but do you want to talk about it."

"Yes and no." Eric dipped a noodle in the duck sauce before placing it in his mouth. "I lost one of my accounts today."

"I'm sorry to hear that. Would I be crossing the line by asking why?" Toni asked, feeling relieved knowing why Eric had been in a bad mood earlier.

"Not at all."

The waitress placed the drinks down on the table. "I'll be back with the Pu Pu Platter in a bit."

"Thank you." Toni raised her coconut. "Here's to a nice night."

They clanked the shot glass and coconut together before Toni took a sip of her extra strong drink while Eric drank down his shot in one gulp.

"That was my limit, Eric said, placing his glass down. I very rarely drink."

"Thank you. I'll let you know when I'm ready for another one."

Eric leaned back against the cushioned booth. "My last stop at the medical clinic is usually one of my favorites. They welcome me with open arms with coffee and some sort of dessert that one of the extra-large nurses or receptionist had brought in earlier in the day. But today I felt the difference in their mood."

"Really?"

"I usually give the girls behind the desk samples of aspirins, never any prescription drugs. But today, the cute one, Wendy, asked if I could slip her a couple samples of painkillers. She explained her back hurt and the doctor wouldn't give her anything, telling her she had to go see her own doctor."

"I can understand that. Staten Island is known for the high use of prescription drugs. I'm sure the doctor was covering his behind."

Eric raised his hand, and then dropped it onto the table. "I'm glad someone else understands. This is the reason why I couldn't give her any samples. What would have happened if she had an adverse reaction to the medication?"

"You would be sitting in jail."

"Exactly. So I politely told her no."

"I see nothing wrong with that," Toni said, taking another sip from the straw.

"Well things didn't go like that. I got thrown under the bus. The other woman told the doctor I always gave them samples."

Toni's eyes bulged open. "No."

"Wendy made such a big deal, drawing both doctors out into the reception area. She told the doctors I always gave them samples. Once Wendy told him what happened, of course padding the story, the two doctors went ballistic, throwing me out of the office, pulling their account."

"I'm sorry, Eric. Is there anything I can do to help?"

"Unfortunately not. Tomorrow I'll have to go to the corporate office to report the incident. My boss is going to be pissed. That clinic was one of their biggest accounts."

"You just have to tell him the truth."

"Tell her," Eric corrected her. Working for a woman is the pits. I see the way she looks at me when I'm sitting in the office. Her eyes are always on my butt and crotch."

"Do I have anything to worry about?"

"Nope." He sipped his seltzer out of the straw. "She's old and overweight. I hate that look. I love my women tall and thin."

"Then what do you see in me?" Toni leaned back, pointing at herself. "I'm not that tall."

"You know what I mean. Men like to look, just the way you girls do. I'm sure you look at your friends' husband and boyfriends, with their athletic forms."

Toni shook her head. "No. I don't. We all grew up together. I think of Richie as a brother," she snapped.

"Okay. I didn't mean anything by that," he held up his hand. "My previous girlfriend I dismissed because she always checked out my friends. The last time we went out dancing, she shook her ass in front of all of them. I'll tell you that put me right over the edge. So I said bye to her."

Actually Toni didn't see anything wrong with looking at other people. She always looked at other men and she was aware that Eric had wandering eyes, but she never thought twice about it because she did the same thing.

"Sorry to hear that. I'm sure it was hard for you."

"Not me. Didn't bother me in the least. There are plenty of women out there. I settled once, and don't plan on settling again. Who knows? Maybe you'll be the one to change my mind."

Toni crossed her arms on the table. "Maybe I might be. No one knows what the future holds."

"I know what it holds. Our Pu Pu Platter."

The waitress put the platter down in the center of the table. "Can I get you another drink?"

"I'll have another Mai Tai."

"Another seltzer with a twist of orange."

Toni took a miniature eggroll off the tray. So far the night had been going pretty well, until the conversation started to go south. She really didn't know what to talk about with him, their interests being so little.

Eric broke the silence. "I thought maybe one day next week we could go shopping in Manhattan. I would like to pick up a nice pair of snakeskin boots."

"I love going to Chinatown. I can always find myself a new handbag or two. I love when they bring you into the back of the store and open a camouflaged door into another room of designer bags."

"Don't worry," he winked. "I will make sure you get everything you want. You deserve to have only the best."

Toni was speechless, this being the last thing she expected to hear. Gazing up at him, their eyes met. His tight lips turned into a grin.

"Thank you. I'm not used to anyone being so nice to me."

"I told you from the beginning, I would be like no other man you have ever met."

"I couldn't agree more. That's what I like about you."

"What do you say we finish the last few pieces and go back to my apartment for dessert? I bought a peach crumb pie earlier."

"I'd like that."

Eric slid out of the booth. "I'll be right back. I'm going to take care of the bill."

Within a few minutes, Eric returned to the table, extending his hand out to her. They held hands as they walked to the car. This time he opened the door and waited for her to get in before closing it.

The ride back to his apartment didn't take long. Driving straight down Hylan Boulevard anytime after rush hour would get you back to the other side of Staten Island in less than fifteen minutes.

Eric pulled the car into a spot in front of an old house. He came around to open the door for her, leading her up two stones stairs to the front door. After fumbling a few minutes looking for the key, he unlocked the door and flicked on the lights.

Toni followed him into the living room, placing her handbag on his black leather sofa. "You have a really nice place here."

"Thank you. I did all the decorating myself."

"You have a good eye. I love the way you used the different colored paintings to break up the white walls."

"I like to keep things simple. I hate when you walk into people's houses and there are so many colors causing me to get lost in the room."

"Ha. Are you making fun of my living room?"

"Yes and no. You have potential. I'll help you. You have so many mismatched pieces and colors going on all over the place, especially the throw pillows you have on your sofa."

Toni laughed. Everyone always made fun of her taste in furniture and colors. She didn't care if the pieces matched. Most of the furniture in her rooms was antique. The cocktail table belonged to her grandmother on her mother's side, and the end tables belonged to her father's mother. The pieces were a part of her childhood, which always brought her happy memories.

"Let me show you the rest of my place." He took her hand walking her into the kitchen. "My kitchen is fairly plain. I hate things being all over the counter."

"Your kitchen looks great." Toni was impressed with Eric's taste. Now getting an inside look at his apartment, she could understand why everything in his life was so simple. Snow-white walls were throughout the living room, dining room and kitchen area. The floor had ivory tiles with matching floor molding. Burgundy and charcoal gray colors accented the rest of the rooms throughout the apartment.

"This is the bathroom," he opened the door. "The room at the end of the hall is my bedroom."

"You have a nice big airy place here."

"I try to keep everything simple. Less is better. Excuse me for a minute."

Eric walked down the hall into the bathroom. This gave her a chance to take a quick look around. Even though the rooms were beautifully decorated, the one thing it lacked was personality. No pictures or knickknacks of any kind were on any of the tables or walls. The only things lining his counter were a toaster, breadbox and coffeepot, drain board and a white microwave over the stove, which got lost in all the white.

The bathroom door opened. Eric's footsteps went in the opposite direction. Within a few minutes, Eric returned dressed in a black sweat suit.

"Now this feels better. I have to wear a suit and tie everyday to work. I hate the way dress pants cling. Forget about wearing silk briefs under it. It makes it even worse. I don't know how you ladies do it."

"Is there anything I can help with?"

"Just relax, make yourself at home."

Toni felt uncomfortable just standing in the middle of his kitchen. She wasn't sure if she should sit at the kitchen table or on the living room sofa. Instead of sitting down, she joined Eric at the kitchen counter.

"Are you sure there isn't anything I can help you with?" she asked sliding her hands into her back pockets.

"Why don't you take the fresh fruit out of the refrigerator. In the cabinet above the microwave, grab us two of the blue and gold small square dishes."

Toni opened the cabinet, taking out the dishes, placing them on the table. Next she spotted the napkin holder on the counter, grabbing two napkins to put next to the dishes. She returned to the refrigerator and pulled out the container of iced tea.

"Can you pour some in this glass pitcher?"

"Sure."

Toni took the navy blue and gold glass pitcher from him. Lifting the full gallon of iced tea had turned into a challenge for her. When she went to pour it in, the plastic container fell from her hands, landing all over the floor and them.

"Shit. Look at the mess I made. I'm so sorry." Toni grabbed the roll of paper towels off the counter, dropping to her knees.

"It's all right. Let me get the mop. I'll clean it up."

A few minutes later, Eric had everything clean. Numerous times, she tried to take the mop from him, but he wouldn't hear of it.

"The floor might be clean, but I'm soaked and so are you. I am such a klutz."

Eric rested the mop against the closet door and approached Toni. "This isn't a problem. I'll get you some dry clothes. If you'd like, you can take a shower."

"I think I'll take you up on that."

Eric leaned into Toni. He lifted her chin until their eyes met. "If you don't mind, I would love to take that shower with you."

Toni stood on her tippy toes, reaching her lips to his. As she kissed him, Eric opened the buttons on her shirt, dropping his lips to her neck. Toni didn't resist. She had made him wait long enough. "I'd like that," she whispered.

Eric took her hand leading her into the bathroom. He put on the water and closed the shower curtain. "We have all night."

"Yes, we do."

Chapter Sixteen

As the season progressed and the closer it got to Labor Day, Richie became antsy. Vic had finally got him back into the bullpen to throw everyday. Despite being on the DL list, he had been traveling along with the team. He continued to call Francine daily telling her about his progress. When she had spoken to Vic, he assured her his recovery had been on schedule, because he stayed on the strict schedule he had made for him. If everything went according to plan, Richie would be back in the pitching rotation in a couple of weeks. His fastball had been clocked at eighty-three miles per hour. With the Pelicans leading the league by seventeen games, there was a good possibility they would be in the playoffs. For that, the team wanted Richie to be in top form. Vic wanted to make sure Richie was one hundred percent.

With the restaurant almost done, Jason had left the final touches for the girls. They needed to pick out dishes, tablecloths, flatware and stemware.

The official football training camp had opened a few weeks earlier. Jason had practice everyday, and now the preseason schedule began. Jason assured Francine that once he got the final inspection, they would be ready to have the grand opening after the baseball season. Richie and Jason decided one of them should be in the restaurant at all times until they found a staff that could be trusted.

Francine and Amy assured them that one of them would be there, along with Angelina who would be there every morning baking the bread and desserts. With Richie coming home in a couple of days, Francine needed to go food shopping to pick up a few things for the romantic welcome home dinner she had planned. She tried to focus, but couldn't.

The basement nightmare had been that, a nightmare. Everyday for the past few months, Francine or Amy would check downstairs. Nothing had changed or was moved. Francine decided to use the oldest trick in the book. On the top of every door, she placed a piece of tape that hadn't been broken. Couldn't this have been something else abandoned by the previous renters? She would try and remember tomorrow to change the locks on the front doors.

Earlier, something told Francine to stop by the restaurant. She had a feeling, and her instinct was correct. In the pantry, the tape on the door had been broken. Without hesitation, Francine took the flashlight on the counter, pulled the pantry door open and walked down the stairs.

At the bottom of the stairs, she pushed open the door and the light went on. She walked around until she spotted three big black garbage bags in the far left corner of the room.

Walking over to them, she unraveled the rubber band on one bag and found it full of designer handbags. In the next bag, she hit the jackpot. It was filled with shoes. Without dillydallying, she rifled through the bag, pulling out a pair of shoes. *Screw it. My restaurant, my shoes. Hmmm...a matching handbag too.* She closed the bags and snooped around the rest of the room, checking the back door. Tape broken. Someone had to have stopped by last night. Francine locked up and drove back to the office. Looking through the bag again, she didn't know if she should laugh or be scared, knowing someone was in the restaurant the night before. *Hell—shoes!* She'd deal with things for the time being.

Francine leaned forward in her chair at the office, looking through the new listings to see if anything new came in for one of her top clients. The time had come to make a decision on what to do about the basement. This situation wasn't going to go away. Maybe she needed to speak to someone at the police precinct, and have the police get involved.

"I'm here," Amy sang as she walked in. "What the hell are you doing here so early?"

Francine jumped. "Early? It's past lunchtime. I think you're late."

"Yes I am. That's because I just came from a meeting with Tigerlion Contractors." Amy reached into her handbag, pulling out a folder. "I got the signed contract on a two hundred family community off Arthur Kill Road."

"Woo hoo." Francine high-fived Amy. "This is fantastic. We're talking commission on two hundred sales. This is great news."

"Yes, it is," Toni said walking in holding a folder in her hand. "On the way here, I drove through Lighthouse Hill. I saw a For Sale sign by the owner. I got out, rang the bell, and here you go. Another signed contract for a one point two-million-dollar home."

"I'm thinking a big celebration is about to happen," Francine said. "Let's go back to my house for a swim."

"That sounds great."

"I was thinking in terms of a Mojo Colada," Toni said.

Francine grabbed her handbag, throwing it over her shoulder. "You always liked those colada things. I find them too sweet. I prefer a frozen white Russian."

"I'll forward the phones. Do you want me to drive?" Toni asked.

"No, that's okay. I'll drive. I have the truck. We need to stop at the store and pick up some dishes for the restaurant."

"That's right. Jason mentioned the dishes to me this morning before he left for training camp."

"I envy you two," Toni said.

"Why?" Francine and Amy said together.

"I feel like I'm not fully involved in the restaurant. Sometimes I feel left out."

"Why?" Francine asked.

"Because you're always together working on it. The last time I've been out there was when we found the cellar door."

"You've been asked to come with us each time. But lately you've been spending all your time with Eric," Amy stated.

"I know. Thing are going so well with him. I think he might be the one."

"Yeah, the one who alienates you from your friends," Francine snapped.

Toni spread her arms open. "What are the two of you going to do, gang up on me?"

"No, we aren't." Francine leaned down to wipe dust she spotted on the front of her shoes.

"The shoes," Amy pointed. "Don't even tell me you took evidence out of the basement."

"Evidence? When did you turn into police woman?"

"By you touching things, you are compromising the investigation."

"What the hell are you talking about?" Toni asked.

Amy stood. "We need to go to the police."

Francine detected a slight smirk on Amy's face, which she knew all too well. Amy had already made a few phone calls. Leaning back in her chair, Francine rested her feet with her brand-new shoes on her desk, keeping her eyes on Amy.

"Don't look at me like that!" Amy shouted.

"When did you make the call? And, what information are you holding back from us?" Francine asked, crossing her arms tightly to her chest.

Amy walked across the room, before turning to face them. "You have to swear not to breathe a word of this to anyone. If word gets out, it could botch up a sixteen-month investigation."

"Oh shit. This sounds serious." Francine dropped her feet to the floor. "Do I have to put back the shoes and handbag?"

"A handbag too?"

Francine dropped her gaze to her feet, extending her bottom lip. "Yeah, matching."

"No more going down there."

"When did this come about?" Toni asked.

"Yesterday. I'm not sure but I think the police and FBI are close. That's what my neighbor told me. He also advised us to go about our lives as usual." Amy turned to Toni. "Not a word to anyone. Not even Eric. We have to all stick together."

"Not to abruptly change the subject Toni, but you never come out with us anymore. You always make excuses when we ask you."

"Francine's right. You either outright tell us you can't come or just don't show up, calling us with a ridiculous excuse."

"It's not me. Eric feels so uncomfortable around Richie and Jason."

"Then you have to talk to him about that. You two have been dating for months now. I can't understand why you can't do something you want to do. He doesn't even want you to come to the ballpark with us," Amy said.

Toni put her head down. "Please understand, it's not me."

Francine stood. "Let's get out of here." Once everyone put their seat belts on in the truck, Francine pulled away from the curb. "We know it isn't you. I think Eric is insecure and becoming way too possessive of you."

"At times, I feel the same way. But then he'll do something sweet or tell me how much he cares about me. You of all people should know how that feels, Francine. My foster family took care of me, but there was never any compassion toward me. Now I have it, so I have to overlook some things Eric says or does."

"I would seriously think about what you're getting yourself into."

Amy turned around in her seat to look at Toni sitting in the back. "You have to do what's best for you. But if you ask me, he's trying to control you."

"Nonsense. He's just generous. Many times he's on the road looking for new clients, so when we are together he spoils me. I don't see anything wrong with that."

Francine made the decision not to say anything else. She remembered what Richie's mother did to her. It took her over a year to win her trust. Toni had to live with him, not them. Thinking back, Richie did the same thing to her, showering her with gifts, and buying her clothes. He did this because he loved her, not because he was trying to control her.

"I thought we'd stop by here before we go back to my house," Francine said, pulling into the parking lot of the Richmond Restaurant Discount Store.

Toni unbuckled her seat belt. "Works for me. I love this store. You can find things here you can't get anywhere else."

"Do you know if they deliver?" Francine asked.

"I'm pretty sure they do," Amy said, closing the car door.

Once inside the store, Francine acted like a little kid. There were so many different sets of dishes. Francine had a vision of what she wanted. Earlier, Richie suggested the simpler, the better. After picking up a few wine glasses, she understood what Richie meant, the plainer the design, the heavier the glass.

"I like these." Francine handed a wine glass to Amy, and a tall beer glass to Toni. "I'm going to find a salesperson to help us."

Francine wandered off. Along the way, she spotted square navy dishes in assorted sizes. Even the soup dish was square. These would fit in with the white porcelain dishes that were left by the previous owners. Lifting a dish, she walked around making her way to the front of the store. Before she made it to the counter, an older gentleman approached her. His nametag read Andrew, Manager.

"Good afternoon, Mrs. Raggalio. How are you today?"

"I'm fine thanks," she hesitantly said. "Do I know you?"

"Not really. I met you and your husband Richie at the Little League fundraiser over the winter. Your husband, and Jason Maddock, were the only two athletes who not only showed up but stayed the whole time signing autographs, taking pictures with the kids."

Francine stood taller. "That's my husband."

"How's he feeling? When is he coming back?" Andrew asked like a Little Leaguer.

"He's doing much better, thank you. He started throwing the ball again. If his rehabilitation goes according to plan, he should be back in the pitching rotation in a few weeks."

"That's wonderful. So what can I help you with today?"

Francine handed him the dish. "Richie and I are opening a sports restaurant and bar in a few weeks. I need to pick up a few things. I especially like this," she said handing it to him.

"I have these in stock. Do you know how many you need?"

"Hmm. I'd say around ten to twelve dozen place settings."

"Wow," Andrew jerked his head back. "That's a lot of dishes. You're opening a big place."

"Big enough. I'd rather have too many in the event some break along the way."

"I have to agree with you."

"Can I interest you in some white dishes?" he asked.

"No thank you. The previous owners left us a few dozen sets of plain white dishes which we plan on using at the bar/pizzeria side of the restaurant."

"Please let me know when you guys are open."

"I will."

"Anything else I can get you?"

"Yes. If you follow me, my friends are over in the glassware department. I found some really nice heavy duty glasses for the bar."

The sound of a broken glass and the word, "Shit," echoed through the store.

"That would be where I left my friends," Francine said holding back her laughter. She could hear the two of them giggling from aisles away.

"Hey, we're over here," Amy waved.

"I heard you." Francine bit her bottom lip while walking over to Amy. There was glass all over the floor. "What happened?"

"I went to swing my handbag over my shoulder." Amy dropped her eyes to the floor. "And this is the result."

"Ladies, it's okay, it's only glass. What can I get you from here?"

Toni held up two glasses. "Tall and short bar glasses."

"The perfect choice. I expect a delivery of these today. Are you looking to take the dishes home with you today, or would you like me to have everything delivered at the same time?"

"I'd love for them to be delivered. The guys are all tied up today," Francine said.

"I'll call you when I get the glasses in. Anything else you'll be needing?"

"Not right now." Francine opened her handbag. "Here you go. Put them on my charge. While you ring up the order, I'll look around."

After a quick stop at the ladies' room, they were back on the road, making their way down to Amy's during school rush hour. The normal ten-minute ride turned into a half hour when they got stuck on a one lane street behind a school bus.

Francine pulled into her driveway. They got out of the car and walked into the house. Francine plopped her handbag on the chair by the door before joining the girls in the kitchen.

"I'm going up to change," Francine said. "Your swimsuits are in the pool house along with towels."

"I can't remember the last time we did a girls' afternoon," Amy said. "I miss them."

"A lot has changed since last summer," Toni said. "Last summer neither one of us was in a relationship."

Amy raised her hand. "I'm feeling an argument about to come on, so let's forget about last summer and concentrate on the present." Amy raised an eyebrow to Francine who just shrugged.

"I'll meet you by the pool," Francine said, walking out of the room.

By the time she reached the top of the stairs, she could hear Amy and Toni bickering about Toni's absence from their friendship. Francine closed her bedroom door, shutting it out. All she wanted was to have a quiet afternoon with her friends playing catch-up. Since it was just the girls, Francine chose her bronze two-piece bathing suit. An afternoon floating on a raft was her idea of the perfect day.

As she walked back down the stairs, her cell phone went off with a text from Sophia Larsen, saying she was outside. Francine opened the door. "Sophia, how are you?"

Sophia greeted her with a hug. "I'm doing great. You're looking good."

"Thank you. You too. It's been a long time."

"Too long especially with our husbands on the same team."

"Yes. We must get together soon."

"I hear you." Sophia handed Francine an envelope. "I thought since I was in the neighborhood, I'd drop you off your invitation to Scott's surprise birthday party."

"How's Richie doing? Scott said he rejoined the team for the road trip."

"Yes, he has. I spoke to him earlier. He's been throwing the ball. If everything goes according to plan, he should be pitching by mid-September."

"Honestly, I don't miss going to the games. You know what it's like to be married to a pitcher."

"Tell me about it. And then they talk about women having mood swings."

"How's Scott? Richie told me he's working as a coach."

"Yes, it's the best thing that could have happened to him. Once he retired, he moped around the house all day long. When he got offered the job as bullpen coach, he came back to life. As it turns out, our husbands don't know anything else but baseball."

"Oh, you are so right there."

"Has Richie given any thought to what he's going to do once he retires?"

"Yes. We're in the process of opening a sports bar and restaurant down on Page Avenue."

"That is awesome. You guys know how to run a restaurant?"

"We're learning. So what brings you to Staten Island?

"I had a meeting down at The Finn. I'm working freelance for them."

"At least it keeps you busy while Scott is on the road."

"Yes, it does." Sophia opened her handbag. "Excuse me for just a minute."

Sophia walked toward the front door talking on the phone. As she strolled back, Francine heard her say, "I'll tell her," before slipping her phone back into her handbag.

"Sorry, but I have to run. That was Scott. He said hi. He's with Richie as we speak."

"Let's get together when the season is over. I would love for you guys to be at the restaurant opening."

"When is it?"

"We decided to wait until the season is over."

"Let me know." Sophia hugged her. "Send my love to Richie."

"Same here to Scott."

Francine strolled onto the deck and smiled when she saw Amy and Toni sitting on the side of the pool with their legs dangling in the water, giggling. Seeing her friends happy made her happy. Sometimes there would be some tension between Amy and Toni. They were always bickering about the stupidest things. Neither one of them would drop it. But today, they both seemed to be in extremely good moods. Maybe love did make a difference in their lives.

"Hey. I see you two are having fun." Francine sat down next to Amy. "I could hear you from inside."

"What took you so long?" Amy asked.

"Sophia Larsen stopped by with an invitation to her husband's birthday party."

"Really? That's strange. Why wouldn't she drop it in the mail?" Toni asked.

"Not a clue ladies." Francine slid into the pool and dunked her head under water.

"What did Sophia have to say?" Amy asked. "She's never been overly friendly to me."

"I have a feeling something might have been bothering her. After she received a phone call, she ran out of here."

Francine waved her hand. "I'm not losing any sleep over it. I was really not very friendly with her."

"I know she did attend some of the parties you've had during the years," Amy said, joining Francine in the pool.

"Yes, she did. But I was never one of those baseball wives. I had the business to run. Besides, I trust Richie. I didn't have to show up on the road to make sure he wasn't doing anything inappropriate."

"You two are vintage," Amy said.

"We've had our ups and downs through the years. Don't forget, we've been together since high school. The good thing is we grew together."

Toni continued to dangle her feet in the water. "I'm hoping me and Eric become vintage too."

"What's with you?" Francine asked Toni. Francine noticed Toni acting somewhat antsy. Toni kept glancing over her shoulder toward the house.

"Nothing."

"Aren't you coming in? This is our girly downtime," Amy said.

"I don't want the two of you to be upset with me."

"Why would we be?" Amy asked.

"Because Eric asked if he could meet me here. I told him to come through the back gate."

"Okay. So why would we be mad?" Amy asked. "Eric could have joined us to eat."

"Because I know Francine wanted this to be a girls' afternoon."

"Please." Francine swam over to Toni.. "You're falling in love with this guy."

Toni blushed. "I think I am. There's just something about him. Besides, you know how much I love men who wear business suits."

"Just as much as I love men in uniform." Amy giggled.

"I wish Richie would come home with his uniform on. That's why I love getting to the park early, just to see him.

It's hard to imagine, after all these years, the uniform still does it for me."

"You two are crazy," Toni said.

"Who's crazy?"

Francine looked up and watched Eric walk over to Toni. Eric stood at the edge of the pool grinning.

"We are," Amy said. "We were just talking about how we love men in uniform."

"And I told them, I'm a business suit kinda gal."

Toni stood up and led Eric to the mosaic top table. "Can I get you anything?"

Eric's eyebrows narrowed. "No thanks. I just had lunch." Eric sat down and Toni joined him.

"If you'd like to take a swim, there's a few bathing trunks in the pool house." Francine pointed to the left of the yard.

"No, thank you. I'm not a big pool person. My mother forced us to go to the beach everyday because we lived in an apartment building. So needless to say, I'm not into water activities. But I can see you ladies love the life of leisure."

"Today we do," Amy said. "We work very hard. Tomorrow is another day."

"I wish I could say the same," Eric replied. "But tonight it's all about Toni.

Toni grinned. "What do you have planned for us for the rest of the day?"

"I thought we'd stop at the mall to pick up those shoes you were telling me about last night on the phone."

"Are you kidding me?" Toni asked, her eyes beaming.

"Nope. And hopefully they have a handbag to match them too."

"Looks like you found Toni's weakness." Francine laughed. "You should see her closet. She is a shoes and handbag fiend."

"That's my girl. I love seeing her face when we pass the shoe stores. Her eyes roam the front windows, always zeroing in on a pair or two of shoes."

"That's our girl," Amy said, getting out of the pool with Francine.

Francine wrapped a towel around her and joined them at the table. "Can I get anyone something?"

"We're good," Amy answered for all of them.

Eric stood and reached his hand out to Toni. "Why don't you go and change back into your clothes so we can go shopping."

In a flash, Toni went into the pool house to change. The moment Toni returned, Eric was ushering out of the backyard. Francine couldn't understand why he didn't like spending time with Toni's friends. They always made him feel at home.

"What's on the agenda for our night?" Amy asked.

"Exactly what we're doing now, sitting by the pool and being carefree!"

Chapter Seventeen

Francine had prepared all of Richie's favorite desserts. During the past few weeks, Francine and Angelina had worked on the dessert menu. They had both agreed a separate menu for dessert would be the best way to go. While they composed the dessert menu, Francine suggested another menu for appetizers and drinks. She had run the idea past Richie and Jason, last time they had been in town, with both of them agreeing it was a great idea. Richie admitted that while he sat at a bar watching a game, he would rather have chicken wings and mozzarella sticks, the things you rarely had at home.

Earlier in the day, Angelina stopped by. As they went over last minute things on the menu, Francine couldn't be any happier with the design Angelina came up with. Once Richie and Jason saw the menu, she would bring it to the printer. They were so close to opening up. In two weeks both Richie and Jason would be in town, that being the weekend they were talking about having the grand opening. Richie had a Saturday afternoon game, while Jason's team was on the schedule to play Monday night football.

The sound of Richie's car pulling up into the driveway sent Francine into full speed. She dimmed the lights in the dining room, and lit the candles.. The click of the key in the door sent Francine walking into the living room.

"Babe, I'm home."

Francine's raced into the center hall. Richie stood with a beautiful bouquet of purple lilies in a glass vase. What she didn't like was the frown on his face. Usually, he was chipper, smiling, sweeping her in his arms.

"They are beautiful. Thank you." Francine touched his cheek. "What's wrong, Richie?"

"Go put the flowers down and we'll talk."

Francine's heart palpitated. This wasn't the greeting she expected. Richie looked so upset that she doubted he would be interested in talking about the dessert menu. Placing the flowers on the kitchen counter, she turned to see Richie wasn't standing behind her. "Hey where did you go?"

"I'm in the dining room. The scent of vanilla candles and this assortment of desserts is a great combination."

"What's wrong?" Francine asked again.

Richie slowly turned around. The frown on his face had turned into a huge grin. "Oh, there isn't a single thing wrong." Richie gathered Francine into his arms. "Baby, I'm coming off the disabled list next week."

"Get out of here. That's great news. I am so happy for you."

"Thanks." He kissed the top of her head, before stepping back to face her. "Vic and Doctor Weston said they would give me the clean bill of health. My fastball is right on the money. I've been throwing everyday."

"I can't wait. You know how I get turned on seeing you out there on the pitching mound." Francine licked her lips. "Looking at you in uniform, to this day is still a turn on, always will be."

"Don't even go there yet. I want to hear about the dessert bar you transformed our dining room into."

"These are all on our dessert menu, specifically made by your mom. We have pies, cakes and pastries." Francine pointed to each one. "I'll pack these up later on. You can bring the goodies down to the ballpark tomorrow. If they stay here on the dining room table, I can assure you I'll be eating these all day."

Richie chuckled. "I should have known my mom would be behind this. She is so excited about this business venture. With my father retiring at the end of the year, I think this will be the perfect thing for her. If they spend too much time together, you know they will be fighting nonstop."

"Your father is going to be looking to do some work around the restaurant too."

"He already is. Jason had him do all the brick outside," he said.

"If you had gotten home two hours earlier, the apple crumb cake was hot. She wants to do some baking in the kitchen before we open."

"I think that's a great idea. Mom is the only one who knows what she needs."

"Believe me, she is already set. She hired a young baker out of the Culinary Institute and ordered cake and Bundt pans, cookie sheets, mini and big muffin pans and a few commercial appliances."

Richie smiled. "That's my mom. Not only does she call me everyday to ask about my pitching arm, but now she calls asking when the grand opening is."

"We're almost there. I'm waiting to coordinate with Jason so we are both in the restaurant that night."

"That would be at the end of the regular season. I already looked at both calendars with Jason before he left Texas." Francine lifted the dish with the tiramisu. She took a forkful and slid the fork into Richie's mouth.

"Oh my. My mother outdoes herself every time."

"Yes she does. A few days ago, she interviewed a couple of chefs but didn't like anyone. She insists on making the pot of gravy, meatballs, sausage, marinara sauce and fried eggplant. I assured her running a restaurant is a lot of work with long hours. Inasmuch as we'd love to do all the cooking ourselves, it will be literally impossible."

"It will be. The last thing I want is for this to be a burden on anyone. I don't want you wearing yourself out. We will be a family owned establishment. Jason and I are going to hire a few college kids as waiters and waitresses. Besides hiring a master chef, I have contacted a few of the culinary schools, extended paid internships for chefs."

"That's a wonderful opportunity you're giving."

"I believe in giving others an opportunity to explore their dreams."

Francine grinned. "Your mom is living out her dream too."

"I hear you. She told me the both of you were not only working on the dessert menu, but you also started the food menu."

"Yes we did. What she didn't tell you is I'm working on a cocktail menu."

"That's a different twist."

"Oh yeah. Each drink is named after the baseball diamond."

Richie gave Francine a peck on her lips. "Sounds quite interesting. Care to elaborate?"

"A Homerun is my own special mixture of Kahlua, Bailys Irish Cream and a splash of marshmallow vodka. They can have it regular or as a frozen drink."

"Wow. I have a feeling we are going to do much better with the bar service than the restaurant, especially during the summer months."

"Exactly. Everyone loves frozen drinks on a hot summer night."

"I couldn't agree more."

"This is going to be our time to shine together. Tomorrow, we can go down to the restaurant. I can't wait for you to see what Jason did. That man has hands of gold. He also had the televisions installed a couple of days ago. Next Tuesday, I have the cable company coming to run the cables inside."

"If you're going to be there, I'll put in an order for liquor. I don't think we have enough on the shelves."

"You think of everything." Francine licked her finger. "Can I get you anything?."

"No, " Richie waved his index finger. "I have been on the road for two and a half weeks. What I want right now is to spend time with my wife." He pulled her into him. "Just you and me. We can talk about business later."

Francine stuck her finger into the whipped cream on the chocolate cream pie. Immediately she had Richie's attention. Slowly, she reached her finger up to her lips and sucked the tip of her finger before circling her tongue down the rest of her finger, making sure she removed all the whipped cream off.

"There will be no teasing tonight. What I want to do is sweep you into my arms and carry you up the stairs, but I don't want to take any chances."

"I agree. But no one said I can't race you up the stairs." Francine grinned, placing her hands on her hips, licking her lips.

"You're playing dirty."

"First one upstairs and undressed in bed runs the show tonight."

"You already win," he nodded his chin toward her. "I want you to be the first one ready."

"Why?"

"Because when you're in this playful mood, the sex is always phenomenal."

The next morning, Francine reached her arm over to hug Richie, but he wasn't there. She turned onto her back, taking a deep breath. The scent of Richie's cologne drifted into the room.. Richie always knew how to put a smile on her face first thing in the morning.

The sound of water in the shower became silent. Within a few minutes, Richie came into the room with a towel wrapped around his waist. God, how she missed seeing him everyday. The tiny microscopic cuts in his shoulder from the surgery had almost disappeared except for the tiny scars that hadn't tanned from the sun.

Francine whistled. "Yummy. I love when you stand before me with a towel wrapped around your waist, makes we want to attack you."

Richie held up his hand. "You drained me last night."

"Hmm." Francine licked her lips and pushed the covers down on his side of the bed. "Can't you just come and lay down with me?"

"Oh no. "Richie waved his finger. "I have to be full of energy and alert. Vic isn't going to let me work out today."

"I wouldn't do that to you. I just want a kiss from my drop-dead gorgeous husband who looks just as delicious as the first day I met him."

"I got up early to spend time with you and talk about the restaurant a little before I leave."

"I'd like that. When you leave, I'm going to the office. I have a lot of paperwork. Amy and Toni have been really great, doing more than their share of the work. I don't want them to think I'm taking advantage."

Richie pulled his head back. "No one would ever think that of you."

"That will all end soon. Once we open the restaurant, we'll be spending all our time together. I'll come down to the stadium later on."

"No," he shook his head. "I won't be pitching, not yet. Vic says not for another week or two."

"That will be the end of the season."

"Babe, I'm lucky if I pitch one game before the end of the season." Richie ran his fingers through his hair. "I didn't want to retire like this. I wanted to go out on top of my game."

"You will. In my heart I know you will be back for the last month of the season. And then there is post season. It looks like you guys are heading to the championship."

"Nothing is etched in stone. We are only leading by five games. I need to get back to help my team."

"Yes, you do. Hmm." Francine rested her finger on her lips for a few moments. "Do you think Vic would put you in to relieve?"

"I thought about it. Even brought it up to Vic, but he said he wants me to be a hundred percent and take the mound from the first inning."

"He's right. I don't want you out there teasing the fans, especially the young girls who scream your name from the outfield into the bullpen."

"Jealous?" He chuckled.

"Never. Proud, yes. You are an icon, a role model for young boys. I have an idea." Francine got out of bed and slid Richie's T-shirt over her head. "We can offer discounts to the little leagues when they come here after their game."

"That's a wonderful idea. We'll keep it simple, making a plain cheese pie. Free soda for the kids." Richie slid a black golf shirt over his head.

Francine slowly approached Richie, placing her arms around his neck after buttoning the bottom two buttons on his shirt. "I guess I'll be making another menu," she said before leaning her body into his.

"There's plenty of time to work on that."

Francine could feel the warmth of his excitement resting against her stomach. "I think it's time I jumped into a cold shower. I don't want to distract or mar you in anyway when you go to the field because my libido is in overdrive."

"That I can see." He leaned into her, kissing her lips before taking a step back. "I will take you up on your proposition tonight, that's if you don't fall asleep on me again."

"Never. I promise to wait up for you."

Richie slid on his briefs and then his jeans. "Do you want to meet me at the stadium restaurant around six?"

"Is that kind of early?" she asked following him downstairs into the kitchen.

"I don't think so. The game starts at two. After the game, there's supposed to be a team meeting."

"Oh geez. The last time you had one of them it lasted close to two hours."

"That's why I think six would be perfect. See if you can get a ride from Amy so you can have a couple of drinks."

"If she isn't going, I'll jump on the express bus and take the train out there. It isn't a big deal."

"Whenever you use public transportation, you wind up having lots of shopping bags with you."

Francine giggled. "You know how much I love shopping in Manhattan. I also get something for you."

"That you do."

"Always."

Richie's cell phone beeped. Looking down, he nodded his head in agreement. "Babe, I have to get going. Vinny LoMaro," he lifted his phone, "texted me. He's in Staten Island, wants to pick me up."

"Perfect. I will see you after the game. This way if Amy doesn't want to go, I don't have to guilt her into going.."

"What time you heading out this morning?" he asked.

"When you leave I'm going to take a shower and head to the office around lunchtime."

The phone beeped. "That must be Vinny. I'll see you later."

Francine took her shower and dressed comfortably in jeans and a T-shirt. She looked forward to going to the stadium. With Richie not pitching all year, there was no need to sit there in stiletto city. She was an old hand at this, dressing the same way when Richie first came up to the majors. But as the years went on, she didn't have to prove to anyone she could sport around in a convertible and stilettos.

Her cell phone went off with Amy's face flashing to the music.

"Hey. What's going on?"

"Not much. I'm doing some paperwork at the office."

"Sucks to be you." Francine laughed.

"Yeah," Amy mumbled.

"What's wrong? Did someone back out of a deal?"

"Eh, not really. I forgot my wallet at home. Will you be coming into work soon?"

Francine knew immediately something wasn't right. Amy never left the house without her wallet, and if she realized she left it at home, she would have locked up and went back to retrieve it. "Not a problem. I'll be there in a little while."

"I wish you would come now. There's an account I'd like to talk about."

"I'll be right there."

Francine clicked her off, grabbed her handbag off the counter, got into her car and sped down Hylan Boulevard to the office. She opened the door to the office. When she went to walk in, Amy stood in her way.

"You can't believe what's going on. I'm just about ready to shit my pants." Amy spoke quickly in a whisper.

"What the hell are you talking about?"

"There are two detectives in the office wanting to speak to the both of us."

"Why? We didn't do anything illegal... Oh, the shit in the basement."

"That's what I'm thinking." Amy sighed. "Richie and Jason are going to kill us. We should have reported what we found to the police from the beginning."

"How could we? Richie made me promise not to do anything that will cause attention to us in the media."

"Fine time for you to take his advice."

A deep grunt caused Francine and Amy to turn around. A short overweight man in a business suit stood in the doorway of the reception area.

"Are you two ladies about ready?"

"Yes, we are," Francine said. "Can I get you a cup of coffee?"

"That's okay. Miss Mills has given us coffee and cookies."

"Jason brought cookies?" Francine asked Amy as she eyed the two detectives.

"Yes."

"Oh let me see what he brought," she said, stalling.

"Mrs. Raggalio we aren't here for a social call." One of the detectives held out his badge. "I'm Detective Morris and this is my partner, Detective Seawood."

Francine looked at the younger of the two, who sat silent. If she had to place a wager, she'd bet he was the new detective on the block. He didn't seem as confident as Morris.

"Nice to meet you." Francine shook both their hands before sitting down behind her desk. "What can we do for you today?"

"Mrs. Raggalio you and Miss Mills are in quite an unfortunate situation. You should have come to us when you first found the illegal contraband in the basement." Morris pointed to her shoes. "I see you helped yourself."

"I knew we should have gone to the police," Amy whispered.

Francine dropped a glance down to her lap. Her heart palpitated and she nervously grinned.

"This isn't a joking matter," Detective Seawood sternly said. "These men are dangerous. They won't think twice about killing you if they found out you located their secret hiding place."

"Call me stupid, but I don't understand what's going on."

"You are in the middle of a year and a half investigation. We are so close in nailing the bastards. That's why we were surprised when you started doing work on the old restaurant."

"I'm sure I don't have to tell you how I wound up with the property."

"Not at all. We were just surprised that you kept it. But that isn't why we're here," Morris explained.

"There's no way to tell you how things are going down. You're in extreme danger and your friend Miss Belluci is in bigger danger," Seawood added, readjusting his tie.

"Why Toni?" Francine asked. "We're all in this together."

"Miss Belluci's boyfriend is the ringleader of the operation."

"Are you kidding me?" Francine glanced at Amy who sat with a blank look on her face. "Eric?"

"Yes Mrs. Raggalio. When you all came to the restaurant, that first day, Eric and his cronies were in the basement. Hitting on Miss Belluci was his way of having an in. Knowing when you would and wouldn't be in the restaurant." Morris opened his pad. "Eric isn't a pharmaceutical representative. Everything he has given Miss Belluci is stolen."

"How could it be? Toni said he brought her on a shopping spree in the mall," Amy said, tapping her fingernails on her desk.

"Yes, he did. But everything he bought her was with stolen credit cards. He brought her to the stores that he knew didn't check the cards. And with the new technology, a lot of the stores don't require signatures," Morris explained.

"He also has items being sent to numerous houses in the area, knowing that merchandise under five hundred dollars doesn't require a signature."

"Oh my, God." Francine covered her face with her hands. "This isn't good. What can we do to help?"

"There isn't anything you can do but be careful. Stay away from the restaurant at night. He only goes in when he knows you aren't there."

"Please detectives, I can't tell my husband what's going on."

"We are close to making an arrest. What we ask is you keep clear of the place. You have a cute little business here. And try to keep Miss Belluci away from Eric."

"That's going to be quite hard. She is totally smitten by him."

"Try your best without letting her know what's going on," Seawood said.

"You can't breathe a word of this to anyone. We are that close. Do you understand?"
Francine and Amy nodded their heads, while both detectives stood, handing them their cards.

"If you have any concerns, call us immediately," Morris said.

"We will."

Francine didn't move from her chair. She kept her eyes on Amy as she walked the detectives to the door. Within a few moments, she heard the door lock and Amy walked in, her arms crossed, just shaking her head.

Silence lingered over them for a couple of minutes. Francine watched Amy sit down behind her desk. This was a lot to comprehend. How could they have gotten themselves caught up in such a mess? Funny, how trouble always seemed to follow Francine. Even when she minded her own business, she got involved in something that never in her wildest dreams she could have ever imagined.

Flipping a tissue out of a small square box, Francine wiped the sweat off her forehead. She didn't know what to say to Amy. No words could express how she felt.

"Say something," Amy cried. "How could we have gotten ourselves stuck in the middle of this bullshit? I've never gotten into trouble…"

"Never?" Francine's eyebrows rose up.

"Okay, through the years we have gotten ourselves in trouble, but that was minute compared to what we are entangled in now."

"What are we suppose to do about Toni? I'm sure everything we tell her she repeats to Eric."

"I agree. That was always the one flaw in Toni I couldn't stand. We have warned her time and time again about not sharing any of our secrets to a boyfriend until we all got to know him."

Francine stood, crossing her arms against her chest. "I hate that this loser is using Toni. She can be quite vulnerable at times when it comes to love."

"Not in her defense, but we all are. I know I am, especially with Jason."

"But Jason is different. We've known him for a long time."

"What does that have to do with anything? You should know better. You watch those investigative shows all the time. Sometimes it's the person you are the closest to that uses you the most."

"Let's not go there." Francine dropped her hands to her sides. "We can't start second-guessing everything we do. What we can do is figure out how to live our lives like nothing is going on. From here, I can see an unmarked cop car across the street. Richie is going to kill me."

"This isn't your fault. How could we have known that there was something illegal going on in the basement? At least now we know and we can stay alert to what's going on around us."

"And keep a watchful eye on Toni. We will have to give her things to do to keep her busy without causing suspicion."

"Then we better start thinking and fast."

Chapter Eighteen

Toni and Eric walked around Clove Lake Park. This was always Toni's favorite place to schlepp. She knew Eric wasn't too happy about strolling, since he always dressed in a suit and dress shoes. But when he asked what she'd like to do, this was exactly what she wanted.

For the end of September, the weather was quite brisk. Usually she would jog through the park into mid-December and some years throughout the winter with just a heavy sweatshirt. Today, she had on a blazer and the chill went right through her.

Her favorite time of the year had been the fall with the different colored leaves. That's why when Eric asked her what she wanted to do, she said walk around the trail of the park. After much hesitation on Eric's part he eventually said yes.

"Isn't this beautiful?" She pointed up at the trees.

"Just lovely." He frowned.

"You're not enjoying this?"

"I'd rather be sitting home having a cup of coffee and watching a movie."

"I'm sure you would. But walking out here is absolutely irresistible. The fresh scent of the trees and flowers are breathtaking."

"Don't forget the scent of dog shit, too. I can't tell you how many times I just missed stepping in it."

"Oh come on. The best things in life are free." Toni circled her arms. "I don't need anything fancy. I'll take doing this anytime instead of going out to eat."

"No one is saying you have to come out to eat with me. You can stay home whenever you want."

Toni glared at Eric. What he had just said was a complete insult. Every time she said something he didn't like, that would be his favorite saying.

There was so many times that she bit her lip, when what she wanted to do was break up with him. Sometimes he got her to the point that her right eye would start twitching. Why would she want to stay with someone like him? Before she met him, she did fine. But now with Amy dating Jason, it left her out in the dark, alone.

Toni reached over to slide her hand in his, but he pulled his hand away. Eric wasn't in the least bit romantic. He didn't believe in any public display of affection whatsoever, total opposite of her. They had walked around the park twice with no conversation at all, which bothered her.

This time when they passed the bathroom, she stopped in. She didn't have to go. What she wanted to do was revamp, and figure out what to say to him. Even though she liked him, she needed to get out of their relationship. It had taken a toll on her and she was ready to move on without Eric. She would like a break, staying on her own for a while.

When she walked out of the restroom, Eric turned to face her.

"What do you say we go to Vegas for a couple of days?"

Toni's mouth dropped open. "Really?"

"Yes. I thought we would go and have some fun." He winked. "You never know what happens in Vegas."

"I'd love to go. When are we leaving?"

"How about next week?"

Toni parted her lips to say yes, until she realized that next week could possibly be the World Series. This would be the perfect way to get out of this relationship."

"What's wrong? You seem hesitant." Eric reached into his jacket pocket, taking out a cigarette.

"I would love to go next week."

Eric lit his cigarette, taking a long inhale, blowing the smoke up into the air. "But?"

"If the Pelicans win tonight, then they're going to be going to the World Series and I want to be there."

"And what does that have to do with you? It isn't your husband pitching."

"No, it isn't," she snapped. "But I've always been a part of it. Besides, we have all been together since high school."

Eric stopped walking to face her. "And?"

"And I don't want to miss it."

"You're kidding me."

Toni watched the corner of his lip twitch. One thing Eric didn't like was when he didn't get his own way. She didn't know what else to say to him. She wasn't going to change her mind about the games. Maybe they could work out a happy medium.

"What if we leave the beginning of next week and come home on Thursday?"

"Are you kidding me? I'm asking you to come to Vegas with me. Now you're telling me when to go."

"If it's really a big deal, I'll go whenever you want to go." After she answered him, she regretted giving in to him, yet again.

"No." He shook his head. "Things don't work like that. To be quite honest, it seems your friends are more important to you than our relationship." Eric took a step back, sliding his hands into his pants pockets. "I am not going to put up with this. These are the things that annoy me about you."

"Annoy you? Are you kidding me?" Toni raised her voice causing two joggers to turn around to look at them.

"You may not see it, but you have a lot of flaws that you choose not to deal with."

Toni threw her hands up in the air. "I can't believe what I'm hearing. After all these months you're telling me there are things about me that you hate."

"That's exactly what I'm saying, starting with your friends. You will have to make a decision. It's either them or me. You can't have it both ways. I am not going to live my life around your friends. You're going to live my life the way I want it, nice and simple with no complications."

Toni stepped back from him. "You are sick. How can you ask me to choose between you and my friends? And why would you want to alienate me from them?"

"Because they take up too much of your time. You are with them all day at work. There is no reason why you have to gallivant out to ballgames every other day. That is sick."

"What's sick is that you don't respect the things I love to do. I can't understand why you can't accept me for who I am," Toni lashed out.

"I see the way you look at the men on the field. Your tongue is hanging out of your mouth."

"You're an idiot."

"Is it safe to assume you are going to tell your friends that you won't be seeing them anymore?" he asked.

"You are so confident in yourself." Toni rested her hands on her hips. "What I'm telling you is I have no intentions whatsoever on making a choice. There's no way I'm giving up my childhood friends for anyone, let alone you."

Eric slid his hands out of his pants and pointed his finger at her. "You're not thinking rationally. But I'm going to tell you one thing, you walk away from me, it's forever. I will never take you back."

"Please." Toni laughed. "You aren't that good. You're a nightmare to deal with and you suck in bed. So, don't be standing there giving me ultimatums. I think you're the one who is dysfunctional."

"I'm not going to stand here listening to anymore of your shit. I'm out of here. You lost the best thing that has ever happened to you."

"Eric, the best thing that has ever happened to me is right at this moment, letting you go. You have done nothing but put me down and tell me what to do. I don't need you."

"That's it." Eric waved his hand, pivoted on his shiny polished loafers and walked down the path out of the park.

Toni kept her eyes on him until he was out of her sight. She felt no remorse letting him go. The past few weeks he had been grating on her nerves with all his nonsense. Every time she went to do something for herself, he would call her or show up at her house to stop her from going out. She knew her friends saw it but didn't want to say anything. A few weeks ago, she wouldn't have listened to them. But after what he pulled today, all she could think was goodbye and good riddance. She'd rather be alone then put up with his monstrous demands.

After a few moments, she realized that he left her at the park with no ride home, which was just great. She had no money on her and left her cell phone on the kitchen counter. Glancing at her feet, she sighed. Walking home or to the office wouldn't have been a problem if she had on a pair of sneakers. There weren't many choices except for taking her time walking home.

Once she made her way to Clove Road, she stood with her hands on her hips, assessing the easiest way to go home. Out of the corner of her eye, she spotted a navy car with darkened windows sitting at the curb. If she didn't know any better, she'd think the car was following her along Victory

Boulevard. Once she crossed the street to walk along Clove Road, the car pulled up right next to her. She walked quicker and the car continued to follow her. The passenger window opened and an officer held up his gold badge. "I'm Sergeant Thompson, this is Officer Bova. Please get into the car."

"I didn't do anything," Toni said holding her hands up. "I don't even have I.D. with me."

"It's okay. You'll be safer in the back seat of our car than with Eric Summers."

"What does Eric have to do with this? Did he call you?"

"No. Please get in. Summers is a dangerous man."

Toni hesitated for a moment. As much as she didn't want to believe what Thompson was saying, she had a gut feeling his words were correct. Just that he left her in the park proved he had no respect whatsoever for her. Even though they had an argument, he should have never left her in the park without a ride.

She reached for the metal handle, opened the door and slid into the back seat, which was separated from the front of the car with thick Plexiglas. The car pulled away from the curb and Thompson opened a small window between them.

"What do you know about Eric Summers?"

"He was my boyfriend. We broke up about ten minutes ago."

"What else did he tell you?"

"He works for a pharmaceutical company as a rep, going to all the doctors' offices bringing samples."

"I'm sorry to tell you, but he's a fraud. He is not a pharmaceutical rep. He's a criminal."

"I don't believe it." Toni ran her fingers through her hair. "Criminals don't get dressed up in suits and carry around leather briefcases full of samples."

"Did you ever see any of his samples?"

"No."

"Did you ever meet him at a doctor's office or run into anyone he knew while you were together?" Thompson sternly asked.

Toni put her head down. "No," she cried.

"Eric Summers is dangerous. He is involved with the distribution of goods and drugs."

Toni slid to the edge of the seat, resting her arms along the small opening. "I don't understand."

"Your friends, Francine and Amy are also in danger."

"Wait. You are scaring me. What's going on here?"

"Summers is storing all his illegal contraband in the basement of your friends' restaurant."

"Oh." Toni raised her hand to wipe the tears from her eyes with thankful that I just broke up with him."

"Yes we know. We have been following Summers for months. I need you to stay far away from him."

"What about my friends? Are they going to be okay?"

"Everyone will be okay as long as you follow our instructions."

"Okay," Toni whispered.

"Do you want us to drive you home?"

"I'd like to be dropped off at the office. I left my handbag in my desk."

"Not a problem."

As they drove down the block, Toni saw Francine and Amy crossing the street. The car stopped in front of the office.

"Thank you." Toni opened the door. "I promise to be careful and stay away from Eric. I'm through with him. He is too damn controlling for me." Toni shut the door. She pivoted on her shoes to thank them again, but they were already gone.

"Hey, isn't that Toni?" Francine pointed across the street.

"Yeah. Go see what's going on. I'll meet you there in a few minutes," Amy said.

Francine crossed the busy street. Toni stood in front of the office with tears in her eyes, fumbling with the keys in the lock.

"Hey, are you all right?"

Toni turned, shaking her head no.

"What happened?"

"You'll never believe me."

"Try me. But let's wait for Amy. She went to pick up her prescription at the drugstore."

Francine unlocked the door and made her way to her desk. How could she tell her about Eric, when apparently something happened to push her over the edge? Just when everything seemed to be going good for Toni, things were about to explode even more.

The bells rang on the door. Amy came stomping in with a small white bag. "That place is so out of control. How can there be only one person working with a line extending throughout the store? Once I get settled in, I'm making a call to the corporate office," she said placing everything down on Francine's desk.

Toni's sniffles brought both their attention back to her.

"What's going on?" Amy asked. "You told her already?"

"Told me what?"

"Oh." Amy bit her bottom lip.

"What's going on here? What are you keeping from me?" Toni asked.

"What we have to tell you can wait. I want to know what happened to have you so upset," Francine said, sitting on the edge of her desk.

"The day was going great. Eric picked me up and we went for a walk in Clove Lake Park. One minute we were holding hands, the next he took off leaving me in the park with no way to get home," Toni cried.

"Oh my God. What a jerk off. Why did he do that? How did you get here?"

Toni began sobbing again. "I was picked up by two police officers." Toni covered her face with her hands and went hysterical.

Francine looked at Amy shaking her head. Francine slid off her desk and put her hand on Toni's shoulder. "It's going to be okay."

Toni wiped her tears away with a couple of tissues before standing. "I am so confused. Every time I meet someone, they turn into bastards. Once again I opened my heart and was taken for a total fool."

"What are you talking about?" Francine asked, crossing her arms under her breasts.

"I had a huge fight with Eric. He told me that I cared about my friends more than him. He threatened if I didn't stop being friends with both of you, then our relationship was over."

"What nerve," Amy said.

"He's such a bastard. I knew it from the beginning," Francine uncrossed her arms.

"He was so sweet in the beginning. But that's not what has me so upset."

"Then what is it that has you so worked up?" Amy asked sliding her desk chair to the front of her desk.

"The police officer who picked me up told me Eric is a criminal and is the one storing the drugs and illegal contraband your the restaurant's basement."

"We were told the same thing right before you got here. Two undercover officers came in here to tell us. They also suggested we don't go anywhere near the restaurant, especially by ourselves. If he finds out we know what's going on, there's no telling what he will do," Francine said as she stood up.

"I always make the wrong decisions when it comes to men. Every time I find someone I like, it always turns into a disaster."

"I think you need to take a short hiatus from men for a while." Francine rested her hand on her shoulder. "Let us fix you up with someone who we know something about."

"I would like that. But yes, I think you're right in saying I need a break from dating. But what do we do about the restaurant? This isn't good."

"Everything is ready to go with the restaurant. The grand opening will hopefully be after the World Series, providing the Pelicans get that far. But first we need to get through tonight's game."

"I'm so sorry, Francine, but I haven't been keeping up with the standings,"
Toni said.

"It's fine. The Pelicans have to win tonight's game to be in the World Series."

"I bet Richie is pissed that he can't pitch."

"Pissed is saying it mildly, Toni."

"I was hoping you two could come stay with me tonight. I'm so scared Eric is going to come knocking on my door."

"We were going to the game tonight. Are you up to going?" Amy asked.

"Yes. This is a big game. I want to be there if they are going to win to become the National League champions."

"Wonderful. You'll see. Everything will work out," Amy said.

"And I wouldn't worry about Eric. The police are out there watching him. I'm sure they will be close by."

"What time do we have to leave?" Toni asked.

"I need to stop home to change into jeans and a pair of flats."

"Can we stop at my house too? I'd like to get out of these dress clothes and take a jacket with me." Toni asked.

"We'll stop at your house first since it's on the way. I want you to know we're here for you, no matter what happens. Nothing will ever break us up."

"Let's close up the office and get going. I don't want to get caught up with all the traffic going out to the stadium. I'd rather get there early and watch batting practice with a glass of wine," Francine said.

"That sounds perfect. But I won't be doing much drinking, since I'll be the designated driver tonight," Amy pouted as she slid into her car.

"We can take my car," Francine said, "or we can take car service to the game."

"Where's Jason?" Toni asked clipping her seat belt on.

"He's in Colorado. He wants me to keep him updated throughout the game."

Toni smiled. "I'll be your date tonight."

Francine slid into the front seat of Amy's car. "I'll drive tonight. This way if you want to stay after the game or go out for a drink I don't have to hang around."

"You don't want to hang around if they lose," Francine frowned.

"You're right, but that's not going to happen," Amy nodded her head.

Amy put the car in drive. Their journey was about to begin.

Chapter Nineteen

The usual forty minute trip to the ballpark took over an hour and a half. The traffic was backed up from the Brooklyn Queens Expressway through the Grand Central Parkway, all the way to the stadium. The closer they got to the stadium the more vendors stood on the side of the highway selling New York Pelican's T-shirts. The vendors walked from car to car when the passengers waved them over with a twenty dollar bill out the window.

Finally, they arrived at the stadium, which was packed with people tailgating with their charcoal barbecues and coolers full of drinks. The scent of a grilled hamburger made Francine want to jump out of the car and ask for a cheeseburger, cooked medium. Instead, she directed Amy into the players' parking lot. The security guard opened the gate for them. Francine handed him a ten dollar bill. He pointed to a stop close to the gate making it easier for Amy and Toni to escape quickly if the Pelicans lose.

Francine led them through the side entrance into a tunnel that split into two different directions. Going right brought you into the bullpen, going left to the elevator up to the box seats behind home plate. The elevator door opened the second Francine pushed the up button. All three of them got onto the elevator dressed in their Pelicans' shirts. Francine sported Richie's jersey with Raggalio in capital letters on the back with the number forty-eight underneath.

They sat in their usual seats in the section to the left of the dugout. Batting practice was over. Francine searched the field looking for Richie. Usually he was working out, sitting in the grass stretching his legs and his back.

Two members of the ground crew came onto the field to place two microphones between home plate and the pitcher's mound. Again Francine looked around for Richie. This time she spotted him coming out of the bullpen, jogging toward the infield with his catcher, Chad Hartman following behind him. Before going into the dugout he stopped by the right side of the dugout to sign a couple of autographs.

"Hey sweetheart."

Francine looked up. Richie stood at the railing grinning. Francine walked down the four steps to meet him. He leaned over the railing to give her a soft kiss on her lips.

"Sweetheart, tonight is do or die."

"I know. I am so excited. Hopefully you'll pitch the opening game of the World Series."

Richie took her hand. "I'm pitching tonight."

"Really? Are you sure you are okay? I heard you this morning on the phone with Jason saying your shoulder is still bothering you."

"I came here early. Vic worked on the shoulder, and I sat in the whirlpool. I have to give it a shot. The other two pitchers have been doing a great job, but between you and me, they aren't experienced enough for the pressure of tonight's game."

"Please promise me one thing."

"Anything."

"If your shoulder starts bothering you, please tell Vic and come out of the game. The Pelicans has one of the best bullpens in the league. Don't damage your arm or else you won't be able to pitch in the World Series."

"I promise."

"Good luck. Love you."

Richie gave her another peck on the lips. "Love you more," he said before disappearing into the dugout.

Francine sat back down. "I need a drink. Richie is pitching tonight."

"Get out. I'm so excited," Amy said. "I feel better knowing the game is in Richie's hands."

"I feel the same way," the girl sitting next to them said. "He is the best pitcher in the league."

"And the hottest," her friend sitting next to her said.

"Shh. That's his wife," she whispered.

Francine laughed. "It's okay." Francine reached into her handbag and handed each girl a business card. "Send me an email with your name and address. I'll send each of you an autographed picture and a T-shirt."

"You'd do that?"

"Sure I would."

"Thank you. I. . ."

"Good evening. Welcome to game seven of the National League playoffs. Tonight we have a special guest singing the National Anthem. Please welcome Michael Gio of These Machines," the broadcaster announced.

The stadium went wild. These Machines was the hottest band with the hottest summer song. The crowd was on their feet, singing along. By the last line of the National Anthem, the crowd roared. They continued to roar while management made the usual announcements about no smoking, jumping on the field, obstructing a play, et cetera.

Just as the roar of the crowd died down, Richie took the pitcher's mound and the crowd went crazy again as Richie took his eight warm up pitches. Richie looked over at Francine, smiled and blew her a kiss before his face went serious.

"Are you all right?" Amy asked, squeezing Francine's hand.

"I'm nervous as all hell. I'm probably more nervous than Richie. I just hate when he pitches these important games."

"He'll be fine," Toni said, squeezing her other hand.

"I'm so lucky to have my two best friends sitting at each side of me."

"Play ball," the home plate umpire hollered.

The first baseman rolled the ball the infielders were throwing around the infield into the dugout. Richie took a deep breath. He got the signal from Chad, went into his windup. He released his first pitch.

"Strike," the umpire said.

As the crowd roared, Francine remembered Richie telling her that he learned to block out the noise with his concentration only on Chad's sign and his windup. Richie shook his head no, before nodding. The next pitch he threw, the batter swung at. The ball went to the third baseman who leisurely threw it to first for the first out. *One out, twenty-six more to go.*

The next batter brought the count to three balls and two strikes. Already Francine was sitting on the edge of her seat. The next pitch was popped to the second baseman. He caught the ball and they threw the ball around the infield before returning it back to Richie. Next came Wayne Bergman, one of the hottest batters in the league. He led the league with home runs and extra base hits. Usually he had at least three hits in every game.

The first pitch to Bergman he let pass him for a strike. The next pitch he hit a bullet to the shortstop. The ball hit his glove so hard Francine could hear it from her seat. The inning was over. Eight more to go.

The excitement from the crowd grew louder as each inning went by with little action. This pitching duel had the fans sitting on the edges of their seats until the bottom of the seventh when third baseman Gary Thompson hit a fastball, sending it over the left field wall. The fans went wild, clapping, cheering and stomping their feet.

With a one-run lead, Francine was able to take a deep breath and take in the scent of freshly popped popcorn. Being such a close game Francine didn't want to leave her seat in fear of missing a beat.

Richie was pitching okay, but it wasn't one of his top games. By this time he usually had at least eight strikeouts, but today he only had two. Watching Richie come off the field in the top of the eighth, she knew he was at his limit. Pain was written all over his face. All she could hope was that he put his pride to the side and told Vic and Scott, the pitching coaches that he had enough.

But that didn't happen. Richie took the mound at the top of the ninth. The first batter hit a ball over the shortstop's head for a double. By now, Francine's legs were shaking as both her friends held her hands. They didn't have to say a word to her. They knew exactly how she felt at that moment. The tying run was on second. A base hit would bring him home to tie the game. With a three and two count, the next pitch Richie threw was ball four. The stadium went silent. Now the tying and go ahead run was on first and second.

The catcher walked out to the mound. They exchanged words before Chad slapped Richie on the ass and returned behind the plate. He dropped the catcher's helmet over his face, dropped his hands to his thigh to give Richie his sign. Tim Elliot walked to the plate. He swung and missed the first two pitches. *Come on, swing and miss again.* But the next pitch never made it into the catcher's mitt. Elliot bunted, making it to first. The bases were loaded. This sent pitching coach Scott Lawsen to the mound.

Whatever he was saying to Richie kept causing him to shake his head no. Francine squeezed Amy and Toni's hands. Francine closed her eyes and said a prayer to Saint Anthony to help Richie get out of the inning. This situation wasn't good.

Richie walked around the mound before taking his place on the pitching rubber. He took the sign from Chad. The first pitch was up the third base line. The third baseman scooped up the ground ball, stepped on third and pivoted on his cleats and threw to home plate for a double play.

The crowd went wild. Francine jumped to her feet yelling, "You can do it, Richie."

The Pelicans still had another time to get up in the event Saint Louis scored a run. They were one out away from winning the National League Division.

Francine clutched her fists to her chest. Her heart was palpitating. Looking out at Richie, she could see the sweat dripping down his cheeks. The stadium had gone silent. Everyone stood.

Richie went into his windup releasing the ball from his hand.

"Ball one," the umpire called.

Richie bit his bottom lip. Francine couldn't see the front of the plate, so chances were that the ball had been very close to the strike zone. Richie took a deep breath. He lifted his left leg. The ball flew like a bullet for a strike.

The crowd went wild. Everyone was repeatedly chanting, "Let's go Pelicans," until Richie again stood on the pitching rubber. That's when the stadium, filled to capacity at over sixty thousand fans, went silent again.

Richie played with the ball in his hand behind his back. She watched as his two fingers gripped around the red stitching of the ball. Again he went into his windup. The batter made contact with the ball. The ball flew way back into deep centerfield. Bill Lightman ran back as everyone's eyes were on the ball. Bill was up against the centerfield wall. He jumped up with his right arm extended above his head. The ball flew right into his glove. By the time his feet touched the ground the whole stadium had gone wild.

Francine jumped up and down, hugging Amy and then Toni. "We are going to the World Series."

"I know, I can't believe it!" Amy yelled so Francine could hear her.

The fireworks started. Over the PA system, *New York, New York* blared out leading into, *We are the Champions.* Photographers and reporters covered the infield. Francine looked for Richie, but with the crowd of people covering the field she couldn't find him.

"This is awesome," Amy shouted above the crowd, who continued to cheer.

"What a ninth inning!" Toni hollered over Amy.

Amy pointed. "Here comes Richie."

Francine walked down to the railing throwing her arms around his neck. "I'm so proud of you."

"I almost blew the game in the ninth."

"Almost doesn't count. We won."

Richie reached over the railing in one forward motion and lifted Francine over the short gate. This time he hugged her tightly before a reporter pushed a microphone in his face.

"Congratulations on a superb pitching performance," the young reporter said.

"Thank you."

"What was going through your mind when the bases were loaded with no outs?" the young reporter, Jerry Simons, his press badge read, asked.

"Absolutely nothing. When I pitch, I focus on each individual pitch, I'd be lying if I didn't admit I became somewhat nervous. Every pitch I threw had to be on the mark. I had no doubt my fielders would give two hundred percent to make the play."

By the time Jerry finished the short interview, five other reporters had surrounded them with notepads, taking notes on each word Richie said.

"Richie," someone shouted. "Go to home plate."

Richie took Francine's hand leading her toward home plate. As he walked, Chad handed him a championship T-shirt along with one for Francine. Not to lose hers in the chaos, Francine quickly slid the shirt over her head.

At home plate, reporters from the major networks greeted them. A few of the players stood around the small podium holding their younger kids who already had on toddler-sized championship T-shirts.

Gary Pixton, the Pelican's general manager stood in the center of the podium with team manager, Jeff O'Donnell, standing alongside him. When Gary spoke, the stadium went silent.

"We are the National League Champions," he said, causing the whole stadium to go into a roar again. "We are the Champions." He sang the first four words of the Queen song, driving the crowd crazy again.

Richie squeezed Francine's hand. Francine gazed up at Richie. His face beamed, but beneath his excitement she saw the pain in his eyes. Every so often his shoulder would jerk, indicating his shoulder hurt him. All he had to get through would be two more games before his official retirement at the end of the season.

Francine turned her attention back to Gary, who held the MVP (Most Valuable Player) award in his hands.

"This year's MVP goes to Richie Raggalio."

Richie leaned over to kiss her. The smile on his face extended well past his broad shoulders. Receiving the MVP award was one of the most prestigious awards following the Cy Young, which Richie had won four times, along with Rookie of the Year.

The flashes of cameras clicked all around, leaving Francine with white dots in front of her eyes. Each year she started a new scrapbook filling it with pictures and articles about the games he pitched. In the morning she'd have a lot of newspapers to buy, and would be surfing the Internet for pictures to add to the latest scrapbook Francine had for this year.

"Thank you for this honor," Richie's voice echoed throughout the stadium. "This is an honor to be shared by the whole team who backed me up, especially in the top of the ninth."

The stadium roared.

"I'd like to thank Jeff O'Donnell for having faith in me to let me finish out the game. I can't thank you enough," he pointed around the field, "our fans for all your support throughout the year. And lastly, to my beautiful wife, Francine, who has always been there for me." Richie held up the trophy. "Thank you and God bless America."

The rest of the night was a total blur. The activities on the field lasted for another hour before the players all retreated back into the clubhouse for more partying and reporters. During the time Richie spent in the dugout, Francine brought Amy and Toni across the street for cocktails and a couple of orders of appetizers.

By the time the guys made it across the street, they were hungry and tired of answering questions. Every time a reporter would ask what they thought about the upcoming series against the Connecticut Brown Dogs, Francine was convinced the players were just answering around the question. The Brown Dogs had the best record in baseball, hell they had the best record by any team in the last nine years. They were on fire. They swept the American League Championship in four straight games. The Pelicans were the underdog in the series. From a conversation she had heard earlier from the three guys sitting behind them, they were talking about how the bookies had already adjusted the numbers.

Richie finally made his way to the oversized booth in the corner of the room. They always took this table allowing for some of the other guys whose wives were with them to sit and join them.

Francine wanted to get Richie alone to make sure he was all right, that his shoulder was okay. If he overexerted himself and wasn't able to pitch in the World Series he would hate himself for retiring without finishing out the post season.

Since Richie joined the team, they only won one World Series ring, which she always wore on a long thick rope chain along with her grandmother's wedding band. Lifting the chain on her neck, she looked down at the two rings. She hoped the Pelicans would win the World Series and make it the perfect way to end his career.

"This is so exciting," Amy said. "I wish Jason was here for the celebration."

"Did you call him?" Francine asked.

"Of course I did, while you were on the field."

"This had to be one of the best games I've been too," Toni said. "I was on the edge of my seat the whole entire game."

"Tell me about it," Gary Thompson, the third baseman said, sitting down next to Toni.

"I wanted to close my eyes." She laughed. "Honestly, I wanted to go to the ladies room and return when the inning was over. If Francine squeezed my hand anymore, she would have broken it."

Gary chuckled. "You are funny. Richie always talks about you and Amy, her partners in crime. I personally like the word cronies."

"That's what our teachers called us. But I tell you one thing, we have always stuck together."

"You can't find loyal friends like you anymore. I really don't know what's going on in this world today. But…" Gary lifted a small black plastic bag off the seat next to him. He reached in and pulled out a championship T-shirt. "I brought this for you."

"Really? Thank you." Immediately she pulled the T-shirt on over her navy shirt. "I love it."

Francine kept one ear open to the conversation taking place next to her. It looks like Gary had finally taken Richie's advice to strike up a conversation with Toni, which she hoped would lead to them going out to dinner to get to know each other better. Once Francine knew Toni was in a good place, she could stop worrying about her too. When Amy met Jason, she couldn't be any happier for her friend. Sometimes it's just a matter of pushing things along.

"Do you know the World Series schedule?" Francine asked.

"Yes. The first three games are in Connecticut, then we return home for two, and hopefully we don't have to go back to Connecticut for the last two games," Richie said.

"Once you get the pitching schedule, I will make certain to be at the games you pitch."

"You don't want to come for the three-day series?" Richie asked.

"I do, but if you aren't playing the first game or two, I can get some work done at the agency before heading to the game."

"Oh, okay."

Francine lifted her wine goblet and took a sip. "If it means that much to you to be there for the entire series, I will put everything on hold and join you."

"I hope you'll be bringing Toni," Gary said.

"Yes, I'll be bringing Amy and Toni."

"You think Jason will be around?" Richie asked. "I can get a ticket for him along with my mom and dad."

Amy tipped her glass toward Francine. "Looks like a family outing is being organized."

"It's going to be a tough series," Richie said. "The Brown Dogs are on fire. They're coming off a sweep of the Cali Spirit."

"You guys are going to rock," Francine sang. "Tonight was just the start. It feels great to be a winner."

"And we're going all the way," Richie and Gary said together, raising their beer bottles.

"Yes, we are. When you get this far, then it's time for everyone to take their time giving two hundred percent concentration on the game. The last team that played the World Series in Connecticut got swept in four. We are going to put up the fight of our lives," Richie said. "I want to go out in style with another World Series ring."

"So do I," Gary said.

"We have to show the league that even though we are a fairly young team, we can still play against the best and win the whole thing. Now all you have to do is keep healthy for a few more days," Chad said.

"I'd like to work on the screwball with you tomorrow," Richie said.

"You know how the manger feels about you throwing too many screwballs. It's not worth overexerting your arm, especially when it's possible you can pitch a second game in the series."

"I promise to take it easy. I'll work with you on the pitch, but I won't be giving you the sign very often."

Richie extended his arm across the table and shook hands with Chad. "It's a deal."

"We're going all the way," Gary shouted, holding up his beer bottle.

A fan yelled, "Let's go Pelicans," causing everyone in the restaurant to go crazy again. The fans kept chanting as they stomped their feet on the floor and their hands on the table. Francine squeezed Richie's hand. She loved the feeling of victory and loved the fact that her husband came through and pitched a great game. Richie's eyes shined each time a fan came over for an autograph or to high five him.

Once everyone quieted down, Francine leaned into Richie. "How are you feeling?" she whispered in his ear.

"I'm okay."

Francine rested her hands on her hips, frowning while staring at him. "Okay. Tell me another story."

"Shh." He touched her lips with his finger before planting a kiss on them. "I'll be fine. I just have to rest my shoulder for a couple of days. Please don't make a big deal out of it," he whispered back.

"Okay. I'm not going to bust your chops over this. I just don't want to see you hurt."

"Hey, why are you two getting serious on us?" Gary asked. "This is a night of celebrating. We are the National League Champions."

"We worked our asses off," Chad added. "And to think, at one time during the season we were in last place, seventeen games behind first."

"We deserved this. We are a young team with only a handful of us veteran players. The young players did their job. The second-string players never let us down. Their bats were on fire. If I'm not mistaken, Jeff made mention at the team meeting this morning that the pinch hitters led the league in home runs and extra base hits," Chad said.

"What makes this so surreal is that in my rookie year we won the World Series. And now that I'm retiring, we are a few games away from doing that again," Richie said.

"I want another World Series ring," Francine said, causing everyone at the table to laugh.

"She isn't kidding either," Amy pointed to Francine. "She wears the World Series ring around her neck on a chain every single day. I don't ever remember her not wearing it."

"If I'm not mistaken, I think I got to wear it for a week." Richie laughed. "But Francine earned it just as much as me. She sat at every home game I pitched."

"I'll never forget the day we sat out in the rain," Toni said. "The umpire refused to call the game and Francine refused to leave her seat."

"I'm going to miss you ladies at the games," Chad said. "I love when all three of you start yelling, 'you can do it Richie'. You can't imagine how many times I walked out to the mound in tears. Every time Francine made one of her brash comments, I could see the steam in the batter's eyes as I held back from laughing."

"I put my time in. Now the younger wives can take over for us," Francine concluded.

"I wouldn't put money on that. The young girlfriends and wives, sit there annoyed the world. I say if they don't want to be there, then they should just stay home," Gary said.

"I went because I love watching my husband. Maybe it was different for me because Richie was a pitcher and didn't play everyday."

"Who are you kidding?" Richie asked. "I know you. You would be at every home game if I played everyday. I have never seen a woman more committed to coming out to the ballpark."

"That's because they started selling wine at the refreshment stands." Toni laughed.

"How about, if truth be told it's because we didn't have to move from our seats. We placed our order for cocktails and food and within ten minutes it is delivered right to you." Amy laughed. "If we had to get up to get our own wine and food, we would have waited for you guys over here in the restaurant, watching the game on the fifty-two-inch television."

"Is this true?" Gary asked Toni.

Toni blushed. "Kind of. We were never the wait in line kind of girls in our younger days."

"Amy almost got us banned from the bakery on New Dorp Lane about ten years ago," Francine said.

"Really. I'd love to hear about it," Gary said.

"I thought we were talking about the World Series." Amy laughed. "Go ahead and tell the story."

Francine sat back in her chair. "Here I am trying not to cause any undue attention to me because of Richie, and there is Amy dragging me into the middle of yet another situation causing attention to us."

"Chill out," Amy said, lifting her wine glass. "Bottom line is everything happened so fast that no one had the chance to take notice of us."

Gary took a slug of beer. "I'm interested. Tell me what Toni's part is in all of this."

"Let me set the stage so you can understand why we did what we did." Amy giggled.

Francine looked over to Gary, who had rested his arm along the back of Toni's chair. This was exactly what Toni needed. A good, normal man, that is, if there were any left. She hoped Amy didn't tell too many stories to scare him off, since through the years they have done things that were totally out of control. Francine was lucky that most of the time she wasn't recognized as Richie's wife.

"Picture making the left off New Dorp Lane onto South Railroad Avenue," Amy began.

"I'm really not familiar with Staten Island, but I'm following you."

"It's Francine in the back, Toni sitting in the passenger seat and I'm driving. As I drive down the street, there isn't a spot to be had. I drive around, not paying attention to what's going on around me."

"Of course, as usual." Toni laughed.

"Shh. Let me tell the story."

All four of them laughed.

"Just as I rounded the corner, someone pulls out of a spot. I say thank God. But of course because the car that pulled out was small, I had to go with the whole parallel parking thing." Amy wiped the back of her hand on her forehead. "Believe me, what a pain in the ass. It had to take me over twenty minutes to pull into the spot."

"Don't you think you're exaggerating just a bit?" Toni asked.

"Okay," she shook her head, "maybe five minutes. But that's beside the point." Amy repositioned herself in her chair so that she faced all of them. "We get out of the car and walked down the block toward the bakery. We had to walk past at least twenty-five people standing along the side of the building. I didn't give it a second thought as I walked into the bakery with Francine and Toni following behind."

"I don't see anything wrong with that," Gary said.

"No, however, the line of people was for the bakery."

"No way. What did you do?"

"We ordered our pastries and cake and walked out of the store."

"And that's when all hell broke loose," Toni said.

"I never ran so fast down the street. Richie would have killed me if he knew we cut in front of all those people standing in line."

"Babe," Richie squeezed her arm, "don't forget to tell him that the whole incident is on YouTube. The only thing that saved the three of you is that the person only taped the back of you three nuts running down the street with boxes of cakes and pastries. "

"That's awesome. You ladies really do know how to have fun."

"These ladies know how to give you a heart attack," Richie said.

"Don't embellish the story." Francine placed her hand on top of Richie's. "The bottom line is that we didn't get caught."

"That's true, until next time."

Chapter Twenty

Francine woke up to the scent of coffee. Glancing at the clock with one eye she couldn't believe Richie let her sleep to past ten. They had a lot on their agenda before they left to go to the city. She threw her feet over the side of the bed and stood. Bending down, she lifted Richie's T-shirt off the floor and slid it on over her naked body. As tired as Richie was last night, they still had celebration sex. Most people said makeup sex was the best, but in their case, they rarely fought so celebratory sex after Richie won a game had been their equivalent. By the time Francine reached the bottom of the stairs, Richie stood there with a mug of coffee in his hand.

"Just the way you like it, fake sugar with a tad bit of hazelnut creamer."

"Thank you." She gave Richie a quick peck on his lips. "Sorry but I didn't brush my teeth before I came down. I know I have morning breath."

"I don't care." He leaned into her, softly kissing her. "You're my good luck charm going back from our high school days. I still love how dedicated you are to my career."

"I wouldn't call it dedication. I supported you because I love you. We've been through a lot together. Now it's all coming to an end."

"I have mixed feelings about retiring."

"I'm sure you do." Francine took a sip of coffee. "You can change your mind."

Richie dropped his gaze down to the floor. "I wish I could." He sat on the barstool next to Francine at the granite island in the kitchen.

"Plenty of players announce their retirement and change their mind."

"Yes they do. But those players don't have the shoulder problems I have."

"I thought the surgery repaired the damage."

"It did, but I think I still have more damage that I'm keeping quiet about. I want to finish what we started this year. The Pelicans are going to be World Series Champs."

"I want that for you so badly. I don't want you to cause anymore damage to your arm."

Richie turned sideways in his chair to face Francine. He took both her hands in his. "We have a whole new chapter in our life about to unfold."

"And no more living out of a suitcase and team bus when you're on the road. I always hate when you're on the road."

"Looks like I only have one more road trip left before I am officially retired."

"I look forward to you being home. I can lighten up my load at the real estate office so we can spend our time at The Perfect Pitch."

"Speaking of which, I'd like to take a ride down there with Jason. We are good to go. I'm thinking the grand opening being the day after the World Series."

"Sounds like the perfect choice."

"I think so. But I wonder after all these years, will I be able to adjust to my new life?"

"We won't have time to think about it. Running a restaurant isn't going to be easy. I'm sure we will be on our feet all day long."

"Maybe you will," Richie said, "but I will be sleeping in."

Francine laughed so hard she had tears in her eyes. Richie had no idea of the work they had ahead of them. Running a restaurant was a full-time job with unlimited overtime with no extra pay. Their lives would be at The Perfect Pitch.

"We need to make some decisions on what we want to do."

"As in?"

"Do we want to be open seven days a week, or do we want to close two days during the week?" Francine asked.

Richie sat back in his chair, his eyes closed deep in thought. Francine would bet Richie never gave any thought to that.

"I think we should start small as we build the business, so we can hire a good staff."

"I agree. Your mother is going to make sure everything runs smoothly."

"I'm afraid of what my mom is going to do."

"Why do you say that?"

"She calls everyday telling me about a new dessert to add to the menu."

Francine giggled. "You haven't seen anything yet."

"No, what has my mother done now?"

Francine slid off the barstool and reached to the top of the refrigerator, taking down a hot pink folder. Opening it, she took out two laminated dessert menus, one in the shape of a baseball, the other in the shape of a football and handed them to Richie.

"I don't believe her." Richie dropped his gaze to the menus. He looked from one to the other, nodding his head. "I must say, she went all out this time, however, I must admit I love them. The idea is so original. I really think this is going to work out perfectly, but don't tell mom yet. We don't need her head to swell."

"Stop it. Her business skills are phenomenal. And come to think of it, I think she's right in saying we should keep the menu simple. While people are watching games, they don't want to be eating spaghetti or lobster tails. They want finger food. We also need to utilize the pizza ovens. Men love pizza."

"I agree. Let's take things easy. Less is more."

Francine slid another laminated page out of the folder. "Here you go. This is another menu. Your mother has everything under control."

Richie took the menu. "I must admit this is good. What do you think?"

"We should go with it. We can always add or take off as we go along. If we feel we want to get fancy once a week or once a month, we can have the special of the day."

"Oh, I agree."

"I think the only thing missing from the menu is salads. I know for myself I'd rather have a salad than pizza."

The doorbell rang, startling both of them.

"Were you expecting anyone?" Francine asked.

"No. I haven't spoken to anyone this morning," Richie said as he walked to the front door.

"Rise and shine," Jason's voice echoed in the hallway.

"Hope you're up and ready to roll," Amy said, walking into the kitchen smiling. "I just got finished telling Jason that we should all take a ride down to The Perfect Pitch."

"We just got finished saying the same thing."

"I say we stop at Katie Lingerie. I called her yesterday and she couldn't talk. She said she had gotten a huge delivery in of new merchandise. What do you say?" Amy whispered.

"You don't have to ask me twice. We'll have the guys drop us off at the store. We can walk down to the restaurant to meet them when we're done."

"Works for me."

They both giggled, causing Richie and Jason to walk into the kitchen.

"What are you two conniving in here?" Richie asked.

"Nothing," Francine answered.

"Every time those two giggle like that, it winds up costing me money." Richie tapped Jason on the shoulder. "Welcome to my world."

"I hate to say this, but I'm so happy to be a part of all this conniving and manipulating."

Richie slid his hands into his front pockets. "You're kidding, right?"

"Not at all. I have finally found myself an awesome woman."

"Newlywed stage," Richie and Francine said at the same time.

"Go grab your wallet," Francine said, "and let's get going before all the good things are gone at Katie's."

"Oh boy. Jason, my man, you better take your bank book with you. These two are totally out of control when they go in there. One minute they are talking and the next she is ringing them up for close to a thousand dollars."

"All right, stop exaggerating," Francine warned. "We don't get that crazy."

"Really." Richie tapped his foot in rhythm. "In case you forgot, it wasn't too long ago that you came home with blackberry body lotion and sex dice."

Francine covered her mouth as she giggled. "Okay, I get your drift. I promise not to go overboard. Maybe a matching bra and thong along with some body paint."

Jason held up his hand. "Come on guys. I'm still in the newlywed stage. I get excited just thinking about it."

286

"You can use the guest room if you like," Francine teased.

"I think we better all get out of here. I'd rather spend the money than have these sex conversations," Richie said.

"He's still a stickler when it comes to talking about sex." Francine pinched Richie's ass. "I know how much you love it. That's probably all you guys talk about in the locker room."

"She's got us there," Jason admitted. "Your darling husband is always talking about sex."

"Richie!"

"Don't even go there," Richie blushed. "Of course I talk about sex, but it's different talking about sex in a men's locker room. I don't feel comfortable talking about it in front of other women."

Francine raised her hand in a stop sign gesture. "Don't even go on. I never for one second thought you didn't talk about boobs and butts in the locker room."

Richie lifted his keys off the kitchen counter and jingled them. "I'll drive."

"I'm calling shotgun." Jason laughed. "No way am I going to continue this conversation with the girls."

"You two are just jealous. You can buy lingerie in the store too," Francine said.

"Yeah. There's nothing wrong with you buying silk boxer shorts or briefs."

"This conversation is officially over," Richie said, sliding into the front seat. "I will drop you two off at Katie's. When you're done, you can walk over to the restaurant."

"That works for us," Amy answered for both of them.

"I'm going to text Katie and let her know we're on our way. This way if she isn't in the store, she'll have time to get there," Amy said.

"She'll have plenty of time to grab a bite to eat, and get a manicure/pedicure. Look," Jason pointed.

Francine looked up. "Shit. Why is it there's always traffic on this damn expressway no matter what the time of day?"

"Beats me," Richie said. "If it were up to me, I'd move off this Island."

"I wouldn't want to miss when you tell your mother." Jason chuckled.

"That's why that conversation will never take place and we will continue to sit in bumper to bumper traffic."

After crawling in traffic for close to forty-five minutes, they finally got off the West Shore Expressway at Page Avenue. But again to their surprise, when they went around the curve up to the light, the traffic again was backed up.

"This is like a nightmare. Just for the inconvenience of sitting in the car for so long, I think I'm entitled to an extra negligee or two," Francine said.

"*Brrrring.* That's another seventy-five dollars." Richie laughed.

Finally they turned onto Page Avenue. What they didn't expect to see were a half a dozen police cars, yellow tape and swat trucks.

"What the hell is going on?" Francine asked.

"I'm not sure. It looks like something happened at the restaurant. Let me pull over."

Jason pointed. "There's a spot over there."

"If this traffic ever moves, I'll pull in there."

"Why don't you girls go over to Katie's while we check things out," Richie said.

"Like hell I'm not going to see what's going on. This is our business. The lingerie will have to be put on hold for the time being."

Francine opened the door before Richie put the car in park.

"Be careful sweetheart. This looks like something serious happened."

"Probably just a car accident…"

"Hope it wasn't a shooting," Amy added.

As they got closer to the restaurant, it was evident something major had taken place in front of the restaurant. Francine pushed her way through the crowd of people standing behind the yellow police tape.

"What's going on?" Francine asked, bending down to go under the yellow tape.

"Miss, what are you doing? This is private property under police investigation," a police officer asked.

"This private property happens to belong to me."

"I don't care who it belongs to. This is now closed."

"This is unacceptable..."

"Sorry, sir." Richie stood at her side. "My wife is right. This is our restaurant, along with our partners, Jason and Amy."

Detective Morris walked over to them. "Well I'll be damned. Richie Raggalio and Jason Maddock." He shook both their hands.

"Can you tell us what's going on?" Richie asked.

"Follow me into the restaurant where we can discuss it."

Richie took her hand, following Detective Morris inside. Once inside, all Francine saw were police officers sitting at tables counting merchandise.

"Where did all those handbags and shoes come from?" Jason asked.

"From your basement," Detective Morris said, "along with over half a million dollars of prescription drugs. I have a feeling there was also cocaine stored down there too because we found residue of white powder on the table."

Richie scratched his head. "Oh my God. I don't understand. This restaurant doesn't have a basement. I saw the blueprints myself."

"You're right. It was closed off. They made an entrance in the backyard, and hid the stairs in the storage closet."

"How does one hide stairs?" Jason asked.

"There's a hidden door behind the back wall of the shelves. There wasn't any way you would have known that unless you took the shelves down."

"We would have found the entrance outside when we built the outside café," Richie said.

"Thank God you didn't. These are dangerous men with extensive arrest records. We have been watching them for months. Summers and his crony have been covering their tracks perfectly, until today."

"What made today different?" Francine asked.

"Summers? Are you talking about Toni's boyfriend?" Richie asked.

"Ex-boyfriend," Francine spat out.

After she spoke, Francine glanced over to Amy. Amy blinked her eyes once. Francine nodded her head once, letting her know they were both on the same page. Before the detective could speak, an officer in uniform walked out of the kitchen with Eric and another man in handcuffs.

"We have a lot of work to do here." Detective Morris reached into his pocket and handed Richie his business card. "I'll call you next week to let you know when you will be able to return to the restaurant."

"What do you mean?" Jason asked.

Francine threw her hands up in the air. "We have to prepare for the grand opening. That's why we came down here today."

"If I'm to be honest with you Francine, we will be doing our investigation over the course of the next week. There is a lot of merchandise downstairs."

"Are you kidding…"

Richie cut off Francine. "You have a lot of explaining to do," he whispered. Turning to Detective Morris, he said, "It's not a big deal. This might turn out to be a blessing in disguise. What's the difference if we have the grand opening at the end of the World Series or a week later?"

"You're right." Jason slid his hands into his pockets. "The last thing we need is to have any undue distractions, especially during the World Series."

"I absolutely agree with Jason on that." Francine turned to walk toward the front door. "Let's get out of here."

Richie and Jason led the women outside. Francine sighed in relief. She would suggest going to The Finn for a cocktail.

Once they were on the opposite side of the police tape, Richie stopped walking and turned to face Francine. "Do you have something to tell me?"

"No. Why?"

"How did the detective know your name?" he asked his tone going up an octave.

Francine raised her gaze over to Amy who shrugged her shoulders.

"Look at me," Richie said, raising his voice even higher. I want you to look into my baby blues and tell me you have no idea how the detectives knew who you are."

Francine dropped her gaze to the ground, shuffling from one foot to the other.

Jason crossed his arms. "I don't like where this is going. Amy?"

"Yes…" Amy whispered.

Francine bit her tongue. She had to tell the truth. All along Amy was the one who insisted she tell Richie. Once again, they got themselves into a big mess.

"Okay, okay. We knew," Francine blurted out. "We found out by accident."

"Are you two kidding me?" Richie pushed his hair off his face, a nervous habit of his.

"Do you realize that the two of you could have gotten yourself killed?" Jason asked, looking from Amy to Francine.

"It's not Amy's fault. She wanted me to tell you. I'm the one who said no."

"Are you crazy?" Richie yelled in a tone Francine had never heard before. "That explains why the shoes and handbags didn't show up on my credit card bill."

"I'm sorry. I…"

Richie raised his hand, stopping her. "I can't believe you would put all our lives at stake."

"I totally agree," Jason added.

Francine stomped her feet. "Okay. I should have told you. Please don't be upset."

Richie shook his head. "No more secrets," he said, grinding his teeth loud enough for her to hear.

"Promise."

Richie walked to the car door, opening the backdoor for her. 'See what I mean, Jason. Welcome to my crazy world, which is about to become yours too!"

The first six games of the World Series were exciting, with each game going into extra innings. Tonight's game was do or die. The Pelicans had to win. Richie insisted on pitching on only three day's rest.

Francine knew how much pain Richie was in. When he pitched three days ago, the pain had been evident in his face. After the game, when they got back to the hotel, Francine couldn't even go near his right side without him letting out a holler.

The first seven inning of the game went scoreless. Richie threw bullets. His fastball had been clocked at one hundred and three miles per hour. The only thing Richie had in his favor was his retirement at the end of the game. Francine doubted his arm could take much more. From where she sat, with each pitch Richie threw, she knew the pain had to be so bad that he had become numb to it.

There were two outs and the count was three balls, two strikes. The next pitch Richie threw, the batter got a piece of and the ball flew over the left field wall. From where she sat, she could hear Richie cursing, repeatedly using the "f" word.

The next batter he stuck out on three consecutive strikes, leaving him standing at the plate in shock.

The bottom of the seventh, the Pelicans came out swinging. They scored three runs giving them a two-run lead. All Richie had to do was throw strikes and have two, 1-2-3 innings. But the Brown Dogs weren't going down that easily. The top of the eighth they added three more runs when their second baseman hit a three-run home run. This brought pitching coach Scott Lawsen out to the mound.

A little pow-wow took place. After a few minutes the home plate umpire walked out to break it up. Everyone returned to their positions. Scott handed Richie the ball before jogging back to the dugout. Richie got out of the eighth and pitched a perfect inning in the ninth. Now it was up to the Pelicans to score a run to tie the game. But instead, the first two batters stuck out. The stadium went silent.

Gary Thompson came up. On the first pitch he hit a rocket up the third base line, making it to second. The crowd went wild. There still was hope. Francine tried to remain positive, keeping faith in her husband and the Pelicans.

Francine knew Richie stood in the dugout, leaning against the metal railing watching every pitch. She was certain his heart was palpitating so hard that he could hear it beating. Next up to the plate was Chad Hartman. Francine took a deep breath. The whole series, Chad didn't have a single hit. If anything, he led the World Series in strikeouts. The first pitch to him was a strike. The catcher threw the ball to second and the second baseman missed the ball. Gary took the opportunity to run down to third base.

The pitcher took his time, walking around on the mound. The tying run was on third base. He walked back to the pitching rubber, looked over to Gary on third who kept wandering off third base and called a timeout.

The Brown Dogs catcher walked out to the mound. They talked for a couple of minutes before the home plate umpire started walking toward them. The catcher returned to his post and placed the catcher's mask over his face. He gave the pitcher his signs a couple of times with the pitcher shaking his head no. Finally, when he shook his head yes, he took his position with both his feet on the pitching rubber.

The stadium was silent. Everyone was on their feet as this was what the whole season came down to. The pitcher played with the ball in his hand for a few seconds before going into his windup. Chad took a step forward and swung his bat. The ball hit the top of his bat. Everyone watched as the ball flew through the air. The right fielder kept running back until he reached the wall. He leaped up, but the ball went ten rows into the right field stands. The fans went wild. By the time Chad reached home plate, the Pelicans were out on the field waiting for him. He stepped on the plate and the stadium erupted. *New York, New York* blared over the PA as the cheering went on for over the next hour.

Francine stood beside Richie on the podium as he received the MVP award again. She had already slipped the World Series Championship T-shirt on. This was the perfect way for Richie to retire, on such a high. As much as she was excited, she still felt sad that this part of their lives had just concluded. Now they would have a different life style to get accustomed to. The restaurant had been a fabulous idea, but she wondered how successful it would be. She guessed only time would tell. If things didn't work out, it really didn't matter. They were set for life with money and wouldn't have to worry at all. If anything, they could sell the business and use the money to purchase a summerhouse at the shore.

"I'll meet you upstairs in the players' lounge. We'll have a quick drink with everyone before heading home for our own private celebration," Richie said before going into the dugout.

Richie and Francine pulled up in front of their house. Richie took his duffle bag out of the car, and carried it in.

Francine could see the sadness in his eyes, and knew it was hard for him because he just pitched the last game of his career. Being the winning pitcher of game seven of the World Series and winning two MVP's in his last year was an honor that he would always remember.

Amy and Jason had left right after the game. They had already placed the congratulations and happy retirement signs in the living room and kitchen. On the front lawn was another sign that read 'World Champs.' Once Toni and Gary arrived, Jason opened the bottle of champagne and handed everyone a glass.

"Time for a toast," Jason said, holding up his glass. "We are all here because of these three lovely ladies." Jason pointed to Francine, Amy and Toni. "Their friendship has expanded into a wonderful new world for all of us. With today's win, my dearest friend Richie is officially retired and has already revamped his life with us. I wish you nothing but happiness. I am so happy to be onboard with you on our new business adventure. Salud."

They all clicked glasses.

"I'd like to add to your toast," Francine said, lifting her glass. "I want to say that these past years have been hectic, but the end result is I have my husband back. We still have the rest of our lives left to explore the world." Francine turned to face Richie. "I love you more than anything in this world. Through the years our love has just grown stronger. Here's to living the rest of our lives full of love and happiness."

Instead of clanking glasses, Francine kissed Richie. She had her reservations about the success of 'The Perfect Pitch,' which she would keep to herself. It was better to let things play out and see where it led them.

"Now with all that said, I think that a vacation would be in order," Gary said. "We had a long season and broke our asses to win."

"I agree. But Jason is still playing," Amy said.

"That's okay. But I want all of us to go together," Richie said finishing off his champagne.

"Where is Jason playing next week?" Francine asked.

"Florida," Jason said.

"Then Florida it is. We will all go. Amy, book us the hotel Jason is staying at. Even though he will be practicing during the day, we can still go and grab dinner at night. What do you all think?" Francine asked them.

They all shook their heads in agreement.

"Then it's set," Richie stated. "We will all go to Florida. When we get back the investigation should be over. We'll put the finishing touches on the restaurant and take an ad out in the Staten Island newspaper announcing the grand opening on December first."

Toni wrapped her fingers through Gary's fingers. "That sounds like the perfect way to kick off the holiday season."

"Then it's a plan." Richie lifted up his champagne glass. "To my beautiful wife, friendship, my retirement and new beginnings."

"Salud," they all said together.

THE END

AUTHOR'S BIO

Karen Cino has been writing since she was fourteen years old. She started her career by writing poetry, short stories and writing article for her high school newspaper. After reading Jackie Collin's *Lovers and Gamblers* and Jacqueline Susann's, *Valley of the Dolls,* Karen found her niche. She wanted to write women's fiction and wrote her first book during the summer before she started college. Her daily walks down at the boardwalk are what gets her muse going. It clears her mind and helps her find realistic plot ideas and the characters boosting up her muse. Karen loves writing about local places that people can relate to. The late Paul Zindel's books took place in Staten Island and reading them, especially *My Darling My Hamburger,* still brings back many memories for her.

Karen loves the summer, loves the beach. Her books are written in Staten Island, and take place in various places across Staten Island. Karen relocated to Barnegat, New Jersey in 2015. She traded in the Staten Island Boardwalk for the shoreline in Long Beach Island.

Karen is a member of Romance Writers of America, Women's Fiction Writing Association and Liberty States Fiction Writers.

Karen has two children, Michael Giordano who's a singer, songwriter and producer and Nicole Giordano who works at Home Depot and is also a photographer. In 2014 Karen married John Gatti. Her husband is an actor, teacher and attorney.

Currently, Karen is working on a new series.

Visit Karen at: karencino.com. You can email her at: karencino@aol.com